The Tory's Daughter

Angela K. Couch

The Tory's Daughter

Contact Information: titleadmin@pelicanbookgroup.com

Scripture quotations, unless otherwise indicated are taken from the King James translation, public domain.

Cover Art by *Nicola Martinez*

White Rose Publishing, a division of Pelican Ventures, LLC
www.pelicanbookgroup.com PO Box 1738 *Aztec, NM * 87410

Publishing History
First White Rose Edition, 2018
Paperback Edition ISBN 978-1-5223-0085-4
Electronic Edition ISBN 978-1-5223-0083-0
Published in the United States of America

Dedication

To all my readers and their love for this series.
Thank you!

Books by Angela K. Couch

The Scarlet Coat
The Patriot and the Rebel
The Tory's Daughter
The Return of the King's Ranger (coming soon)

What People are Saying

I felt as though I was in this small family, in this big war. I truly have a loss for words to describe how this book read for me. All I can say is that anyone can pick this book up, and they will fall in love with the book. They will want more. I want more. ~ Bibliophile Reviews for *The Scarlet Coat*

The Scarlet Coat...is captivating in the dilemmas it presents, in the characters it introduces, and in the romance it embraces. The history of the era becomes personal and dimensional, and there are moments so wrought with tension that it takes your breath away. ~ Reading is my Superpower reviews

1

May 1781, Mohawk Valley

Nine months...and he still felt like a rotted-out stump. Hollow. Joseph Garnet lowered to his knees on the soft soil and glanced at his baby girl, nine months old today. She sat at the foot of her mother's grave, gnawing on the end of the twig her brother had just handed her.

James, now two-and-a-half, searched the immediate area for more treasure. A pebble came to hand, and he brought it to Joseph. "Papa, look."

Joseph took the smooth rock and placed it near the roughhewn cross bearing Fannie's name. "Should we leave it here for Mama?"

Little James, named for his grandfather, nodded. "Want Mama."

"You and me both." Joseph filled his lungs. The air was laden with the scent of moisture and earth. Spring. The season had done little to dull the loneliness winter had festered within him. He was busy with planting, but that also meant he had less time with his children.

"Joseph!"

He sighed. Rachel had probably forgotten something for the children. His sister worried too much. Did she not trust him to manage his own young'uns for a couple of hours? That was all he'd asked for this Sabbath day.

His name echoed closer now.

Joseph stood and plucked Martha and her twig from the ground. He didn't need Rachel to find him here. Again. Judging from her frantic tone, he'd best hurry. A child in each arm, Joseph breached the edge of the grove to see Rachel rushing across the freshly turned earth of the garden, skirt pulled almost to her knees.

"The raiders. They're back."

Joseph faltered. "What? Where?"

Rachel pushed strands of blonde away from the perspiration moist on her face. "Down river, maybe ten miles. A boy came riding. They need help."

"The Frankfort area? Where's Andrew?"

She motioned behind to where her husband stepped from the small barn—hardly more than a shed—their own little girl in his arms. "You'll meet the others at the old fort." Rachel reached for the baby and James. "I'll stay here with the children."

Thoughts taking flight with his pulse, Joseph managed a nod before sprinting past her and shoving into the cabin. He grabbed the musket from over the door, and then snatched up his pistol and powder horn. His hunting knife he slid into his boot. Would there ever be an end to this fighting–this war? Joseph's stomach already turned. Hadn't there been enough bloodshed? Years ago he'd learned to despise this waste of life–even before a British officer became his closest friend…and family.

Andrew Wyndham met him outside with the horses. "Otetiani's raiders by the sounds of it." The rich tones of England still rolled from Andrew's tongue despite his four years' residence in the Mohawk valley. He handed Joseph the reins to Hunter, and then swung aboard the younger horse. "They rode from the lakes and have been killing and burning their route southward."

Joseph mounted and clenched the reins.

The locals had come to call the Mohawk chief Bloody Bear for the death his warriors brought to the valley. The thought of the raiders coming anywhere near his home and family wrung a cold sweat from the back of Joseph's neck. Last summer had become so dangerous, they'd set up makeshift shelters in Old Fort Schuyler, only venturing out during the day to work and harvest the land.

Winter's reprieve was at an end.

With Joseph's baby daughter in one arm and little James holding his younger cousin's hand, Rachel shooed the children into the cabin, before she glanced back. Her free hand rose, but didn't quite manage a wave. Rachel's brown eyes mirrored Joseph's fear…and his weakness, exposing him.

He spurred Hunter toward the road.

"Please be careful. Come back to me. Both of you."

"We shall," Andrew said, and then clicked his tongue.

Joseph beat him to the road, having saved himself from answering. He would not make promises that couldn't be kept, and he'd learned all too well the extent of control he held over death.

The ex-British captain brought the sorrel gelding alongside Joseph's stallion and kept pace with the dust-churning gallop. He looked at Joseph with a gaze far too searching.

Joseph ignored him and encouraged Hunter's gait. Lives and farms were at stake–no time to wonder what went through the other man's head.

Minutes later the trail broke past the thick spring

foliage and the log walls of the old fort, a remnant of the French and Indian War, rose from the grassy meadow. The rush of the nearby river did nothing to drown out the raised voices of the seven men gathered near the gate.

"What's going on?" Joseph reined Hunter into the center of the foray.

"The raid is all the way down near Frankfort," Cyrus Acker grumbled. His grown son was also present, but, as always, remained in his father's shadow. "By the time we ride that far, Bloody Bear and his renegades will likely be gone. Meanwhile, we leave our families unprotected and our fields unplanted. How do we know he's not riding under Brant again?"

Even Brant's name was enough to chill Joseph's blood. No other Iroquois leader had caused so much devastation in the area, often commanding many of the other chiefs, and their warriors, against the Patriots who remained in the valley.

A couple of the men mumbled their agreement with Acker.

Others made known their opposition.

Benjamin Reid, Joseph's father-in-law, shook a finger at them. "And what of those families down river? Do we simply ignore them until the raiders reach our own settlement?" His hand rested on his cane which hung alongside his musket.

Voices again rose, and Joseph jerked Hunter's head, spinning him away.

"Where are you going, Garnet?"

"To fight some Iroquois." He kicked the animal to a run. He'd fight whoever came against this valley until there was no one left to fight. Talk wouldn't save lives. Whoever felt the same way would follow or…he'd worry about that later.

By the time he slowed to ford a stream, Andrew was again at his side. The others followed behind. Frigid water splashed as they trotted through the knee-high current.

Andrew's head dipped forward.

"Praying for us?"

A moment passed before he glanced up, his green eyes sincere. "Always."

"Good." Joseph redirected his focus to the trail ahead. *We definitely could use Thy help, Lord.* Whether or not God would hear him remained in question. He believed in God, tried to do what was expected of him as a Christian, but had yet to see the hand of God work directly in his life for good. Not that he'd noticed, anyway. God hadn't stepped in to stop the life bleeding from his wife. Hadn't stopped Pa from being hacked to death by a tomahawk at Oriskany. Or Mama from failing with illness.

But Joseph had seen a British captain survive a devastating blow to the head, two musket balls, and dangling from a noose. Andrew Wyndham had not only survived, but had married and now had a daughter with the woman he loved so well. Was it his never-faltering faith that made the difference…or merely luck?

The path wound not far from the river, following the current through the valley. The chilliness of morning gave way to the warmth of the sun rising higher overhead.

If only he could blame the sun for the moisture on his forehead and soaking his shirt, but even the exertion of racing his horse toward a skirmish with the enemy was not wholly responsible. The real reason he hadn't been able to stop and argue with the men who wanted to remain behind–the one hundred of his own excuses not to go.

The popping of distant musket fire rose above the rush of the river and the pounding of hooves. Only a matter of time before one of those balls, an arrow, or a tomahawk found its mark. How many times could a man ride into battle before death became inevitable? What would become of his family then?

A pillar of smoke billowed over the tops of towering spruce in the east, flanked by two more.

The band slowed, and men stuffed powder and musket balls down the long barrels of their muskets. Others loaded their pistols.

Joseph hitched his musket under his arm and glanced at Andrew who gave a nod.

They again sped their horses forward.

A gust of smoke carrying the stench of burnt animal carcasses assaulted the riders just before the woods gave way to the soft earth of freshly plowed fields. The Weber homestead. Joseph directed Hunter over the straight furrows toward a barn ensconced in flame. They were still three or four miles from Frankfort—six or seven from home. Only one wall of the cabin fed a blaze. The raiders could not have gone far. If they didn't lurk somewhere beyond the wall of new foliage.

"Whoa, boy." Joseph swung from his saddle and searched the surrounding woods for any sign of motion. He couldn't shoot an old tree at ten paces from off his horse.

"It is too quiet," Andrew said from beside him.

Other than the growing roar of the fire, Joseph had to agree. All the more reason for caution.

"Look there."

He followed the motion to large mounds laid out between the barn and cabin.

A cow, her coat a light brown except for the stream of red from the arrow protruding from her neck, and two pigs lay dead. No horses in sight. Either Mr. Weber had fled with them or they'd been stolen. The answer came as a lower, longer form came into view. The corpse of a man.

"Where is the local militia?" Benjamin had also dismounted, his cane in full use as he neared. "Where are the men?"

Not the question tormenting Joseph as he surveyed the area. "What about Mrs. Weber and the young'uns?"

They'd had three or four children. Had others come in time and pursued the raiders? Or maybe the men of the area were too busy trying to save their own farms and families. How far had the raiders already come today? How much farther would their destruction reach?

Thoughts of Rachel alone with the children sped Joseph past the blond-haired corpse to the cabin door, still untouched by fire. He yanked up on the latch and shoved his shoulder against the dense oak. Not a budge. The inside bar remained in place.

Someone was still in there.

"Mrs. Weber?" Joseph plowed his hip into the door. Pain jolted through him. "Are you there?" The solid planks only vibrated. Again and again. Even Andrew's added force did little. And the single window was much too small. But if they didn't get them out in time…

"Lord, help us," Andrew prayed.

With one motion, they slammed against the door.

Something snapped.

The sensation of falling ended abruptly, jarring the air from Joseph's lungs. The packed dirt floor felt almost as solid as the door. Not giving himself time to recover, he rolled to his feet. His arms rose, but did little to shield his head and neck from a blast of heat. His cocked hat, with its brim stitched up on three sides, was equally useless against the scorching air pressed against him. Joseph's eyes watered from smoke as he scanned the small room.

The woman huddled with two boys and a young girl beside the bed. They peeked out from under a tent of blankets.

Joseph grabbed for their arms. "Get out of here."

The mother struggled free of his grasp. "*Nein*. Not gone." Her eyes appeared wild in the light of the flames behind Joseph.

Andrew ripped one of the boys from her. "We have to–"

A shout from outside spun Joseph back to the door.

Guns discharged.

The section of the blazing roof over the table crashed down. Sparks flew.

Joseph coughed, and he lunged for the older boy. "Get them out!" he yelled over the roar in his ears. Better to face the possibility of an arrow, than the surety of being roasted alive. A gulp of air did little to dissipate the fog hovering over Joseph's brain. He was only partly aware of the woman and children being rushed around the cabin and out of sight.

Most of the men crouched wherever they could find cover and fired into the nearest stand of trees.

Joseph hit the ground and peered past the branches, searching the shadows.

Nothing.

"Let's not let them get away from us," someone cried, and men rushed their horses.

Joseph followed, but wished he knew what they were riding into. Had the raiders been watching the burning cabin for any survivors? He'd seen enough since the beginning of the war to know they would not have hesitated to kill even the youngest child, but would have no desire for an actual battle. They only wanted to terrorize. To murder.

With Benjamin and Andrew still behind with the woman and her young'uns, Joseph brought up the rear as the band charged into the forest. They met dense brush, fallen logs, and the ground heavy with deadfall and debris. Joseph broke his speed to safely navigate the maze. He checked his musket. Maybe this time they would catch up with the Tory raiders and make them answer for their crimes.

~*~

Lungs burning from deprivation, Hannah Cunningham watched from the shaded gap under a half-rotted log. Tiny red ants tickled her arm, but she didn't dare move even enough to bush them away. Not until the band of farmers were far from her hiding spot. If they found her…

Hannah gulped back the terror and buried her face in her cloth sleeve that already smelled of earth and decay. She should have listened to Otetiani and stayed far from the raiding. Or perhaps she should have never disguised herself as one of the raiders to follow them back to the valley. But Otetiani, the son of her mother's brother, had refused to help her. She'd had no other option.

Still, she should have kept her distance—ignored the smoke rising like beacons, and put aside her curiosity for once. It wouldn't be long before her mare was found by the farmers, and then how would she find her brothers? Or survive this wilderness, miles and miles from her home among her mother's people? Any soul she could call a friend had long ago been driven from the Mohawk Valley as her own family had. She could expect no help, or even mercy, from those who called themselves *patriots*.

They rushed past, muskets raised and fury on their faces. For the anger, she could not fault them. She knew it well enough—had felt the same when her family's cabin had been put to the torch. And so many times since.

The farmers disappeared through the woods, and Hannah wriggled out of her hiding spot. She brushed the leaves and dirt from the shirt she had traded her feminine tunic for. Though designed for a man and hanging large over her frame, the belt she'd furnished out of a strip of rawhide kept it from encumbering her movements. She kept low and followed the direction the patriots had gone. Hopefully they'd somehow overlook the small mare.

The hush of the forest was cut by the familiar thunk of an arrow biting wood. And then a cry and the booming of guns.

She dropped and scrambled against the wide trunk of the nearest spruce. Knees hugged to her chest, she listened. Men yelled. Branches snapped. Guns fired. Had Otetiani and his warriors returned on her account? She had not stayed put as he'd ordered her to after discovering her identity. If men died, it would be her fault. Hannah crept from her shelter. She needed to know what was happening, but every twig that snapped under her moccasins, every brush of leaves against her leggings, sounded in her ears. Her heart pounded.

Most of the farmers had dismounted and ducked down wherever they could find cover, but it already looked as though the warriors were withdrawing. The Patriots had likely taken them by surprise.

A low nicker startled Hannah, almost dropping her on her back end, and she twisted to a tall chestnut not ten feet away. His large brown eyes had a gentleness to them, and a familiarity. She knew this horse, had always admired him. James Garnet's stallion.

Her passage away from here.

Without pause, Hannah sneaked to Hunter and unwrapped his reins from a branch. "Easy. You remember me, don't you?" Her fingers trembled as they slid down his thick neck to the saddle. After slipping her toes into the stirrup, one smooth motion lifted her onto the animal. She hugged his neck and nudged him away from the skirmish. One step…then two. Almost safe.

2

The musket bucked against Joseph's shoulder. A cloud of smoke billowed back on him. He dropped behind the log and scrambled for more powder and another ball. The ramrod made smooth time down the shaft and out again, but before he could slip it back into place, a motion drew his gaze to where he'd tied Hunter. Reins hooped the animal's neck and turned him away. A buckskin clad leg hung from the saddle—almost the only thing visible of the Mohawk brave astride.

"No." Joseph almost jumped to his feet to pursue the renegade, but that would make him an easy target for the man's friends. And he couldn't shoot without risking the horse. He dropped his musket and scrambled along the length of the log. Under cover of the new foliage that surrounded him, he raced to intercept Hunter and the brave.

The man hunched low over the saddle was in the motion of kicking Hunter into a run when Joseph caught up, coming at them from the side. He gripped the shirt hanging around the man's middle and yanked him off the animal's high back.

The brave proved quite a bit lighter than anticipated, and his body flew against Joseph's, slamming him to the ground. With a twist, Joseph threw him off and aimed a fist into his face. The warrior, not more than a youth, reeled back, and

Joseph rotated over him to pin him to the ground.

Like a bobcat, claws slashed across Joseph's face.

He caught the offending hand, while his own dropped to search the boy's person for a knife or other weapon. The waist was surprisingly slim compared to the hips and... A decidedly feminine gasp jerked Joseph's hands back.

A mistake.

The brave's knuckles wiped across his face, followed by a sharp knee to the ribs. Joseph grunted and pushed himself away. Worse mistake–the equivalent of holding a cougar by the tail, leaving all other appendages free to attack. All he could do was fall on his back in an attempt to fend *her* off. The little Iroquois warrior was female!

How was he supposed to fight a girl? He almost felt bad for punching her, and probably would if she wasn't determined to return the favor a hundred fold.

Abruptly her attack broke off. She grabbed toward the knife in his boot.

"No, you don't." Joseph tried to jerk his leg away, but only succeeded in helping her draw the blade. He lurched backward just as a shot rang from only yards away.

The girl spun and fell in the same motion.

"Joseph?"

Even Andrew's call couldn't pull his gaze from the girl as she pawed at her sleeve and the growing crimson stain. Her hand shook as it hovered over the wound, never actually touching it. High pitched squeaks, like an unhappy mouse, were the only sound she made despite the obvious pain. The problem was, she didn't do anything to hinder the bleeding, and it wouldn't stop on its own.

Joseph grabbed the knife from where she'd dropped it, and stooped over her. She flinched as he reached for her sleeve.

"I won't hurt you."

Andrew pulled his horse up short and swung down.

It had never bothered Joseph until now that one of them had decent aim from the saddle.

"Thank goodness you are alive. When I saw that..." Andrew looked down at their captive and frowned. "Oh, dear. A woman? I thought–"

"And you were probably right." Joseph sliced through the heavy sleeve and peeled it away from the chunk of missing flesh just above her elbow. The ball had barely caught her, but enough to leave a deep gash. "She was, no doubt, trying her best to kill me."

She gave a bit of a squeak as though about to protest, before clamping her mouth shut. Big brown eyes watered as he cinched a strip of cloth over her arm, and he couldn't quite push past a twinge of regret. What was a little thing like her doing out with a raiding party anyway? Besides stealing horses?

"What do you intend we do with her?"

He pushed to his feet. "You figure it out. You're the one who shot her."

Andrew glared. "In order to preserve your life."

Joseph slipped his knife back where it belonged and stole another look at the girl and her painted face. Black hair hung over her shoulders almost to her waist, feathers braided throughout—along with several twigs, plenty of dried leaves and spruce needles. She didn't look at him in return, instead stared at her arm and the makeshift bandage. "So you're suggesting I couldn't defend myself against a little girl?"

The young woman's head snapped up, and she leveled a glower at him.

He'd have to keep in mind that she understood at least part of what they said.

"You were the one flat on your back while she wielded the knife," Andrew stated flatly. "*Your* knife. The fact remains, we need to do something with her. And quickly."

Joseph had no answer.

"She is both injured and without a horse. Surely you do not think it best to leave her out here?"

Of course not.

Her friends were hopefully riding hard in the opposite direction.

"You're right, she may go back to burning farms," Joseph said.

"Perhaps Mr. Reid or one of the other men will have an acceptable solution."

Turn her over to a bunch of angry frontiersmen? Better for them to never know she existed. "No. No one else need be involved." It was too easy to lose control of a situation.

The frown on Andrew's face deepened. "So you suggest we take her home, perhaps hide her there until she recovers..." His eyes took on a twinkle. "Something in this rings with familiarity."

Joseph wiped his wrist against the moisture dripping from his forehead. "Which makes it completely unacceptable." They didn't need a replay of events from four years ago. No matter how well that had finally ended for his sister and Andrew Wyndham. "Rachel is not to be involved this time."

He turned to the girl and scratched his scalp. Under the red and black paint she appeared completely bereft of color, and her whole body shivered as though she were cold.

Andrew came beside him. "How do you expect to keep her from your sister?"

"I don't know." But Joseph had a few miles to figure that out. "Let's get her on my horse." Before the others found them.

"You will not be able to keep this a secret."

Joseph grunted. He knew as much from experience, but mostly he just wanted to keep things simple. For a little while anyway.

~*~

Strong, calloused fingers wrapped Hannah's good arm, and she flinched. She wasn't sure why. Though her panic had done neither of them any favors, Joseph didn't strike her as the kind of man who would purposefully harm a woman–never had. Her throbbing jaw would have thanked him to realize her gender a few minutes earlier.

Joseph Garnet.

The past six years had taken all his boyishness away. He'd been almost twenty last she'd seen him, but the maturity, the more definitive line of his jaw, the broadening of his shoulders…Hannah shook her head, both to clear the word *handsome* from her head and the sudden blackening of her vision as he drew her to her feet. Thankfully the cloud soon cleared.

"Who are you?"

Hannah dropped her gaze from Joseph's searching one. She should be relieved he didn't recognize her, but instead she felt a little hurt. Why should he remember her? He'd already been a man, while she'd only been a girl of thirteen. Hardly more than a child in the eyes of Joseph Garnet. Even Fannie Reid, three years her senior, hadn't been successful at garnering his attention.

A low grunt merged into a growl. "You understand what I'm saying, don't you?"

She should tell him the truth. He obviously didn't want to be put upon by her, so it would probably be easy enough to convince him to let her go. But then she might never find her brothers. Her cousin would drag her north again to the Great Lakes, leaving her without answers.

"Fine," Joseph stated. "You don't try to kill me, and I won't try to kill you. Agreed?"

She afforded him the slightest nod.

He replied with another grunt.

His large hands embraced her waist and lifted her onto Hunter's back. Again the world swayed and darkened, until his grip returned. He swung up behind her in the saddle and shoved her forward onto the pummel. A jolt of agony speared from her wound, evoking a gasp. He cinched her against his solid chest and reined the stallion away.

The man who had shot her, whom she didn't recognize, soon caught up with them on a gelding she did know. Sorrowful had only been a fresh-broke colt when her family was driven from their home. Joseph had sat tall in his saddle, blue eyes like stone.

"Go on, then, while I inform Mr. Reid of our withdrawal. I shall catch up with you as soon as I am able." His tone was decidedly formal. Very British.

"But you won't say anything concerning her?"

"You do not trust even him?"

Joseph released a breath that heated her ear. "Do

as you see fit."

The man nodded. "I shall."

As the sorrel dug dirt with his hooves, speeding away, Hannah forced herself to relax a little more. Mostly for the sake of her head, as the throbbing in her jaw expanded into her temples. Even the base of her neck ached, either from the fall or the abrupt force of Joseph's fist. All of that, however, proved no rival for the hot agony burning through her arm.

Splashes of sun spilled through the high branches overhead and flashed across her vision as they moved. Hannah closed her eyes. She had to make a plan. Her family's homestead neighbored Garnet's. Did anything remain? Anything that would help her find her brothers? After six years, she'd hoped Myles and Samuel would be released from their bondage in the Continental Army and allowed home. Would they have returned to the valley, or did they seek their family farther north? Or were they dead, too?

Coming across the main trail along the river, Joseph nudged Hunter to a lope.

Though the horse's gait was one of the smoothest she'd ridden, the rocking did nothing for her arm or her head. She gritted her teeth and gripped more of his mane. Anger surged. Joseph Garnet cared nothing for her comfort or lack thereof. Always distant. Always aloof. For all she knew he had agreed with the men who forced her mother to flee their home because of Pa's loyalties to the crown. And compelled her brothers to fight a war that was not their own. No. She wouldn't trust Joseph Garnet to help her. Only his pa.

3

Joseph slowed his horse as Andrew brought his alongside. "What news?"

"The raiders have crossed the river, and Mrs. Weber and her children have been taken to a neighbor. Mr. Reid will stay to see to her husband's burial."

Benjamin was a good man. "And the others?"

"Returning to their homes and fields."

With the fair weather, everyone was in a hurry to sow their fields before the rains came. Or before raids became too frequent.

Andrew shifted his gaze to the girl, and his expression took on concern. "I think it best that Rachel be informed."

"Why? So she can complicate everything?" Joseph shook his head. "Turn our backs, and the next thing we know they'll be sitting down for tea."

Andrew cocked a smile. "And we know how greatly you detest tea."

"Precisely." If Rachel got involved, she would step in and take over the situation, removing any control from him. Just as she had before.

"Then what do you propose?"

Joseph glanced down at the dark head of the girl in his arms. From the way she leaned into his chest, he couldn't be sure whether or not she'd lost consciousness. "You ride in first and collect Rachel and the children. Take them home. I'll wait out of sight with her, or…" The smokehouse was empty. "Stash her somewhere out of sight."

The girl stiffened. It appeared she was still very much aware of what went on around her.

Andrew cleared his throat. "'Pray for us: for we trust we have a good conscience, in all things willing to live honestly.'"

Joseph aimed a glare. Most days he didn't mind his Scripture-spouting brother-in-law, but not when it pricked his conscience. "We're not lying to Rachel."

"Of course not."

"Simply not informing her of certain details."

Andrew chuckled.

"Fine," Joseph said. "If you want me to, I shall tell your wife how you shot this poor little thing."

The Mohawk maid straightened.

Joseph fought down a chuckle. She definitely understood him well enough.

"Rachel will not be willing to leave before seeing you unharmed—all your limbs accounted for. And I am sure James would like to have a few more minutes with you, as well."

Joseph reined Hunter to a full stop at the edge of his land. Little James craved his father's attention and presence. Most weeks, especially since the start of planting, Joseph only saw his children a couple of hours at a time. Sometimes a little more on Sundays, when he joined Rachel and her husband for meals and "church." He needed to give his son what time he could. "The smokehouse, it is."

~*~

"Keep quiet, and I'll be back with food and

bandages." The solid door closed.

Hannah leaned into the closest wall. Not that any of the walls were far. If she stretched out both arms she could probably touch the opposite side of the tiny building that was at least tall enough for her to stand in. She gave the door a little kick and heard Joseph's "Shhh". Not that anyone near the front of the cabin would hear any racket she made.

Hannah kicked the door again. Not as solid as the ones Pa built, but of fine construction nonetheless. Her family's homestead–or what remained–was less than a mile away, and she was stuck here in this tiny crate of a smokehouse. She couldn't help but wonder if she would be left completely to Joseph Garnet's mercy. From what she had gathered from conversation, Rachel was now married to the proper speaking gentleman–he was no frontiersman–and they had children.

Joseph remained on the Garnet farm, his marital state unknown…not that it should matter to her. And their father? No one had so much as spoken his name, and he hadn't ridden with the others. Was he even alive? Or had this war claimed him too?

The whinny of a horse was joined by the murmur of voices. A few minutes later the steady thud of hooves and a sharp creak of an axle suggested a wagon's departure. Soon there was only silence.

Hannah prepared herself for Joseph's return. She would ask about his father. And then she'd question him about her brothers. If he returned. She couldn't very well blame him if he wanted to forget her.

Hannah pressed her head against the ridged wood. Her arm throbbed in time with her heart and the pressure mounting within her skull. Thirst clung to her tongue along with the feeling of having swallowed sand. Gradually her legs gave out, and she slipped to the ash-littered dirt floor. She clamped her eyes closed against the sensation of burning. She'd been told tears were a sign of weakness...and she would never find Myles and Samuel by being weak.

Her brothers. What had become of them?

Samuel had been barely twelve. What would years in the Continental Army have done to a lad so cheerful, a contagious smile stretched across his face? He'd always seen the good in everything. But there wasn't any good in war.

And Myles? Had he heeded his commanders, or made things worse for himself by trying to fight back? Her older brother was a man with too many passions. Too much like Papa. Even in his love for wood and talent of creating something beautiful from it.

But Pa was dead.

She had to believe Myles and Samuel had survived the war that had taken everyone else from her. Hannah pressed a hand over her moist cheeks. Perhaps she should be grateful Joseph hadn't immediately returned. And she was. For a little while.

Silence and the throb of her wound stretched across unmarked time. Still, he did not come back. The sun, showing through cracks around the door, slowly slipped away. Dusk draped the valley with a blanket of blue before the door swung open and Joseph stepped in—tall and broad in all his manhood. A striking image in the fading light.

His voice rumbled in the back of his throat, words spoken under his breath, but she refused to look his direction. Not until her glower was back in place. She narrowed it at him as he stepped to her and stooped. Weariness fed her anger, making it easier to ignore how well he looked with the shadows angled across his clean-shaven face.

He'd rarely gone clean-shaven.

Without hesitation, Joseph scooped her up into his arms and hauled her out of the smokehouse.

How dare he? She wasn't a brainless sack of cornmeal he could shove and haul from one place to another. "Let me down." Hannah ignored the stab of pain though her arm as she squirmed out of his grasp. He tried to maintain his hold on her, but she aimed a swift kick to his shin, only to meet the thick leather of his boot with her soft moccasin.

He hardly faltered or winced. "So you do speak." Joseph grabbed her good arm.

"When I have something to say." She curbed her desire to fight him off again. His face already bore the thin gashes her fingernails had left from their first skirmish. Not the best way to convince him to help her.

Joseph tugged her toward the cabin. "I suppose it shouldn't surprise me that you speak the King's English so well, with how loyal your people have become to him."

He was right in a way. There had been much discussion between British officers, Otetiani, and the other leaders of the Mohawk people. She glared at the back of Joseph's head all the same. "What do you know of my people?"

"I know I'm weary of burying good men. And women and children. And trying to put out fires." He halted outside the door. "Perhaps you will answer me this. Why were you, a mere slip of a girl, riding with Otetiani's raiders?"

She'd like to show him what a *mere slip of a girl* was capable of when angered. Her jaw ached, and she tried to relax enough to answer him. "I wasn't riding with them. I was waiting for them."

Joseph's blue eyes became thin slits. "Why?"

"I..." Now wasn't the time to explain to him about her cousin or her quest. Joseph was as weary and irritable as she. She wanted to speak with his pa, first. Hannah glanced around the farm bathed in long shadows. The barn looked much smaller than the one she remembered, and more land had been cleared, but the two room cabin appeared unchanged. "You live here alone?"

"I do."

A chill dropped through her, and she tipped her face away. James Garnet was likely dead then. After all the death she had seen since the start of the war, she shouldn't be shocked, but he'd been so kind. Especially to her. Perhaps because they had shared a love of horses and an adoration for his chestnut stallion.

"You have nothing to fear from me."

Joseph's crisp tone yanked her from memories of his father.

"So long as you behave yourself." He led her into the cabin and the warmth radiating from the large stone fireplace.

Hannah straightened her spine–though Joseph remained a stately elm to the willow sapling she resembled. "Afraid I'll burn you out?"

He pushed her into a chair, and then hefted a wooden pail onto the table. "Shouldn't I be?" Water sloshed over the rim of a mug as he filled it. "Drink that."

While Hannah's parched throat thanked him, her stomach grumbled for something more substantial. Warmth rose to her face.

Joseph was too busy, however, pouring water into a basin and gathering rags. After a moment, he sat on the chair next to hers and shifted it until he faced her wounded arm. A tug on the ties of the handkerchief he'd used as a bandage pierced through the center of her wound.

Hannah jerked away. The last thing she wanted was his large hands inflicting any more pain. "I don't need your help." Yet, she did. Maybe she should tell him exactly who she was right now and ask what he knew of her brothers. How different could he be from his father?

"Good. Because I don't have time for this." Joseph stood and wiped his palms across the legs of his breeches. "I have seed to get in the ground. Two farms to plant. What am I supposed to do with you?"

Do with her? She was nothing more than a complication in his already busy life. But why should she mean anything more to him? He didn't recognize her. And even if he did, it was not as if he had ever really looked at her—seen her as anything more than a nuisance.

Before Hannah could formulate a response, Joseph again pulled her to her feet. Once in the small bedroom at the back of the cabin, he aimed a finger at her. "Stay."

She followed him as far as the door and watched while he collected the cloths and basin of water from the table. He deposited his load on the single wooden chest set against the wall holding a small window, opposite a large bed. Next, he returned with a bowl of what appeared to be a stew or soup. This time he closed the door behind him, leaving her again in solitude. With no answers.

At least she had food and what she needed to tend her wound. The soup was cold—probably made by Rachel while the men were away—but it filled her stomach.

A hammer cracked against the wall near the door.

The spoon dropped back into the bowl, and she set it aside.

More hammering. And then something heavy slid into place across the door. Joseph's footsteps led away. The outside door closed. When the cabin fell silent, she tried the latch. It didn't budge. She kicked the door, though the futility of the action did nothing for the sudden heat surging through her. Again trapped. Again helpless...and completely dependent upon that man.

Good thing for Joseph Garnet she was locked in here.

She wouldn't always be.

What little light remained cast a glow through the window above the oak chest. The opening was narrow...but so was she.

Hannah looked to the solidly constructed chest. She would find out what was available to her before making any plans. A familiarity lowered her to her knees, and she ran her hand over the smooth top, then down the side where her fingertips found the sought-after grooves. She looked closer at the initials engraved into one of the sideboards. *HC* for Henry Cunningham. Papa had built this chest for the Garnets before tensions in the valley had compelled him to leave.

Why hadn't her father taken their family with him? Had he truly believed them safe? Or had he even taken the time to consider what was best for his wife and children?

"Oh, Papa." He'd been killed that next August at Oriskany. So close to home.

Hannah sat on the edge of the chest to clean and bandage her arm, before setting the basin and leftover rags aside.

Once she cleared off the lid of the chest, she lifted it and turned through several pairs of men's breeches, shirts, and an old pair of shoes. Beneath these laid a quilt, sized for an infant. She pulled up the edge and peered under at the assortment of women's gowns. Surely not Rachel's—she would have taken hers to her new home. And none of these appeared too worn to be still in use.

Hannah withdrew a pale yellow gown and held it against her small frame. She'd never owned any fine gowns and had always envied Abigail Reid's daughters in the frills she had sewn for them. Fannie had worn this one.

Hannah shoved the gown back into the chest. Had Fannie indeed won the heart of Joseph Garnet? And if so, where was she now? The room bore no other sign of a woman's residence. Not that it mattered one way or another if Fannie had married Joseph. Hannah wanted nothing to do with the man. Only answers.

In a corner of the chest a smooth wooden handle and glint of iron peeked from under folds of dyed-blue homespun.

A pistol.

4

Despite the approach of dawn, blackness hovered over the valley. Joseph sat awake in a hard-backed chair and stared with aching eyes at the bedroom door and the bar he had fixed over it. He'd hardly slept a wink all night. He should have listened to Andrew. The man usually spoke wisdom, except for when it came to farming–he being a gentleman and pastor and having no experience whatsoever. But no. Joseph had wanted things done his way. Now he reaped the consequences.

Not only did he feel awful for the shades of purple spread across the girl's jaw, but he'd left her in the smokehouse much longer than intended. He'd planned to curry Hunter and put him in the pasture, but then the cow had reminded him that she was ready to be milked again. One chore led to another, making procrastination far too easy. Especially because he didn't know what to do with her. When he'd finally returned for her, what had he done? Locked her up again without proper care to her wound.

Not that she'd wanted his help.

He'd always been clumsy with his fingers and would have probably done as much harm as good. Joseph groaned. He'd been just plain clumsy yesterday, but something about the girl unnerved him—something beyond the war paint marring her features.

Maybe it was the fact he *still* had no idea what to do with her? She'd come into the valley with Otetiani's raiders for who knew what reasons. After all the bloodshed and burning, he'd be a fool to trust the petite warrior. Given the opportunity, would she hesitate to kill him and burn down the cabin while he slept—leaving his children without any parents?

Yet, despite her sharp tongue–and her incredible use of the English language–the girl had an innocence about her. A vulnerability in those pale brown eyes. And a familiarity.

He leaned forward and scratched his fingers through his hair. Fields to plant. Land to protect. Children who needed their father. "What was I thinking?"

After he finished chores, he'd go discuss plans with Andrew…and Rachel. Perhaps even Benjamin. Anyone who'd take responsibility for the girl. Joseph laid his head back and closed his eyes. And woke to a thunderous pounding in his head.

No. Not just in his head but resonating through the whole cabin. He groaned and pushed up. Pain burned across his shoulders and down his back. He tried to stretch the knotted muscles, but with little success. Not that he had time with the banging of something solid against the bedroom door.

Wrestling sleep's overwhelming hold, he staggered across the room and lifted the beam. Dawn lit the small window and cast a glow over the Indian girl in her rustic garb, tangled hair streaming past her shoulders. Something clanked to the floor, and he glanced to the object she had dropped. Pa's pistol.

"Be grateful you don't store your powder in here." Her lips curled with the hint of a smile as she pushed past him.

"Whoa! You can't go."

"Trust me, you do not want to stop me." She continued out the front door, letting a blast of cool air into the cabin.

Joseph blinked away the last of his need to sleep, the breeze lending a hand. He rushed after her. "Where do you think you're going?"

"All you need to know, is I won't go far or for long." She threw the words over her shoulder. With only the fabric of her sleeves warding off the spring chill, she hugged herself and hurried toward the nearest stand of trees. "And it would be ungentlemanly of you to follow."

Joseph took three more steps before stumbling to a halt, his brain fully awake now. He turned and folded his arms. Part of him almost hoped she would keep walking and un-complicate his life. Within minutes, however, she stalked right back past him and into the cabin. By the time he caught up, she crouched in front of the fireplace, blowing life back into yesterday's coals.

"Now what are you doing?" There was no way he trusted her near fire.

"I'm cold."

"Then wrap up in a blanket."

She stomped back into the bedroom–an impressive feat with soft buckskin padding her steps.

Joseph looked in to see her perched on the edge of the bed, Fannie's side, as she hauled a quilt over her. She shivered and wrapped it tight around her shoulders. Her back remained arrow-straight.

Frustration, doubt, and guilt sat heavy in his empty stomach. He would be a fool to let his guard down, but he'd been too harsh. Joseph picked up Pa's pistol and turned out of the room. He closed the door, but didn't bother with the bar. Not much point to it now that his eyes were open. He might as well brew some coffee for them both. Hopefully it would warm her up. And keep him awake.

She didn't acknowledge him when he brought her a steaming mug and some biscuits, so he set them aside on the chest that contained all his and Fannie's clothes, and a few baby things. Well hidden away. Any other proof of children and a wife had been stripped from the room, taken by Rachel for the use of his offspring. He wasn't sure if the effect made it easier not to dwell on how good their life had been…or added to the emptiness.

This time when Joseph retreated, he dropped the bar back over the door. He would get an early start on his chores. Busy hands helped ward off the loneliness.

~*~

Where was that man? Hannah paced the small room for hours. She eyed the window. Within a mile sat her family's homestead and whatever secrets it held. So close. Only a thin pane of glass away.

She paced.

If she discovered nothing there, Joseph was her best hope of finding out more about her brothers. Would he stop avoiding her long enough to speak with?

Sunlight shone through the small window. The sun had already reached its highest point and here she remained, trapped.

Hannah spun on her heel and strode back across

the room. She'd never liked being contained. Never liked sitting still. And with home and possible clues to finding her brothers lingering just out of reach, this confinement drove her mad.

Enough waiting.

Hannah cleared off the chest and collected the tall wooden candleholder from a bedside table. She climbed onto the chest. Braced against the wall, she turned her head away and rammed the base of the candleholder against the pane. Glass shattered. Careful of her fingers, Hannah cleared out the remaining shards. Folded through the window, a thick quilt from the bed shielded her from any remaining slivers. Her injured arm screamed as she pulled herself up. She had to wriggle her shoulders through at an upward angle, but her waist slid forward easily enough. Until her hips wedged against the solid boards framing the opening. *No.* She squirmed with no effect on her position.

"No!"

She tried to push upward, to go back inside, but her injured arm spiked with renewed agony, and warmth trickled past her elbow. Fresh scarlet soaked her bandage.

~*~

Joseph straightened the sack, slowing the stream of wheat seed. He wasn't sure what he'd heard from the direction of the cabin. As much as he wanted to ignore the nagging in the back of his mind, he also wanted his home to remain intact. He tied off the sack and rounded the barn. All was quiet, but he would check on the girl anyway. He swung open the door and stopped short, biting back harsh words. "Did you need to make another trip into the woods so bad that you could not wait for me?"

Her muffled retort and the momentary flailing of her buckskin clad legs pulled at the corners of his mouth. Until the jagged fragments of glass glinted up at him from the floor. Mama's window. "I should leave you there." He huffed out a laugh. "You don't look as though you're going anywhere."

"Only because of my arm." Her voice tightened, whether from the constriction of her lungs or pain.

"If you hadn't attacked me, you wouldn't have been shot."

"I didn't attack you! You yanked me off the horse."

"*My* horse. That you were trying to steal."

"Because you and your friends…" She gasped a breath.

"My friends and I were trying to preserve life and homes. *Your* friends were the ones burning the countryside."

"You *Patriots* started the burning." Her voice lost strength. "You started this war."

"And we shall finish it." Joseph stepped to the chest. He didn't want to think of war or the lives lost to raids. Not when he had to figure how best to get her back in. "You and your people need to go home and leave us be."

"Home?" The word came with a gust he almost mistook for laughter.

Joseph frowned. She appeared quite wedged in place. He climbed onto the chest, and one of her legs bent up, almost clipping him in the chin. "Hold still."

She kicked out at him. "I don't want your help."

Joseph caught her around the knees and held fast, while averting his gaze. It was wrong for a young woman to be clothed in such tight leggings without the proper tunic to hide her form. Best he think of her as the boy he'd first believed her to be. A difficult task as he slid his hand around her slender waist.

She gasped and froze.

Releasing her legs, he braced against the wall and pulled her upward. He lifted her backwards, and she rotated toward him. Her hand gripped his sleeve and her head appeared through the window. He held her with both arms, steadying her on her feet and against him.

Her eyes widened as they rose to his. Light brown eyes. Surprisingly so, with irises the color of pine sap and framed with long, black lashes.

Her gaze darted away, and she wriggled from his hold.

The force sent Joseph from his already precarious perch, and he dropped off the chest and stumbled back until he fell onto the bed. "You could have said thank you." He pushed up on his elbows and narrowed a glower at her.

She cradled her injured arm. Fresh blood reddened the fabric wrapping it. "Why would I thank you for locking me in here?"

Joseph pushed any guilt away with the sight of his broken window. Pa had brought the glass all the way from Boston for Mama, and he had no way of replacing it without going as far as Albany. What would it cost? "If you want to leave that badly, go ahead." He rolled to his feet. "I don't have time for this." He had work to do.

A muscle ticked in her cheek, and her eyes

sparked. She spun and strode out the door.

"Don't go near any of my horses," he shouted, and then huffed out a breath as his anger abated. Couldn't very well send her away with nothing. He hurried to the table and shoved a handful of Rachel's biscuits into a sack with a chunk of soft cheese, but by time he made it outside there was no sign of the girl. The barn sat silent. Hunter and the black filly he had traded for a year earlier grazed in their separate paddocks. No sign that his life had been disrupted.

5

Her struggle in the window had been unkind to her wound. Hannah tried her best to ignore the live coal planted just above her elbow and the sticky wetness down her arm...and the memory of Joseph Garnet's arms around her as he'd braced her against his chest. He'd smelled of fresh turned soil and a wheat field ready for harvest—a fragrance that lingered in her thoughts and confused her. She wasn't a young girl anymore watching her neighbor's son groom the horses or plow a field. Her heart shouldn't race, and her stomach should have held steady. She'd had a chance to face him, to beg him to tell what he knew of her brothers' fates.

Instead, she'd lost her mind and ran.

As Hannah neared the homestead where Papa had settled their family, thoughts of Joseph faded. A strange sort of nostalgic excitement tightened her insides. A lifetime had passed since they'd been forced from their precious valley.

The afternoon sun warmed the chill from the air but not from the breeze as Hannah stepped into the small clearing where she had worked beside Mama and played with her siblings. Tall grass and weeds already claimed the once well-tamped path leading to the cabin Papa had so painstakingly constructed for his Mohawk wife and their four children. Now only blackened boards and smoke-stained stones of the fireplace marked what had been home.

Hannah's steps slowed. Ash. Only ash. What had she expected to find? Her brothers had been taken away the night the Patriots had set torches to the cabin. They were old enough to serve the rebel cause and would be compelled to do so. Old enough? Yes, Myles had been almost a man at sixteen, but Samuel was two years her junior. What sort of brutes forced a mere boy into their army?

Joseph Garnet.

Memories of him rose despite her attempts to push them back. He'd ridden with the men that day, along with his father. But James Garnet's face had worn a different, kinder look. He hadn't been there to evict a woman and her children from their home. Joseph, however, had looked down at her family with his blue eyes glazed with cold disinterest.

So similar to the look he'd worn when she'd fled his cabin.

Hannah climbed through the charred ruins. She sank to the black and crumbling beam that had held up the roof, facing what was left of the fireplace, eyes clamped closed against reality and the utter loneliness burrowing through her. She'd been foolish to return here. Nothing was left.

Nothing that would help her locate her brothers.

Doubt strangled her. After so many years forced to fight a war, what were the odds Myles and Samuel were even still alive?

Hannah swiped a trickle of moisture from her chin. She didn't try to keep her cheeks dry. Though only five or six when Papa built this cabin, she remembered him taking his time to fit the logs tight so little chink was needed. He'd always hungered for adventure, and maybe that was the reason he had gone to fight for the King, but his skill had been with wood. Now, most everything he'd created for his family was reduced to ash. Even the doll and cradle he'd made her, and she'd passed to her little sister.

In the shelter of the meadow, the sun's heat beat down on Hannah's head without the interruption of a breeze. She opened her eyes to blackened hands and wiped them across her shirt. Time to say goodbye and begin her search in earnest.

At the river's edge, Hannah washed the black from her hands, the paint from her face, and the blood streaks from her arm. Her shirt and leggings still wore the dirt and grime of three days' travel. The glistening water beckoned. She gasped at the cold as she waded out to her knees in a cove protected from the main current. She was in no condition to swim. Shivers worked through her body as she submerged herself, clothes and all, in the icy embrace.

Though well over a month since the last of the snow had melted, the sun had little effect on the temperature of the water. She scrubbed out her shirt and hair as quick as she could with one hand, but by the time she stepped back onto the bank, her body trembled like a frightened colt and her teeth chattered. She rested on a rock in the sun for a few minutes to warm, before turning back toward the Garnet homestead. As much as she didn't look forward to facing Joseph again, he was her best hope of finding her brothers.

The twitter of birds and soft whoosh of her feet on the littered ground followed her to the acres of cleared field lined with the deep furrows Joseph planted. Shirtsleeves billowing and his cocked hat nestled low on his head, he dropped seed with steady rhythm from the sack looped over his shoulders.

Hannah hesitated at the edge of the woods though her heart continued racing. She would not blame him for running her off, but she needed to leave her pride and anger behind. She squared her shoulders and started toward him, her focus alternating between him and not rolling her ankle as she made her way over the deep ridges of earth. The closer she got, the harder it became to look away from him, the breadth of his shoulders and the wheat-blond locks tied at the nape of his neck. If possible, the last few years had only made him more handsome. But they were enemies. And he had married Fannie.

Joseph's head jerked up, and he narrowed a look at her.

Hannah stopped and braced for what he would say.

Waited for it.

From the top of her wet head, to her moccasined feet, he studied her. Then, with only a bit of a grunt, he twitched his head toward the cabin.

She reminded herself of a skittish foal as she scampered past. This time she would wait until he was ready to talk. Only a few paces from the door, she dodged out of sight.

The jangle of harnesses and thudding of hooves accompanied a wagon as it turned onto the property. She peeked around the corner of the cabin to make out the gentleman from the day before, and a woman, babe in arms, on the seat beside him.

Rachel Garnet—or whatever her name was now—and her family.

Hannah darted into the cabin and pressed the

door closed. How had the years and this war changed Rachel? Though probably not as informed as her brother, perhaps she would make an easier ally.

The ends of Hannah's hair dripped water down the back of her shirt. A man's shirt. And a man's leggings. She would have more success winning over the sister if she didn't still look like a member of a raiding party.

~*~

Joseph stood in place, his fist closed around a handful of seed, the image of the Mohawk maiden frozen in his mind. She was the last thing he had expected when he'd raised his gaze to the horizon. A deer, a hare, or fox scurrying over his freshly plowed field. Any rodent would have made sense, but instead *she* was there, wending her way toward him.

Why?

She'd wanted to escape bad enough to wedge herself in a broken window. Why return?

And why was there a familiarity about her–even more so now her face was clean.

Joseph emptied his hand back into the sack on his shoulder. No doubt she had made it as far as the river and gained an appreciation of her predicament. Had she actually tried to swim with her arm as it was? What else would account for her saturated appearance? While his conscience eased, his gut tightened with the fact he still didn't know what to do with her. And that she'd looked far too beautiful.

Joseph groaned and pressed his fingers into his temples. The last thing he needed was to acknowledge any attraction to the girl. He'd already given his heart to a woman—a kind, wise, beautiful woman he still yearned for. The months had only numbed the ache, not removed it from the hole in his chest. He turned toward the cabin and compelled his legs to carry him in that direction. He only made it as far as the barn when the chatter of voices met him.

Rachel. And the children.

Joseph dropped his load inside the barn.

"I am no longer accepting of your decision, Joseph."

He swung to Andrew as he rounded the side of the barn. "What? Why on earth did you bring Rachel here?" Not that he didn't agree she needed to be informed, but he wished Andrew would have respected his initial request.

"As much as I attempted to let it alone, this whole situation has not ceased to torment me. It is most imprudent, Joseph. You are a single man, and she is a young woman. For you to remain here alone together–"

"Surely you do not think I would take advantage of her." He bristled at the insinuation. "As far as I am concerned, she might as well be the boy she is clothed as." And yet he couldn't forget the shapely form of her legs undisguised by leggings, or the way her wet shirt had molded to a distinctly feminine figure, her long hair draped over her curves. Joseph looked at Andrew, only to find his penetrating gaze narrowed at him. "What?"

"I think you should to come to the cabin with me and tell your sister."

"Is that why you brought her?" No doubt she would gladly step in and tell him exactly what to do with their guest. And most likely, as with Captain

Andrew Wyndham, she would be correct. And he would be wrong. And the situation would again be out of his hands.

"Joseph, I have not ceased praying since I left you yesterday."

Now even God was against him. "So you're speaking as my pastor?"

"And as your friend and brother."

"Very well." He had already decided to tell Rachel anyway. Hadn't he? He'd been so back and forth it was hard to remember his final thoughts. He waved Andrew toward the cabin.

It appeared Rachel had taken the children inside, so the *introductions* may have already been made. What would his sister make of the wild girl?

Joseph slid to a halt at the open door.

Rachel, his baby girl on her hip, wrapped her free arm around a young woman in a pale yellow gown. Fannie's gown. Moist dark hair had been twisted up on the back of her head, revealing a slender neck…and too much of the dark bruise he'd laid across her fine jaw.

"However did you come to be here, Hannah?"

Joseph jerked to his sister. "Hannah?"

Rachel returned his stare. "Why is she here if you don't remember who she is? And surely you remember the Cunninghams? They were our neighbors until…" Rachel's mouth tightened, and she glanced to the younger woman.

"Cunningham? Hannah Cunningham?" Joseph sounded like a fool repeating her name, but he couldn't help himself. "Hannah Cunningham." How had he not recognized her? They'd been neighbors for almost three years, and she'd always been here, leaning over the fence to watch the horses. He walked to the table and deposited his pistol there. He needed to distance himself.

"I came to visit my family's old homestead." Hannah's lips curved, and her eyes twinkled with mischief. "Joseph was kind enough to give me a place to spend the night."

Rachel smiled. "He has learned a few manners over the years."

A jolt of laughter broke from Joseph. It was only a matter of time before Rachel noticed the brace for the bar he'd built over the bedroom door. Or questioned the bruise on Hannah's cheek.

His sister gave him a searching look, and then reached out to squeeze Hannah's arm. "I'm just glad to know you're safe. What they did to your family—"

A shrill screech broke off Rachel's sentiment.

Hannah bit down on her lip, her hand hovering over her covered wound.

"I'm so sorry. What happened to your arm?"

Hannah waved her away with a sideways glance at the two men. "I gouged it on a branch."

Andrew moaned and stepped forward. "Let us not heap lies upon our wrongdoings."

Rachel twisted to him and hitched the baby higher on her hip. "What wrongdoings?"

He looked to Joseph, his eyes showing a degree of panic.

Joseph shook his head—he already had enough to answer for—and motioned for Andrew to continue.

"Will anyone tell me what happened?" Rachel demanded.

Andrew brushed his knuckles along his jaw and faced his wife. "I shot her."

"You *shot* her?"

He winced. "At the time, I believed her to be making an attempt on your brother's life."

Joseph took that as his cue to come to Andrew's defense. "Which I am quite certain she was." He indicated the thin remains of the scratches down his cheek. "And I had no way of knowing she was a woman at the time."

"It's true, Rachel." Hannah's voice wavered, and she cleared it. "I–"

A yelp of pain echoed from the bedroom. James. In a room still littered with broken glass.

6

Every time Hannah ventured a glance at Joseph she found his gaze steadfast on her, eyes brooding. An attractive expression on him, but she could only imagine the storm brewing inside. Especially since she was the cause of his child's cut finger. Only one more offence added to a growing heap. The broken window. His wife's gown. Returning to the valley after her family had been compelled to leave. Keeping her identity from him.

After they'd washed and bandaged little James's cut, Hannah stood back and let the men explain the events that had brought her here. The young boy hardly seemed affected by his injury now and followed Joseph, pacing the floor with him. When he tired, he hugged Joseph's leg and called "Papa," until he was picked up. Obviously Joseph and Fannie's child—though Hannah still didn't understand Fannie's absence. She might be visiting her family, but reason spoke otherwise. Especially since the baby Rachel now cradled under a blanket to nurse looked much more Reid than Garnet or Wyndham, and what mother would willingly leave her baby for any length of time?

Hannah slipped into the chair closest Rachel, her one ally. The very gentlemanly Andrew Wyndham seemed kind-hearted as well–or at least penitent for having wounded her.

Joseph, on the other hand…a cloud had fallen over

him since hearing her name. His face had lost most of its color, and the blue in his eyes appeared almost gray.

"Perhaps she will now tell us her true intent for coming here." The rasp in Joseph's voice yanked Hannah back to the ongoing discussion. "I can't believe it was to visit the burnt-out remains of a place she once lived."

"Joseph!" Rachel gaped at her brother.

Leave it to Joseph Garnet to remove any sentiment from something once held dear.

"No, Rachel, he's right. Ashes hold nothing for me now." The moment had come, and both fear and anticipation skittered through Hannah. "Though I had hoped, perhaps foolishly, that I might…" She held Joseph's cool gaze, inwardly compelling him to know something about her brothers. "I'd hoped I might find some clue as to what became of Samuel and Myles. I have heard nothing of them since they were taken. And now there is only me. I have to know what happened to them." The words spilled from her and she couldn't dam them. "I must know if they still live. Have you heard anything?"

"I haven't." Joseph's answer was too quick.

Hannah hugged herself, hardly mindful of her arm. She swallowed down a swell of emotion. "But surely someone in the settlement must know where they were taken. Or where they would be now." *If they've survived this long.* She compelled her voice to stay steady. "I won't give up. I won't stop looking until I find them."

Rachel's hand squeezed hers. "Your mother and the youngest are…?"

"Gone. Dead." Hannah swallowed against the tightness in her throat. "The past two winters have been miserable. Hundreds have died. Illness. Hunger." She would never be able to adequately express how it felt to watch those she loved best become victims of this never-ending war. Though pain radiated across the bridge of her nose and behind her eyes, she held the tears back as she centered her gaze on Joseph. "Samuel and Myles are all I have left. Please help me find them. I only ask for a direction—where to start my search."

Joseph turned and wiped his hand down his face.

His little boy studied him, and then patted his cheek.

"No, James, not right now." He set the youngster on the floor and recommenced his pacing.

The child went from his father to the cool fireplace where his fair-haired cousin, probably a year younger, joined him. With frequent glances at his father, James sat on the edge of the hearth. He seemed content enough.

Hannah looked at Joseph. Was he indeed raising his children without their mother? She leaned toward Rachel. "Fannie's dead?" she asked with a whisper.

Rachel frowned and gave a slight nod.

Poor Fannie. Hannah had never had any real care for the Reids, but to leave behind one's babies and a beloved husband–what tragedy could be greater?

"James, no!"

The boy stood with fistfuls of ash–thankfully cold. Instead of dropping his load back into the fireplace, he threw it into the little girl's face, and grabbed for more. The younger child screamed.

Andrew plucked up his daughter, while Rachel brought the baby out from under the blanket.

Hannah caught James's hands, which again

clenched ash.

"I can take him." Joseph plucked James off the floor. "He can come outside with me." He said it as though he'd planned to leave all along.

Perhaps that was his only answer for her.

Joseph stalked from the cabin, boy in arms, gray and black powder sprinkled across the floor. Andrew wrestled to calm the infant while he washed the soot from her eyes and face.

The baby joined in the chorus of wails.

Hannah stood helplessly by. She'd been mistaken to ask Joseph for any help. Obviously his life held no more room for complications.

~*~

His son's dirty hands the least of his worries, Joseph lifted the boy over his head and set him on his shoulders. "We have fields to plant, James. You want to help Papa?"

The exuberant nod banged against the top of Joseph's head. "Help Papa."

"Good." Joseph lengthened his stride. He needed to get away from Hannah Cunningham.

Rachel seemed only welcoming of the girl, but would she remember their long ago conversation when trying to decide the fate of a certain British officer?

"Surely you remember the way it was at the beginning of the war. The Cunninghams and others who professed their continuing loyalties to King George and Britain—they were considered a threat."

Everything short of murder was done until the Tories were driven out. They had fought at Oriskany four years earlier. The ones they had called neighbors.

"I even recognized some of them. Bayonets, the butts of our rifles, and even bare hands. That's how we killed each other."

Joseph's lungs trembled for breath.

Hannah Cunningham.

Her parents were dead. Only her brothers remained. Brothers forced from their family and into a war. One had only been a boy, and the other not quite a man. Had they survived the bloodshed that had drenched this land? Would it be possible to find them? Or would the search only bring Hannah more heartache?

Ducking into the barn so James didn't bump his head, Joseph strode to the satchel that held seed. He would return to the fields so he could provide for his family. He was almost finished with the wheat, but the corn still needed to be planted. And most of the garden. Much of his time would also be spent helping Andrew with their planting. There was too much work to do to sit around thinking about the past.

He set James on the ground and loaded himself down with seed. Now that he knew who she was, it was impossible to not recognize Hannah. Though many of her features were inherent from her Mohawk mother, her bright brown eyes, straight nose and fairer complexion were her father's.

Henry Cunningham.

Swallowing back a wave of nausea, Joseph thrust his hand into the grain and gripped a handful. "Come on, James, follow Papa."

Little James's sandy head bobbed, and he scampered after him. "Papa."

Joseph paused. "I'm waiting for you."

Though James had lost much of his baby appearance, his fat cheeks still jiggled when he ran.

The rutted terrain did not make it easy for the youngster, and more than once James stumbled over the uneven earth. When they reached where Joseph had left off, he filled his son's small hands.

"You help Papa plant, all right? Drop them in the furrow. Like this."

His boy spread his fingers wide, shook the seed free and turned to Joseph. "More."

"Let me finish mine first."

A soft whoosh, like the wind through the nearby woods, slowed Joseph's movements, and he glanced at the solid wall of trees. Nothing. Not even a breeze. Or bird song. Probably a deer, but the hair prickled on the back of his neck as he filled his son's hands once again. His ears stayed attuned to the woods and the silence…and then the snapping of a twig. "Come here, James." Joseph took a slow step toward his son, who had moved farther along the furrow to scatter his seed.

Thwack.

An arrow dug into the soil only inches from where James crouched.

Joseph snatched his son from the ground and pivoted to shield the child. Not that he would provide much protection once he was dead. "Oh, Lord, save my boy." *My children.*

He sprinted to the barn, his pulse choking him as he waited for the razor tip of another arrow to spear his back. But they reached cover before an arrow struck the door they had just passed through. In the nearby pasture the milk cow's sharp bellow announced death. Keeping James tight against him, Joseph stole a look at the crumpled beast. An arrow protruded from low in its neck. A killing shot.

A message. It had to be. They had spared human

lives, but for what purpose?

Only one came to mind.

Hannah Cunningham. They were here for her.

Joseph hugged James and pressed a kiss to the fine hair on the top of his young head. If the raiding party had not missed on purpose, his son would be dead, as would he. And then the fire would come. Though Andrew had a good eye and a straight aim, he wouldn't be able to hold them off on his own. Rachel and the babies would be left to the same fate as the woman they had saved from her burning home. Or worse.

What would save them once the raiding party got what they'd come for?

~*~

The cow's bawl carried a pain Hannah was too familiar with. Death. She rushed to the window, only to be jerked aside.

"Stay back," Andrew ordered, his voice hoarse. He grabbed the musket from over the door and loaded it with a speed she'd not expected from the gentleman.

"What's happening?" Rachel was on her feet, the baby asleep in her arms. "What about Joseph and little James?"

"I cannot tell. Not from here." In a step, Andrew leaned against the wall beside the door and eased it open a crack. He scanned the area. "If anything happens to me, bar the door. If there are raiders, break the windows and fight them off. Do not let them near the cabin." He widened the door as though he planned to slip out.

"Where are you going?" Rachel questioned.

He didn't look back. "To get Joseph." Andrew's knuckles showed white where he gripped the musket.

"Don't." Hannah threw her back against the door, slamming it closed.

"What are you doing?"

What *was* she doing? What did she need to do? Hannah snatched the pins from her hair. She should have anticipated this, planned for it. Otetiani would have returned for her after the Patriots left. He'd have found her tracks that led to Hunter, his large hooves and heavy frame making the trail easy to follow. Her skirmish with Joseph would have said she had not come of her own will. She'd brought him and his warriors here. If Joseph, or his son, or anyone else was killed, it would be her doing. Her sin. "I need to stop this."

"Is that within your power?"

Hannah, glanced from Andrew's questioning to Rachel's wide eyes. Her look encompassed the children. "Let us hope it is."

7

"You need to stay here, and stay silent." Joseph tucked the saddle blanket around his son. In a dark corner, squeezed between a manger and the wall, James would remain out of sight and safe…so long as the barn wasn't set to fire.

"No leave, Papa!" James grabbed his leg when he started to stand.

Joseph crouched back down and gripped his son. *Oh, God, how can I do this?* How could he leave his child here with nothing more than a prayer? "I won't be far. Papa needs to chase the raiders away, and then I'll be back for you. I promise." A promise he was wrong to make. He'd never felt more sure of that. He fished Grandfather Garnet's gold timepiece from his pocket and pushed it into his son's hands. "You hold this for Papa, all right. But you have to stay quiet. Keep quiet so Papa can keep you safe."

And alive.

The little boy whimpered, but his protests ended.

"I'll be right back for you." Joseph tucked the blanket back over his head and kissed his brow. "Papa loves you." He smoothed his hand over the boy's tousled hair. Hopefully his son would survive and remember that much.

By the time Joseph reached the barn door, the raiding party had moved their mounts to the edge of the field, just beyond the reach of the woods. Five warriors–their skin painted in reds and blacks, foreheads shaved high, hair pulled back with feathers and other ornamentation–evoked sufficient horror, but undoubtedly more hid out of sight, bows taut, muskets loaded.

He was weaponless. All these years of training himself to never leave the cabin without a weapon, and yet his pistol remained where he'd set it on the table. Thanks to Hannah Cunningham. He hadn't been able to think straight since learning her identity. Joseph glanced back inside the barn. He didn't have many options.

The door to the cabin creaked open, and Hannah strode across the yard toward the fields, her black hair wild past her shoulders as she pulled the last of the pins from it. Fannie's gown swooshed around her legs with each step.

Joseph's chest clenched. His mind screamed to grab her out of harm's way, but he held himself at bay. These were her people. They would take her north with them to where she belonged.

Would they then be appeased? Or would they seek retribution as well?

He had to get to the cabin. He was of no use to anyone out here. But he would be an easy target without some form of cover.

Hannah paused as she passed the barn, and glanced back.

Or a hostage.

Her gaze froze on his, and he motioned to her. She shook her head.

"Hannah."

"I can't." She turned away.

Couldn't what? Help them? Not that he deserved

her mercy or assistance, but no one else had done anything against her.

He couldn't let everyone he held dear suffer because of his mistakes. Four long strides, and Joseph wrapped her in his arms. Keeping his profile low, he lifted her feet off the ground and hauled her backwards with him. An arrow swooshed past his ear and sank into the wood of the barn door beside the last one. Inside, he loosened his grip on Hannah only to get his chest smacked.

She tried to shove him back, but he wouldn't budge.

"What are you doing?" She hit him again.

"What are *you* doing?"

"Trying to save you and–" Her eyes widened and her head jerked from right to left, searching the shadows. Color drained from her face as it took on a look of terror.

"I told James to hide."

Air whooshed from her lungs and she slapped her palm against his chest again. "Do you have any idea…?" She struggled against his hold. "Let me go."

"Not until you help save my family."

A spark lit in her eyes. "Don't you think I'm trying to?" Her chin tipped up, and sharp pain bit his shin. Twisting away, she rushed the door.

He grabbed her arm.

"You are only making it worse."

Her words stung even more than her kick. What if he was putting his family at greater risk by trying to keep her here? Maybe their best hope was to trust her. "All right." He let go.

She stepped into the doorway. "I remember your mama when she was sick, sitting in her rocking chair at the front of the cabin so she could read her Bible in the sunlight. Your Pa was a believing man, too." Hannah glanced back, her large eyes seeming darker. "I don't know anything about your God, but perhaps you should pray." She stepped out from the protection of the barn. Hem lifted, she strode toward the war-painted Mohawks.

His heart thudded and squeezed so tight he could scarce take a breath. A whimpering cry pulled him to where James huddled, tear stains streaking his full cheeks. "Come here," Joseph whispered. He folded his arms around his little son and bowed his head. "We need to ask God for help." They would soon know with certainly if He took any interest in their lives.

~*~

Hannah could hardly hear past the rush of her pulse in her ears. She wasn't concerned with her own safety. Her cousin's large bay pawed the soft field. She tucked her hair behind her ears and jogged across the deep ruts.

"You did not stay where I told you." Speaking in *Kanien'kéha,* he motioned to the mare he had given her to ride, now with one of the other braves astride.

"I am sorry," she answered in her mother's tongue.

"And these men took you?" He aimed a glare at the barn and cabin, his expression fierce under *onegonsera,* the crimson painted across his eyes and forehead.

"They were trying to help me." Perhaps not the full truth, but not a lie either. "They can help me find my brothers."

"No." He extended his hand. "You will come now. We go."

Hannah only took one step. "But…" Joseph had given her no answer about whether he would help her, but she still believed he could.

"They hate you like they hate us. You are not safe here."

And yet, strangely, that was the one thing she felt sure of. She was safe. "I need to find my brothers."

He glared. It did not seem to matter to him that they'd had no choice but to join the Continental Army. "I will seek them."

"No." That wouldn't work. Couldn't work. Where would they even start looking? How many farms would burn, and people would die before they found any answers? They couldn't walk into one of the forts or settlements and simply ask about her brothers. If anything, Otetiani would only place her brothers in more danger. "I want to stay here. Joseph Garnet has promised to help me. You must leave his home and fields alone so he can do so without fear." *Please.*

Jaw strung tight, Otetiani looked out across the acres of clearing to the homestead. "This Joseph Garnet is a man of honor?"

"Yes." At least his father had been.

"Then I will speak with him."

Hannah froze. Did she trust her cousin with Joseph's life? "No."

He crossed his arms, a smug look on his face. "I will not leave you here until I have spoken with this man."

No other choice remained then, except to leave with him. She couldn't do that. "As you wish." Hannah turned back to the barn.

Joseph's tall frame filled the doorway.

He would probably never agree to her cousin's request. Still, she had to ask, and hope all this could be resolved without anyone dying.

Joseph frowned as she drew near. "What did he say?"

"He wants to speak with you." At Joseph's rippled brow, she sneaked a breath and rushed on. "I told him you promised to help find my brothers, but he says he will not leave me here until he has spoken with you."

"You really believe he plans on talking, or does he merely want an easy scalp?"

"He asked if you were a man of honor. My cousin is, as well." If only she could summon more confidence. Otetiani had given no guarantees of Joseph's safety.

"And if I don't? What do you think he'll do?"

Hannah's fears piled up as she glanced from the cabin to the warriors. "I don't know."

Joseph nodded. "Tell him I will come as soon as I've delivered my son safely to the cabin."

"I'll tell him." She turned to go.

"And Hannah."

She glanced at him.

"If I survive this–if my family survives this–I *will* help you find your brothers."

"Thank you." Though she guessed the promise was made more for his own sake than for hers. If Otetiani did turn to anger, how much did Joseph stand to lose?

Everything.

She raced back, out of breath by time she reached the warriors who had now dismounted. She repeated Joseph's message and watched the ridges lining

Otetiani's frown deepen.

"He has a wife, then?"

"No, his wife died with the birth of their second child." At least that's what evidence suggested. Envy and pity mingled into a feeling she didn't recognize.

Joseph appeared around the side of the barn, arms empty, hat low on his head, and movements stiff.

Hannah tensed. She could imagine what it felt like to walk toward what might be his execution. "You must promise me you won't harm him."

Otetiani's eyes narrowed. "His life matters so much to you?"

Hannah couldn't remove her gaze from the lone figure as he approached. "I gave him my word that you wish only to speak." But she couldn't deny the raw fear.

"Then I shall speak. And you will tell him my words."

"Of course."

Joseph stopped several yards off and raised his hands from his sides so his lack of weapons was evident.

"Waneek says you are a man of honor, and she trusts you to help find her brothers. Is this the truth?"

Hannah translated, leaving her Mohawk name as spoken.

Joseph looked to her, and then back to Otetiani. "Yes. I will do all I am able."

"I ask one more thing–that you take her to shelter and provide for her as your wife."

Only half the words made it past Hannah's throat before it closed off. She rotated to her cousin. "*Yáh*!" How could he demand such a thing without first asking her?

Instead of heeding her, Otetiani spoke to Joseph, his English faulty but clear. "I not leave her unless she your *Tiakení:teron*."

Joseph looked to her. "I don't understand."

Hannah suddenly felt cold. "He says he won't leave unless I am your wife."

8

His wife?

Joseph had been braced for an arrow to the heart, not a suggestion of marriage. What would result if he refused? Something warm tickled his neck, and he swiped at a bead of sweat. He studied Hannah. Surely this was not her idea. Her cheeks flushed with scarlet as she argued with whom he assumed was Otetiani–her relation. He'd seen the man before, but never so close. And never without a weapon in hand.

"What do you decide?"

Joseph forced his hands to remain relaxed at his sides. "I don't think she wants to be my..." He wouldn't attempt the word the Mohawk leader used. "Wife."

The man did not appear pleased.

Joseph glanced from Hannah, hair again flowing down her back and shoulders, to the cabin holding everyone he loved. He couldn't risk their lives. And he did need a mother for his children. *To shelter and provide for*. He owed her that much, didn't he? Joseph gulped back the nagging of his conscience. He couldn't think about that right now. "But I am willing."

Hannah's eyes widened at him, and he managed a nod. What other choice did he have? He was unarmed against over a dozen Mohawk warriors, and his family's fate hung precariously.

Hannah grabbed his arm and dragged him out of

earshot of the others. "He cannot force me to do this. In our traditions, a woman has her choice in marriage."

So she could walk away and leave him to whatever fate Otetiani decided. Not comforting. "Perhaps, but I get the feeling your relation will not take my refusal lightly. Why is he so set on you marrying?"

"He says I am much like my father and would be happier with his people. Where so many of our men have died, and with the clans displaced, he says it is better for me to find a husband elsewhere." She sighed and hugged herself. "And because I seek my brothers…"

"Let me help you find them."

Two creases bunched between her large brown eyes. "You want to go through with this?"

Guilt for his deeper reasoning speared him—reasoning both to take responsibility for her, and remain at arms' length. "I want my family safe. And I want to help you find your brothers."

Uncertainty flickered in her eyes, but she nodded. "I shall speak with Otetiani." Her voice was much more resigned.

A few minutes later, Joseph made his way back over the rutted field toward the cabin. His one request was for who would perform the deed. The door jerked open before he even reached it, and he stepped inside.

"What's going on out there?" Rachel's tone was sharp enough to startle the baby. She rocked the child and lowered her voice. "Joseph?"

"Negotiations."

"Papa!" James attacked Joseph's legs, almost throwing him off balance.

Andrew shouldered the musket. "What kind of

negotiations?"

"A treaty of sorts." Joseph forced air into his depleted lungs as he lifted his son. "We need you to perform a marriage."

"A marriage…" Rachel froze. "You and Hannah?"

"Yes." He looked to Andrew. "Will you do it?"

"If you are certain."

Joseph nodded, though he wasn't certain at all. "I want Rachel and the children to stay here in case anything goes wrong. Bar the door and stay out of sight." He motioned to the gun Andrew held. "You'll probably want to leave that here."

"I imagine so." Andrew laid the musket on the table and kissed his wife.

"Come back to me."

A second kiss lengthened into a third, and Joseph turned away. He missed having someone to kiss like that, but held no hope for this marriage to Hannah Cunningham. If she knew the truth, she would likely never want anything to do with him. Joseph settled James with Rachel and started his return, his pace slower now.

"Are you sure there is no other option?" Andrew asked.

"I'm done fighting. I'm done risking my family." He glanced to where Fannie was buried. "I can't afford to lose anyone else."

"And Miss Cunningham? Is she willing?"

"She wants to find her brothers, and I have promised to help."

"And when she finds them? Marriage is not something to take lightly. You must consider the future."

Joseph spun. "You do not think the future is

foremost on my mind? Perhaps Hannah nor I desire this marriage, but without it I *am* confident there won't be a future. Not for this farm or my family. A future with Hannah is not my concern." He pushed his hat back from his moist brow. "It's the past."

"What do you mean?"

"What I am about to tell you, you must swear, as a clergyman, never to repeat to a living soul." Better for Hannah's sake that she never know.

~*~

Standing beside Joseph Garnet, the warmth of his arm brushing hers, did not seem real. Hannah should have convinced her cousin a marriage was not necessary, but instead she had agreed with him. She wasn't sure if it was the logic he had presented, or the memory of her girlhood dreams. Though her main reasons for visiting the Garnet farm as a girl had been to watch Joseph's horse, Hunter, and learn about horses from Joseph's pa, she couldn't deny her gaze had often followed after Joseph, as well. But he'd seemed so much older and had only ever seen her as a child.

Then Papa had left to fight for the British, her family had been driven out…and Joseph had sat watching with indifference.

She shifted so their arms wouldn't touch.

"I pronounce you husband and wife."

What have I done? Every reason she'd held for the ceremony fled at that final declaration.

Andrew Wyndham nodded toward them and stepped back, his lips pressed thin with evident disapproval.

Did he not understand she was doing her best to save their lives? Her cousin had agreed that as a member of their clan, Joseph would be afforded some protection. Brant had left for the Ohio Valley and Fort Detroit at the request of the British, but the others would be informed, and the Garnet farm would be spared from the raids.

A hand cupped Hannah's shoulder, and she looked at Joseph. Her husband.

He didn't appear much happier than his brother-in-law, but there was a softness in his blue eyes that surprised her. "I'll leave you to bid your kin goodbye."

To see that they left as promised.

Otetiani mounted his horse and signaled his men. Nothing held them here now.

Soon Hannah stood alone, the only one at the spot where she had promised her life to Joseph Garnet. "What have I done?" Setting her shoulders back–ignoring the throbbing of her arm–she steadied her breath. She had done what was necessary to keep searching for her brothers. She had to hold to the hope that Samuel and Myles still lived.

Then what?

Would she live with her brothers or continue on as Joseph's wife? Her heart did a strange sort of fluttery skip, and then a plummet. So many emotions swirled she wasn't sure what she felt. Anticipation, wonder, and nausea. She could only hope Joseph had matured into half the man his father had been. Swallowing down her fears for the time being, Hannah hurried after Joseph, over the field and past the barn.

He stepped to the open door of the cabin and glanced back. His chest heaved as he rotated to her.

She skidded to a stop.

"I suppose there are some things we should discuss." One corner of his mouth crept up. "Hannah Garnet."

Andrew nodded to her and slipped inside the cabin to where Rachel stood with a girl on each hip. Perhaps it was only the lighting, but she appeared very pale.

Joseph looked Hannah up and down before nodding for her to follow.

Panic rose within her. She gathered her hair and twisted it up, only she no longer had any pins. She hooped her hair into a knot and left it at that. She should have braided it again.

They rounded the corner of the barn, and Joseph paused, arms folded. His expression remained unreadable.

"When will we go after my brothers?" She also folded her arms, but immediately regretted the motion with her sore arm. "You promised to help me find them."

"And I shall."

"When?"

"I can't leave until the fields are all planted. You must know that."

She looked across the fields. "Yes. I know." Her father hadn't been much of a farmer—took more to trapping and hunting, but her mother's people were planters. Corn, beans, and squash–she knew the three sisters well.

"But then, I promise, I will go with you, and we will find out what happened to them."

Hannah had no choice but to accept.

"Your assistance would expedite our departure."

"Of course."

Joseph leaned into the log wall of the barn. "It's not just the planting I need help with."

"I expected as much."

"Little James."

Hannah's pulse sped. In the haste, she'd forgotten she'd become the mother of two young children.

"Rachel will keep the baby for now as she's still being nursed, but I think James is increasingly too much for my sister. She hasn't said anything, but keeping up with three children so young has become a challenge."

"Of course."

"But we can worry about those arrangements after your arm is healed. Is there anything else you feel we should talk about?" Something in Joseph's tone suggested a dare.

Several question fought for dominance, but she pushed them aside. One crowned over the rest–one she wasn't ready to ask. She didn't want to know his expectations now that she was his wife.

9

Joseph reined Hunter toward the barn and hurried to unsaddle and curry the weary animal. Bone deep exhaustion dragged his steps as he cared for the stallion and released him into the pasture.

The cabin sat silent and dark.

Perhaps Hannah had already retired for the night.

He couldn't blame her. After cleaning and hanging the dead cow in the barn so the meat wouldn't spoil, he'd insisted upon accompanying Andrew and Rachel home. He'd take no chances with raiders in the area. But what should have been a short ride became hours of discussion with his very concerned pastor and sister. The sun had slipped into its peaceful abyss, and he looked forward to doing the same.

Joseph lit a candle, filled the kettle and hooked it in the fireplace. The coals were banked inside, but the water would be warm enough for coffee tomorrow morning. He dipped water from the bucket someone had filled and took a drink of water before moving into the bedroom. A gust of cold air met him. A quilt still hung through the broken window. How had the wild girl he'd locked in this room the night before become his wife? He looked at the bed, no form apparent in the dim light. Where was his bride?

Smothering a yawn and a groan, Joseph fought the desire to lay down and not think about her. He plodded back outside and glanced around the moonlit terrain. "Hannah?"

Hunter was the only one to answer.

Joseph frowned. Maybe he didn't have a wife anymore? But surely she wouldn't have gone very far. Unless she'd taken his mare. Joseph circled past the well and smokehouse toward the far paddock.

Moonlight glinted off the mare's black coat.

Rubbing grit from his eyes, Joseph leaned into the rough rail fence. Where had the woman gone? That morning he'd considered it a blessing when she'd run out and disappeared. But now? He'd taken responsibility for her—before God and man. "Fool woman," he muttered, then jerked as a shadow moved.

A pale face looked toward him.

"Hannah?"

Black hair met the woolen shawl that draped over the yellow of the dress—no wonder he hadn't seen her in the dark. "What are you doing out here?"

Hannah's eyes, as dark as the night, shifted to watch the mare. "When is she due to foal?"

"Soon." Joseph sighed. He should have known where to look for Hannah Cunningham. This is where she'd always been after sneaking over from her family's homestead to watch the horses. The Cunninghams had owned a mare, but it was an old, swaybacked nag that her father had often taken hunting. The animal had probably been at Oriskany, as well.

"Is Hunter the sire?"

Hannah's question pulled him back from the downward spiral of his thoughts. "Yes."

"Should be a lovely foal then. Do you hope for a colt or a filly?"

It didn't matter. He just wanted to go to bed.

"The mare is a pretty thing, but I hope the foal takes after its father. I've always loved your pa's stallion."

And the stallion loved her in return. Only now did it make sense why Hunter had not balked when Hannah tried to steal him. The animal had known her, just as she'd known him.

"What happened to your pa?"

Weariness poured over his dismal thoughts. "He was killed."

"During a raid?"

"No. An ambush. Near Oriskany. Almost four years ago."

"The battle that summer?" Her voice broke.

Joseph nodded. Thank goodness the raiders had targeted a cow and not either of his horses.

"I was told my pa also died in that battle."

"A lot of men died there." Joseph closed his mind against the memories. He refused to return to that terrible day.

Hannah's fingers brushed his arm. "I'm sorry."

He looked at her, huddled in the shawl, the breeze teasing strands of dark hair against her cheeks. "I am, too. I'm sorry about your pa." He rushed on. "And I'm sorry about what happened to your family after he left."

Hannah stiffened and drew closer to the fence, farther from him. "And yet you were there with those men when they burned our cabin so we had no choice but to leave. You were there when they took my brothers."

Joseph faced the shadowy form of the horse again. How could he answer the question in her words without making her hate him more? He hadn't done anything. He'd simply been there.

The silence hung in the air.

"I thought as much." She pushed away from the fence.

"Pa wanted to make sure things didn't become violent. There was nothing we could do to stop them, but he wouldn't have let anyone get hurt."

"Your pa was a good man. I never questioned his involvement, or that he opposed what they did. But *you*, Joseph. I saw the look on your face. The approval. Why were *you* there?"

A surge of guilt weighed down on him. "I don't know."

"Of course you don't." She gave a shallow laugh. "You were just following your pa."

Joseph bristled. "All right. The truth is I think a man should be able to trust his neighbors." He understood the fears of the men who had driven the Loyalists from the settlement.

"Too bad the same cannot be afforded a woman and her children."

"Your pa was a true blue Tory and your ma's people had taken up arms with the British. And Myles. He was enough of a man to have an opinion, and he made it well enough known."

Hannah's hands went to her hips, and she winced. She glared at him. "Myles was hardly sixteen and his loyalty was to Pa, not the British. How can he be faulted for that? Admit it, even at the ripe old age of twenty, your opinions on the war and your loyalties were only a shadow of your own pa's!"

Joseph bit back a retort. He was too tired to match blows with his bride. Ha! What a laugh that was proving to be. Hopefully her brothers were still alive so they could take her off his hands. He'd probably live longer alone.

Except his children needed a mother. He had to find a way to convince her to stay with him, even if they found her brothers.

"I'm going to bed." She hurried to the cabin.

Joseph followed much slower. He was tempted to make a bed in the barn, but didn't have it in him. And there was no way he would spend another night in a chair. He wanted his own mattress, wonderful stuffed straw, and a heavy quilt—heavy enough to block out the chill blasting through the broken window, because that was one more thing he was too tired to take care of.

Inside the cabin, a dim light glowed from the bedroom. Hannah must have taken a candle with her. He stepped in to find her on the chest trying to hook a blanket over the opening with one hand, her injured arm against her body.

"Here, let me." He crossed the room to take the blanket from her.

Hannah jerked away. "I broke it, I can fix it."

"Unless you are hiding a pane of glass somewhere, you can't fix it. Boarding it up is the best we can do, but I'm not worrying about that until tomorrow. Now get down before you hurt yourself." He set his hands on her waist and lifted her to the floor.

Her palm slapped his arm. "You do not get to tell me what I can or cannot do. I don't care if I am your wife. You do not own me!" She shoved against his chest.

Joseph didn't budge. "Don't you know, a wife is her husband's property?"

She leveled a tight smile at him. "You would like that wouldn't you? Well, among my mother's people, men are the ones who leave their clans and join their wives. *Kanien'keha:ka* women are the heads of their families."

"And yet, you left your clan and joined me. You must take after your pa's side of the family."

Her smile grew as confidence lit her eyes—so similar to her pa's. "I'm enough like both my parents to stand up to you."

"And I..." Joseph looked at the little dark-haired cannonball who had pummeled his life, and all arguments fell away. "I don't doubt it."

What had he gotten himself into?

~*~

What had she gotten herself into? Hannah's pulse tripped as Joseph redirected his intrusive gaze. She wasn't sure if the heat radiating through her was due to their argument, or the realization she stood only two feet from this man's bed, and she was his wife. Her stomach dipped and swooshed, making her grateful she hadn't had an appetite for the beef Rachel had prepared for dinner. Though air flowed from the shattered window, Hannah needed more. She stepped around Joseph and hurried through the cabin. Once outside, she sucked in a breath.

"Don't leave."

She looked over her shoulder. Concern touched not only Joseph's voice, but his matured features. She had always thought him a handsome man, but the years had given definition to his face and sharpened the line of his jaw. Twin creases showed at the corners of his eyes—midnight blue in the low light of the candle he held.

"We should tend your arm after everything you've put it through today." Joseph fished into a pocket and withdrew a small leather pouch. "Rachel sent a salve back with me."

"That was thoughtful of her."

"Rachel has always been the thoughtful one. Unlike her brother."

She stared. Was he apologizing? And if so, for which offence?

"Come sit down." Joseph waved to one of the chairs. "The water in the kettle is already warm. I'm sure I can find some cloth to make fresh bandaging."

She obediently sat, and minutes later Joseph scooted a chair beside her. He touched the cuff of her sleeve and frowned. It embraced the arm too tightly to be rolled up past the wound. The only way she would be able to access the bandage was to withdraw her entire arm from the dress.

"Why don't you go to bed, and I'll see to this." It had been difficult to clean the open flesh or wrap the bandage yesterday, but she'd managed. Besides, he looked exhausted.

"Nonsense. I want to make sure it's not festering." He extended his hand to the top button, the tips of his fingers brushing her collarbone, sparking a fire within her.

Hannah pulled back.

A grunt rumbled in his throat, and he stood. "I'll finish covering the window in the bedroom while you pull your arm out. Wrap the shawl over your shoulders if you wish." He retreated to the other room.

If she wished? As though it made no difference to

him?

Hannah tugged the first button free. Maybe it didn't matter to him. He was accustomed to matrimony and all it entailed, while she…a man had never touched her so intimately before, and that was only the top button! Hannah didn't know what his expectations were for this marriage, but she certainly wasn't ready to be his wife.

She hurried to get her arm out and tucked the shawl over every inch of bare skin above the blood-tinged bandage. It still carried some of the dampness of her earlier bath in the river.

A tapping on the wall preceded Joseph's reentry. He returned to his chair without comment and unbound the cloth from her arm. Pain spiked across the area as he pulled it free from the wound.

"Careful."

He hummed his acknowledgment or apology, poured warm water from the kettle over a cloth, and then cleaned around the open flesh. With two fingers he scooped a generous amount of amber salve from the small pouch and wiped it across the new bandage before pressing it over her wound. Taking the ends of the fabric, he tied it off and stood.

"The area is warm and redder than it should be, so we'll want to replace the bandages regularly. Rachel can keep James until you're done healing. What you need most is rest." He nodded toward the bedroom, before taking up the basin. "I'll clean up."

Keeping the shawl tight, Hannah rushed into the smaller room and closed the door. Mindful of her throbbing arm, she slipped from the gown, put on a shift she found in the chest, and dived under the covers. She pulled the quilt up to her chin.

The door swung open, and Joseph strode across the room. The bedframe creaked as he sat on the edge of the mattress and pulled off his boots.

Hannah tightened the blanket around her as he drew his shirt over his head. "You can't sleep in here."

A harrumph joined the shifting of the mattress as he stretched out. "It's my bed."

And she was his wife, but Hannah didn't want to think about any of the implications. Neither did she dare remove herself, feeling quite naked in the light shift she'd borrowed.

Joseph blew out the candle he'd set on the small table and settled beside her. Not quite touching, but heat radiated from him. He rolled on his side, facing away, and his breathing deepened.

Hannah lay awake, her heart continuing its drumming.

He didn't move again.

Darkness and silence lay over them. Her mind, however, screamed to keep her distance from this man who had only become her husband to save his home and family. She could not blame him, but she would be wise not to develop any form of affection for him.

10

The rooster's early morning serenade grated Joseph's nerves. Or maybe it was knowing he'd overslept. With a yawn, he stretched out his bare arms and settled onto his back. The emptiness of the bed beside him remained a cold reminder of everything he had lost. He looked over at the flattened blankets. The room was dark, the window blocked up with a blanket, the only light a glow through the open doorway.

Hannah.

Where had she gone?

Rolling out of bed, Joseph hit his knees hard on the floor, and flopped his forehead into the mattress. Since he was down here... "Dear Lord, bless this day, bless the planting, bless my family, and..." Hannah's face infiltrated his thoughts, but he wasn't sure what more to say, so he ended the prayer and pushed to his feet.

Boots on and shirt in hand, he walked into the large room. The air still held the night's chill. He'd light the fire before heading out to do chores. But first, what to do with his new wife?

Hannah sat in the same chair she had the evening before, her arms and head draped over the table, eyes closed. The large shawl had slipped from her arm, bearing a shoulder and the bandage.

He tried to focus on the latter. It appeared not to have bled much in the night, but she would never get the rest she needed hunched in a hard chair.

Draping his shirt over the back of the neighboring chair, Joseph moved his hand over her shoulder, skin so smooth.

She groaned, but remained asleep.

He crouched and slid his other arm under her knees. Then lifted.

A sigh lengthened as she leaned her head on his chest and sagged against him. Her long eyelashes fluttered open. A jumble of Mohawk words rolled from her tongue as she jerked upright, almost causing him to drop her. She wriggled. "Let me go. Don't touch me."

"I only meant to take you to bed." He set her down on her feet.

"I don't want to go to your bed. I won't do it."

Do what? Joseph opened his mouth to ask, but shook the thought from his head. "You need more sleep."

She swayed.

Waiting for her to listen was ridiculous. He scooped her up and hauled her into the bedroom.

"Let me down!"

Joseph tightened his grip to keep her from falling. Just as he loosened his hold, a sharp elbow plowed into his ribs and he doubled over, dropping her onto the mattress. His shins met the frame, and his momentum sent him on top of her. He caught himself before he squished her, his arms braced on either side.

Hannah stared up at him.

He shoved away. "Stop fighting me."

"Stop touching me."

Her words stung more than expected, but he gave a smug smile. "You don't have to worry about that." He turned on his heel and strode out of the room—out of the cabin. Goosebumps scurried up his arms and across his torso. He hugged his bare chest. He'd forgotten his shirt.

Just what he needed—something to make him go back inside. Joseph filled his lungs and let the fire in his gut dissipate. He reached near the door and snatched his coat and hat from the peg, but there was no way he was going back inside and chance another tussle. He'd finish the chores first.

~*~

Hannah sat on the edge of the bed, Joseph's last words pricking like hornet stings. Festering. Swelling. Hurting.

You don't have to worry about that.

Because he didn't want to come anywhere near her. Not like a husband or a man in love. She had been the price of his family's safety, and he'd paid, but that was all she'd ever be worth to him. Nothing had changed since she was a girl. No attraction. No feelings. Just as well.

Hannah found her leggings and oversized shirt she'd washed the day before. They were dry enough now. She changed, braided her hair, and put thoughts of marriage—real marriage—from her mind. What did it matter that Joseph didn't want her? She didn't want him, either. She only needed his help to find her brothers. His rejection was merely to her pride.

In the main room, the fireplace coals were banked. She found kindling on the hearth and encouraged a flame to life. Perhaps she would fix one of Pa's favorites and prove to Joseph that she would not be a burden on him.

There was no sign of Joseph when she sneaked out to the barn and found eight eggs and cut a thin slab of meat. The fire was hot enough by the time she returned to start cooking.

The browned meat graced a plate, and she was spooning some of the eggs on beside it when footsteps announced Joseph's arrival. Hannah set the skillet on the table and swept her braids over her shoulders. But she couldn't simply stand there waiting when he walked in. She had to be busy with something. As the door latch dipped, she spun to the fireplace and grabbed the poker to thrust into the coals.

"Joseph?"

The man entered the cabin, his cane swinging with his steps. Benjamin Reid swiped the hat from his dark hair. Questioning marked his brow only momentarily. "You're the bit of difficulty that sent Joseph and Andrew running home with hardly an explanation, aren't you?"

Hannah chose not to answer. Not that she feared Benjamin Reid. It was his son with the temper and reckless behavior who had always concerned her.

"You're one of Henry Cunningham's girls, aren't you?"

A shadow appeared behind him. One of his own daughters—the one her age.

"Pa, are the…" Nora gaped at Hannah for a full minute before wiping her hands across her gown and stepping fully into the cabin. "You look familiar."

"I should." She set the fire poker back in its place. "I lived not a mile from here."

"Hannah Cunningham." Nora smiled—looking far too much like Fannie. All the Reids carried similar traits, dark brown waves and equally dark eyes.

Hannah gave a nod, not sure if she should correct them. Perhaps the Reids would not think kindly of their sister and daughter so quickly replaced. Joseph and Fannie's baby girl looked well under a year.

"What are you doing here?" Nora asked, but not in an unkind way.

"Joseph has agreed to—"

The deep guttural sound of Joseph clearing his throat in the doorway behind them stopped her words. He excused himself to go past the Reids, two eggs in hand. "Morning, Benjamin. Nora."

"Good morning, Joseph." Benjamin followed him to the table. "Our planting is almost finished so Nora thought she could help mind the children. We wanted to check with you first to make sure they aren't here before heading down to the Wyndhams."

"Rachel has them now. But any help I'm sure will be appreciated." Joseph took a bowl from the shelves running along the wall next to the fireplace and set the eggs inside. "Hannah will be staying for the last of the planting as well, but she has an injury she needs to let heal."

Hannah's gaze sank to the floor. No mention of their marriage. Only that she would be here while they sowed the fields. And then what? They would find her brothers, and Joseph would be rid of her.

And she would be rid of him.

"If you want to wait here, Nora," Joseph smiled, "Rachel and Andrew will be along later with the children. You've probably had breakfast already, but you are both welcome to sit down with us."

Nora circled nearer. "We've eaten, but I don't mind lending Hannah a hand." Her lips curved up as her dark eyes gazed innocently at Joseph. Though her features were softer, not as striking as Fannie's had been, Nora was still what men would consider handsome. "Does the cow still need milking?"

Joseph's smile fell. "That's been taken care of."

By me. It was her fault the cow was dead. Hannah started to the door, bypassing Joseph and his guests. "I'll go find more eggs."

A breeze met her outside, but she had no desire to return for the shawl. She lengthened her stride toward the barn, no long skirts to tangle her feet.

"Hannah." Joseph's sandy locks flapped with each step, not yet fastened at the nape of his neck. "I need to talk to you."

"Then talk."

The corner of his lip twitched downward. "I think it best we keep our…"

"Our marriage?"

"I think it best no one know. Not yet, anyway."

Hannah was stoic. "No one? Or just Nora and her father?"

Joseph's brow wrinkled. "Them included. But the whole settlement, really. If they knew I had made such a bargain for the safety of my farm…well, it might not be very safe anymore."

"You have my silence. Is there anything else you want?" Hannah compelled her smile to make an appearance.

He shook his head.

She choked back a bitter laugh.

Joseph Garnet really hadn't changed one bit.

11

The last kernels of corn rolled from the sack. Joseph remained crouched, but looked to the source of happy chatter near the cabin. Rachel and Nora walked together, long skirts swooshing, each with a little girl on their hip. Young James ran along with them, pausing to pick up rocks and twigs on the way to the large area of tilled soil prepared for the garden. Rachel had told him she and Nora would plant the remainder of it today while Hannah rested her arm.

Hannah stood in the cabin's shadow, leaned against the door frame as she watched the other women. Her wound had mostly healed over the past few days and didn't appear to bother her much, but she remained withdrawn. She appeared lonely. And sad.

Joseph rocked back on his heels. He didn't want her to be unhappy here.

"As much as I admire and am somewhat envious of your ability to crouch in such a way for an extended time," Andrew said from behind him, "I suggest we make *some* haste before the Sabbath arrives."

Hannah glanced their way. Her chin lifted a degree before she pulled the door closed and hurried toward the paddock where the mare grazed. Joseph almost smiled at that. She hadn't changed a bit when it came to her love of horses. He well remembered the way she had been, two long braids, wide brown eyes, arms laid over the rail fence as she watched the horses for hours. Sometimes when she was young, she'd venture into the pens and follow Hunter around—his much smaller, two-legged shadow.

Andrew's crisp tones again pulled him from his thoughts. "While your wife is admittedly a becoming creature, she is no longer in sight, negating the need to stare as you do."

Joseph stood and twisted to the man, only to be met by a grin.

"I must admit that if I knew you were this fond of the girl, I would have been significantly less concerned."

"Don't be so quick to get over your concern." Joseph heaved the sack of corn seed over his shoulder.

"That was not attraction I saw on your face just then?"

Joseph kept walking, mostly because he wasn't sure how to answer. He couldn't deny Hannah had grown into a pretty thing, but she was still young and whether or not he was attracted had little bearing on their marriage.

Andrew kept pace until they met the plowed field. "Perhaps you will assist me in choosing a topic for my sermon tomorrow."

Joseph stumbled to a halt. "Tomorrow is Sunday again? Already?" He hadn't made near the progress he had intended this week.

"Already."

"Then I suggest we stop talking and get busy." He didn't want to discuss Hannah any longer.

"You leave me to decide on a topic?" Andrew's words held a good-humored warning. "The second book of Genesis comes readily to mind. 'This is now bone of my bones, and flesh of my flesh: she shall be called Woman, because she was taken out of Man.'"

Joseph glared.

"'Therefore shall a man leave his father and his mother, and shall cleave unto his wife: and they shall be one flesh.'"

Joseph fumbled for a retort. "If I knew the Bible as well as you, I'd suggest you base your sermon on a Scripture about not making your friends hate you."

Andrew chuckled. "Perhaps the fifth chapter of Matthew? 'Agree with thine adversary quickly, whiles thou art in the way with him?'"

"It depends who has to do the agreeing. Because I don't agree with you." Joseph huffed out a breath. "How am I supposed to think of this as a real marriage? I mean, sure I hope I can—we can—someday. But she's not too fond of me, and I'm..." Joseph shook his head, not sure how to continue. He stepped to the rock he had used to mark where he'd left off the evening before. He had planned to be done with this field already, and instead he'd only sown a third of it.

"Still mourning Fannie?" Andrew took a handful of kernels from his own pouch. "It has been less than a year. Seems longer, somehow."

Much longer. The first days and weeks had stretched across endless hours. The shock. Dragging himself out of bed to see to the needs of his family and the farm, though he had hardly slept in the bed now empty of her warmth. The months had passed and gradually he'd become accustomed to the emptiness of both the house and himself.

"The pain will pass." Andrew gripped his shoulder. "Give yourself, and Hannah, time."

Joseph wasn't sure time would have any effect on her.

"I have thought much on it throughout the week," Andrew continued, "and despite my misgivings, I now wonder if perhaps Hannah's coming is a tender mercy of the Lord."

Joseph's shin, still sore days later, begged to differ. There was not much *tender* about the woman. "How so?"

Kernels dropped one at a time from Andrew's hand into the long straight valley of black earth.

"Or are you rethinking your statement?"

Andrew tipped his hat back with his wrist. "I believe Rachel is again with child."

"But…" Martha was still so young. Fannie had not gotten pregnant again until she had weaned James. "Is she certain?"

Andrew raised a shoulder. "I am not even certain she knows. She has not spoken of it to me."

"Then how do *you* know?" Joseph had been oblivious to Fannie's maternity until she'd informed him.

"Her mood. She wearies quickly, and sleeps more. I know my wife."

Better than Joseph had known his…either of them. The corners of his mouth turned down. He had loved Fannie and enjoyed her presence in his life, but he had always been a little envious of many facets of Rachel's and Andrew's affection.

"Do not concern yourself with the children. I know you have promised to help Hannah seek her brothers. If Rachel needs help before you've returned, I will speak to Nora or one of her sisters about minding James regularly."

"No. I'll speak with Nora myself." She loved the children and would no doubt do what she could to help. Joseph clutched another handful of seed. What if Hannah decided to leave with her brothers? Recently, he had begun to consider Nora as a logical choice to help him raise his children. But now…

Now he had Hannah.

~*~

"Don't touch that, James!"

Hannah slipped out between the rails of the fence.

Nora hurried after the little boy who had discovered hard clods of horse dung were excellent for throwing. Rachel had returned to the cabin a while ago with the baby, leaving the children in Nora's care. Rachel's little girl followed James's example, reaching for a fresher mound. Nora left James and lunged for Sarah. The little boy then hurled another clod.

A smile tugged Hannah's lips. Maybe she shouldn't be amused at the child's antics, but she found a strange sort of pleasure in the other woman's frustration. Not that Hannah disliked Nora Reid—only the way she felt beside her. Insignificant. Crippled. And something else she didn't quite recognize, but didn't like in the slightest. A sort of uncomfortable burning in her stomach whenever the other girl spoke to Joseph.

It didn't help that Nora filled out her dress just right, and her rich chestnut locks were in two braids swirled together on the back of her head in such a lovely fashion. She was so very feminine.

Unlike Hannah in her leggings and tattered shirt.

Nora was the wife Joseph would want. The mother

his children needed. *But he's stuck with me.* As was James.

Nora crouched with the little golden-haired girl balanced on one knee, while she pulled James close with her free hand and dusted off his fingers.

The jealousy dug deeper. Whether or not Joseph wanted her, their marriage—as secret as it was—made James her son. Even though she couldn't hope to have Joseph's heart, she might still win the boy's affection. Hurrying across the yard, Hannah extended her good arm to James. "I'll take him and wash him up."

"Why don't you let me? Joseph said you're to rest."

"I don't care what Joseph says." Hannah pulled James onto her hip and started toward the well. Her wound had scabbed over and hardly pained her anymore. Joseph had coddled her long enough.

"At least let me draw the water." Nora stepped around her and set Sarah at the base of the well, freeing up both hands to drop the pail into the sheltered hole. A splash announced the depth of the water, and she soon produced the pail brimming with water.

Hannah perched James on her lap and reached for the water.

Nora beat her to it. "Let me."

Hannah bit her tongue.

As soon as his hands were clean, James threw himself at his aunt, who kissed his sweet little head.

"I'll go see if Rachel needs anything." Hannah swallowed against the swelling in her throat as she hastened to the cabin. She opened the door to silence. A pot hung over the fire with whatever Rachel had been preparing for dinner, but otherwise there was no sign of her or the baby.

Hannah peeked her head into the darkened bedroom, planks now blocking most light from the broken window. Forms were laying on the bed, Rachel with Joseph's little daughter cuddled close. Both appeared asleep. Not overly surprising with how weary Rachel looked that morning.

Back in the main room, Hannah stirred the soup—it seemed a staple in this house—and set bowls on the table. The men would need to be called in from the field soon. First she would better familiarize herself with the kitchen and what was on hand to cook with. Rachel and Nora had been preparing most of their meals, but Hannah hoped that would soon change. A barrel of ground corn sat under the shelves, and beside it nestled a sack of dried beans. A twin barrel held a coarse-ground wheat flour. On the shelf sat a can of honey, molasses, and—

"I don't think Joseph hardly touched any of that this winter." Rachel covered a yawn as she emerged from the bedroom. Sprigs of blonde hair pulled free from her braid and graced her flushed cheeks and neck. "I didn't mean to fall asleep, but the house was so quiet when I went to lay Martha down, I couldn't help myself."

Even the thought of sleep made Hannah ache for it. She hadn't slept well at all the past week and could easily succumb to the comfortable mattress without Joseph's presence beside her.

"You should find everything you need here, but if you can't, just ask. I have a start of yeast at home I can bring you later. Joseph..." Rachel shook her head. "He was never very good at cooking for himself. Most days he comes to our house for supper, and I send him home something to eat the next day. Sometimes he'll go to the Reids, but I think he's more comfortable with us. I cooked for him for years before he married."

Probably the reason Rachel had the children instead of the Reids. With the baby it was understandable as Rachel would have already been nursing her own when Martha was born, but James—

"I think you can make him happy." Rachel crossed the floor to the fireplace where the spoon for the soup hung.

"What?" Hannah sputtered.

"Joseph needs someone. He'll never admit it, but he's no good at being alone. It was ideal when I married that Fannie could step in and fill this cabin with a woman's presence, but she's been gone almost a year now, and I think the silence of this place eats away at him." Rachel looked back. "I might not agree with how your marriage to my brother came about, but that doesn't mean I disagree with it."

"Hardly a marriage." Hannah pushed the lid back over the molasses and gathered spoons to set on the table. She bit her tongue, still sore from the last time she shouldn't have spoken.

"Maybe not yet, but you could make it one."

Not if that wasn't what Joseph wanted.

12

Hannah couldn't quite push aside the bitterness as she helped with preparations for supper. Thankfully, Rachel said nothing more about her brother.

Rachel folded a cloth and wrapped it around the handle of the pot. "Why don't you call everyone in while I move the soup to the table?"

Hannah started to the door. The sun warmed past the cold that settled in every time she thought of Joseph Garnet and their makeshift marriage. What if Rachel was right? What if a real marriage was possible? Perhaps even love…or just affection. That would be enough. Wouldn't it?

The murmur of voices from the far side of the barn drew her around…and then stopped her short. She peeked around the corner.

Sarah sat on Nora's hip, while James had laid claim to his father. Nora said something, and Joseph chuckled. Then he smiled.

Hannah pressed against the log wall.

Perhaps Nora's friendliness to Joseph was innocent—she was ignorant of this week's events—but Joseph was a married man. He had no right to stand so close to another young woman. Especially one as becoming as Nora Reid.

Stiffening her jaw, Hannah stepped into sight. She leaned against the wall and smiled at her husband.

Another chuckle ended with a cough as his gaze

froze on her.

"You'd best come in for supper before it spoils." Spinning, Hannah turned away. She would go visit the horses. She had lost her appetite, and *them* she understood.

The mare had wandered to the far side of the pasture to graze near the edge of the forest. The aroma of pine perforated the air as Hannah laid a hand on the black coat. Loose hair gathered with each stroke, the last of the mare's winter protection being shed. Hannah swept her hand low under the large belly. Soon, Joseph had said. Hopefully before they left to find Myles and Samuel.

If Joseph was earnest that he would help her.

Frustration welled within, and Hannah moved to give the mare a thorough ear rub. She had to gain control over her predicament. But how was she supposed to control a man like Joseph? Hannah lingered with the mare for a while before making her way back to the cabin. The door opened as she approached.

Joseph stepped out. His mouth opened.

Nora came behind him. "There you are. Rachel is putting the soup back over the coals to keep it warm for you." Her smile held only sincerity. "We are going to dig the potatoes in."

"I'll help."

"No," Joseph inserted. "You need to rest your arm."

Hannah returned Nora's smile. "I am sure we can manage on our own, can't we?" She strode toward the garden.

A few minutes later, Nora wielded the spade while Hannah dropped small shriveled tubers into the moist ground. Already they appeared half-grown, some even sprouting tiny green leaves. Halfway down the row, Nora paused to look across the yard at Joseph, who stood near the barn, watching them in return.

Hannah frowned. "I am sorry to hear of Fannie's passing."

Nora nodded. "I miss her. And I can't help but think what a shame when she had so much to live for. All of this, and two beautiful babies."

"And a tall, strapping husband?"

Nora glanced at her, and then back across the field. "A woman would have to be blind not to appreciate that." Her tone held a smile.

It chafed Hannah's nerves. "You are quite fond of him, aren't you?"

"I am." Nora sent the spade deep and leaned around the handle. "But perhaps not as greatly as you."

Hannah tightened her hand around one of the spongy potatoes. How had her interrogation been reversed? She didn't want to think, never mind talk about how she felt toward that man. "I would not call myself *fond* of him." She was fonder of the thought of strangling him—he was way too unaffected and out of reach.

"Oh?" A grin didn't reach Nora's face, but it rose in her voice. She lifted the dirt with the spade so Hannah could drop the tuber in the soil. "My mistake."

Hannah planted her gaze on the dark earth. "I'm only here to find my brothers. That's why I came. And as soon as the planting is done, Joseph has promised to help me." She couldn't become distracted. Myles and Samuel were all that mattered. She picked up another potato.

Nora didn't move the spade. "Are they still with the Continental Army?"

"I believe so." Hoped so.

"While your father fought with the British."

Hannah pushed to her feet. "Myles and Samuel were not given the option of who they should fight for. Otherwise, I guarantee they would have been at my pa's side."

"Then I'm glad they weren't given the choice." Nora's words came out as a whisper, but they might as well have been shouted.

Hannah dropped the potato. She'd tell this girl exactly what she thought about her Patriot friends who spouted rhetoric about freedom, but did not afford the same to others. The happy squeals of children stole her words.

Rachel approached, babe on hip, James running, and Sarah toddling along.

"I should not have said that," Nora mumbled.

"Why not? It's obviously the way you feel." Hannah tipped her chin high and stalked away, past Rachel, to the cabin. Her arm stung anyway. She should have listened to Joseph. Though she definitely wouldn't make a habit of it. She should never have married him—forfeiting her own freedom. He and *any* of the Reid girls were much better suited.

~*~

Bone weary, Joseph didn't wave, he just nodded goodbye to Rachel and Andrew. Behind him, Nora stood with little James cuddled against her chest. The poor lad looked worn out. But no wonder, the sky was darkening, giving them no option but pause for the night…and the Sabbath.

"Here comes Papa now," Nora whispered, swaying with the sleeping child.

Sure enough, Benjamin Reid directed his wagon past Andrew's and into the yard.

"What about Hannah?"

Joseph frowned. "What about her?"

It was just light enough to see the tinge of red rise in Nora's cheeks. "I'm sure neither Mama nor Pa would mind if she stayed with us. I know Rachel doesn't have the room in their cabin, and you…" Concern lit her eyes.

As far as she knew he was now an unmarried man, and Hannah was a lovely young woman with no attachments.

"The barn is comfortable enough for me." Not exactly a lie, though he had no intention of sleeping there. He was tired and stiff and wanted his bed. "I assure you, we have and will maintain everything above reproach." Not hard to do when married to the woman.

"I'm afraid Hannah would probably prefer to stay here. I said something…" Nora shook her head. "But if you decide you should like to return to the comfort of your home, the invitation is open to her."

Benjamin's wagon rolled to a stop and Nora moved to the back.

"I'll ride back here, Papa, so James can sleep. He'll spend the night with us, if that's all right."

"Of course. I'm sure James will enjoy some time with his grandparents. We don't see enough of him or his sister." He smiled and looked at Joseph. "Is there anything else we can do for you, son?"

"No, sir. We got a fair amount accomplished

today, so if the weather holds, all will be well." Especially now that he didn't have to worry about raids against his farm. However, while the rest of the community remained under threat, was he wrong to do what he could to protect his family and livelihood? It wasn't as though he'd sided with the British. He helped Nora into the wagon, and then bid her and Benjamin goodnight. Joseph wasn't sure if he would even have the strength to wash up before falling into his bed. He needed sleep. He set his hand to the latch and gave a shove. The door jerked against the bar and stopped. He tried again. Why would the door be barred? *Unless...*His exhaustion stoked his anger, and he plowed his shoulder into the solid wood. "Hannah!"

"Yes?" Her voice came from the other side of the door.

"Unbar this door."

"Why?"

"Because this is my home, and I want my bed."

"And yet did you not just declare that you are more than comfortable in the barn?" Her tone sharpened, grating against a stone. "I do hope so."

This couldn't be happening. Joseph pressed his forehead into the door. "I beseech you. Let me in so I can go to bed."

"It is no longer your bed."

Or his home, by the look of it. With the door barred, and the windows too small, the precautions he had taken to keep raiders out now worked against him. "What about a blanket? It's already mighty chill out here tonight." If he could get her to open the door for just a second, he would easily be able to force his way inside. "Please, Hannah."

Silence suggested she considered his request, and he held his breath.

"Very well."

Again silence, and he braced himself against the door. Waiting.

"But first I will watch from the window to make sure you're by the barn."

No. He sagged. "Why can't you just open the door, woman?"

She laughed out loud. "So you can plow your way in here? Do you think I'm daft?"

"I wish you were."

"So we'd share more in common?"

Joseph gritted his teeth. "Maybe you're correct. If I had any intelligence, I would have never agreed to help you, never mind marry you."

"Of course you say so now that your family and land are safe. Maybe I should have let Otetiani have his way with this puny farm of yours."

"We all would have been better off!" Joseph pushed away from the door and walked several paces. He threw his hands up in the air. Now what? His anger deflated. Incensing her didn't help his plight, but he held little hope for reconciliation. Better to concede for now and save his energy for warding off the night air.

~*~

His footsteps moved away from the cabin, and Hannah leaned into the door to listen. Was he really leaving? Or was this another attempt to get her to open the door? He was right about the chill, the temperature had dropped steadily as soon as the sun started slipping away. Was she really making him sleep in the barn? Though well into May, and not likely to freeze overnight, it would hardly be comfortable. She should make sure he had at least one blanket.

But that would require her to rein in her pride.

Hannah sagged against the heavy bar, twice the thickness as the one he'd used to lock her in the bedroom the first night. Seemed longer than five days ago. So much had changed. She bristled at seeing him with Nora, and his continued denial of their marriage. If he wanted to pretend they weren't husband and wife, he'd better get accustomed to nights in the barn. She crossed into the bedroom. The quilts lay flat across Joseph's bed.

Their bed.

She sat on the edge. Despite the understanding they had reached, the last few nights she had hardly slept with him beside her. And tonight she'd probably lay awake wondering if he were freezing. As much as she wanted to, she couldn't leave him out there. Not without something to keep him warm. Perhaps if she *accidently* let him back in, she could maintain her pride.

Hannah gathered the two heaviest quilts and plucked the lamp from the table. The night air met her with its cool fingers, and she hastened to the barn. All sat still, laden with a low glow from the short wick. The flame flickered, creating an array of dancing shadows over the straw-littered ground beneath her feet, the single stall, farm tools, sacks of grain seed, and mounds of last-year's hay. Joseph was stretched out, arms folded across his chest, eyes closed. She leaned the lamp nearer. Surely he wasn't already asleep. "Joseph?" she whispered.

He shifted again, but didn't open his eyes.

With another step, Hannah drew closer and

peered down at the man who was now her husband. In sleep, some of the hardness had faded from his features, returning him to the young man she had known. The slight curve of his eyebrows. The slope of his jaw. No wonder she'd been attracted to him as a girl. And yet he had always remained distant, detached from even the efforts of Fannie to catch his attention. Had she finally succeeded? Or, as Rachel had insinuated, had she merely been convenient? Even after marriage to a woman who adored him, did Joseph Garnet understand love? Or did he simply not like being alone and cooking for himself?

Perhaps that was another reason he had agreed so quickly to Otetiani's proposition that they marry. It probably would have been only a matter of time before Joseph asked Nora to wife if his precious farm hadn't been threatened.

Hannah pushed away the souring of her thoughts and set the lamp aside so she could lay the quilts over him and tuck them around his shoulders. The crevice between his eyes relaxed, and his lips parted with an outward breath. Warmth brushed her face, and she paused. What would it be like to be cherished by such a man? To be held? Kissed? Loved?

She hurried to her feet. Better to keep her distance and her anger, or she would lose herself in more ways than she already had. No matter how optimistic Rachel had been.

~*~

Joseph shivered and reached for the quilt, pulling it up over his shoulders. Hay prickled his neck, and tickled his face. He forced his eyes open to the hazy morning light pressing through the cracks in the barn. He blinked and shoved upright. The quilt fell across his lap.

A quilt?

Last evening's events rolled in his weary brain. He'd not had a quilt when he'd collapsed here. Cold seeped through his sleeves as he gathered the quilts and stood. Only to stumble over the milking stool. He kicked it out of the way. He didn't have a milk cow anymore. A yawn stretched his mouth, and he hurried to the cabin. With his hand on the latch, he closed his eyes. "Please, Lord."

The door swung open under his pressure, and he stepped inside to warmth. The fire had been banked but under the layer of ash large logs glowed in the fireplace. He dropped the hay-laden quilts to the table. A second yawn watered his eyes, and he stumbled into the bedroom where his lovely bride slept. He dropped onto the bed beside her and pulled the blankets over his thawing body. She'd likely be the death of him.

13

Daylight stole through the open door into the bedroom and the scent of baking cornmeal roused Joseph and his appetite. He stretched his arm across the empty bed. He'd survived another night without being murdered in his sleep. Small blessing.

After changing his clothes for a clean shirt and pair of knee-length breeches, Joseph sat on the edge of the bed to pull on his long socks. His fingers were sufficient to comb his hair, and he tied it at the nape of his neck before locating his shaving kit. A week's worth of stubble shadowed his chin. He couldn't help but steel himself on his way into the main room.

Hannah danced between the fireplace and the table, first removing the kettle from over the flames, and then the skillet. She barely spared him a glance.

"Good morning." He set the shaving kit on the table and took a basin from where it sat on the flour barrel. He cooled the water from the kettle with some from the pail on the floor.

Hannah set two plates on the table and eyed him.

He gave her a brief smile. With water, a towel, soap and a small mirror at hand, he sat and withdrew his straight razor.

"You never used to shave."

Not exactly the truth, but he definitely hadn't bothered with it often before marrying Fannie. She'd preferred him clean shaven, and he'd sort of taken to it over the last few years. "People change."

Hannah definitely had. He dared a glance at her, and thankfully she looked away to fuss with the dense bread or cake she was sliding from the skillet. Hair in a single braid down her back, nothing obstructed his view of her fine features, long lashes, and honey eyes as they refocused on him.

"Papa always believed it was important for a man to be clean-shaven." Her lips gained fullness with a hint of a smile. "He'd not bother with soap half the time and used his old whittling knife."

The strength fled Joseph's hand, and he lowered it momentarily to the table. Even at Oriskany, Henry Cunningham's face had only shown a hint of neglect. He'd probably shaved the morning before. Strange to remembered that. Stranger still, to sit across from the man's daughter and claim her as wife.

"Papa would approve."

Joseph refused to let his expression change, but approval was something he doubted Cunningham would afford him. What would the man think if he knew Joseph had taken his daughter? Joseph's hand trembled. If he resumed shaving now, he'd probably accidently slit his own throat. If Henry Cunningham lived, he'd almost certainly do the honors.

But Henry Cunningham was dead.

Razor clenched, Joseph focused away from memories and onto the task at hand. Maybe it was a good thing Sunday had arrived. He needed the soothing balm of Andrew's sermons to fortify him for another week. Perhaps this was God's doing, bringing Hannah into his life so he could look after her whether or not they found her brothers. Perhaps it was a way to rectify his sin.

Joseph frowned and scratched the blade from his chin, downward. More likely one thing had led to another, and God sat shaking His head at the absolute mess Joseph had created.

"Here." A plate clanked against the table in front of him with a half-moon of dense cornbread. "You can eat when you are finished." Hannah sat down and nibbled on her own half.

Joseph nodded his thanks. After he'd wiped the remaining soap from his face, he took a bite and chewed. And chewed. The consistency wasn't quite the same as the cornbread he was accustomed too.

"What's wrong?"

"Nothing." But he had to ask. "What did you put in this? Something is…different."

"Beans. I soaked them overnight. They make the bread much more filling. It is well-loved among the *Kanien'keha:ka*. Mama made this for Papa to take on his hunting trips."

Joseph took another bite. The flavor wasn't bad, but would require some getting used to. "It's good. Thank you." He hurried to finish so he could escape her skeptical stare. He'd be quick with the chores and leave right away instead of waiting until the start of the meeting. The last bite of cornbread clung to the back of his throat, and he scooted back his chair to pour a drink.

Hannah plunked a mug in front of him and beat him to the water.

"Thank you." He gulped it back and stood. "I need to look after the animals before I go."

"Go where?"

"Andrew holds Sabbath meetings down at their

cabin." Joseph grabbed his hat and shoved it on his head. "I usually spend most of the day with them." With a nod, he headed to the door.

"And what am I supposed to do all day?" Hannah's tone was soft, but edged with the sharpness of the razor he had left out on the table.

"You should rest." He glanced back, not really wanting to slow his escape. "Your arm needs to finish healing."

"My arm is almost healed. It's fine." A challenge lit her eyes.

He gulped. Whatever happened, he couldn't afford to let her to come with him to a community gathering. He might not have immediately recognized her, but nobody else seemed to have that difficulty.

~*~

Hannah folded her arms across her stomach. How long did he expect to hide her here? And what were his real reasons for leaving her behind? Was it the connection to her family he feared, or her connection to him? No doubt such an arrangement shamed him—not just to be forced into a marriage, but to be married to her.

"It's better you stay here," Joseph reaffirmed. "I don't have time to hitch the wagon."

"I can ride a horse as well as you."

Joseph backed another step to the door. "Perhaps, but…the mare is too near foaling to ride." He shrugged. "That leaves only one horse." Another step.

She matched it, circling around the table. "An easy walk might do the mare some good. But never mind that. Hunter did not seem bothered carrying the both of us back here from halfway to Frankfort." She smiled at Joseph and braced for his next excuse.

"I did not think your family overly religious."

"You suggest I do not believe in God? Mama taught me of the Great Creator, and I believe her words. Is not your God and the Great Creator of my mother's people the same being? And how am I to learn of your God if I am not allowed to be taught?"

Joseph's mouth hung open for a moment. He shook his head. "I'll invite Andrew to come here and you can ask him any questions you have. He knows the Bible better than any man I've met and was an educated clergyman before he left Britain, so I do not doubt he can teach—"

"He's from England?" But of course, that explained so much. "Why is he here?" Surrounded by war.

Joseph sighed, the severity of his expression fading. "He was an officer when the British—"

"A British officer?"

A nod. "He was wounded at Oriskany."

"Your sister is married to a British officer and—"

"*Ex*-British officer."

She made a face. "He fought with them. And yet everyone has accepted him with wide arms."

Joseph wiped a hand down his face. "You don't know how it was."

"I don't care how it was. What matters is how it *is* now." A British officer had been welcomed into the community, but Joseph didn't trust them to welcome her. Not because of her own loyalties—she had none—but because of her father's. Or maybe it was Joseph who didn't want her accepted. It was easier for him to hide her away here and pretend she didn't exist.

Hannah blinked at a sudden surge of moisture to her eyes. She would not cry. Not in front of Joseph.

"Fine." He turned away.

"Fine, what?"

"I'll finish the chores and saddle Hunter. See that you are ready by the time I'm done." Two more steps and he was at the door. "And get out of those buckskins."

She hugged herself. "I don't have anything else."

Joseph waved toward the bedroom. "There is a whole chest of gowns. No one else has any use for them."

"But you seemed…unhappy when I wore one before." And did she really want to remind him of Fannie?

"I wasn't unhappy about that. It's just a gown." He pulled the door closed with too much force.

Hannah looked down at her clothes. She would cause enough of a ruckus without looking so much like those who had been burning homes and killing throughout the valley. But Fannie's gowns…

She had no choice but to make do.

Hannah was still wrapping up her braid and pinning it in place when Joseph shoved into the cabin.

"I'll be leaving." His gruff voice echoed into the second room.

Hannah jabbed the last two pins into place. "I'm ready." Her pulse sped, but she managed to hold her voice steady and give him a coy smile.

His "good" sounded more like a grunt than a word, and he vanished back outside.

Hannah hitched up the hem to keep her feet from tangling on it as she hastened after him. Fannie had been a good two inches taller and the gowns would have to be altered if she was to make regular use of them. She also hoped to make other changes so she didn't have to think of Joseph's late wife every time she dressed. She didn't want him remembering Fannie every time he looked at her, either. She was his wife now. Though, Hannah still wasn't sure what she wanted that to mean.

Her groom stood with Hunter's reins in hand as the stallion ran the side of his nose up and down his coat sleeve. Joseph extended a hand.

Hannah ignored it. She didn't need help mounting. Pulling the layers of fabric up so her foot could find the stirrup, Hannah hoisted herself aboard. Her second leg jerked to a stop halfway over the saddle, giving her no option but to hang there and fight to free her dress from the back of the saddle, or reverse and try again. No way was she reversing.

Joseph's chuckle urged her to hurry, but yards of linen stinted her progress unless she forsook all modesty.

"Here." Joseph braced her waist whilst yanking the skirt free. Up past her knee.

She planted herself in the saddle and jerked down the hem. Gowns were far too difficult, and it had been years since she had spent much time in one.

"It'll be more comfortable if you shuffle back behind me this time."

She scooted behind the saddle and waited for him to maneuver his leg over. As soon as he settled, the horse jerked forward, and Hannah grabbed for something to hold on to. The back of the saddle provided little grip. She had no other option but to clutch Joseph's coat. Even that swayed. Hunter sped to a lope, compelling her to shift her hands to the steadiness of Joseph's waist. Gradually she let her hands encircle him, and they became one to the rock of Hunter's stride.

14

At least they'd arrive early. Joseph always joined Rachel and Andrew for a meal before the services. All he had to do was distance himself from Hannah before anyone else came. While those attending Andrew's sermon might be forgiving of the girl and her family connections, he doubted their marriage would be as acceptable.

The door to the cabin sat open, and he slowed Hunter's approach.

Rachel appeared in the doorway as he assisted Hannah to the ground. His sister's surprise turned quickly to pleasure. "I'm so glad you are joining us," Rachel said taking his wife's arm. She smiled at Joseph. "Why don't you stable your horse while Hannah helps me set the table? I'll send Andrew out."

"Where is he?"

She motioned behind her. "Reading. He's struggling with what he wants to say today."

Joseph frowned. "Trying to figure out the best way to call me to repentance, I reckon."

"That must be it." Still smiling, Rachel led Hannah away.

His frown deepened. His sister and new wife seemed to get along just fine, their temperaments similar. Maybe too similar. It had taken him a while to get used to Fannie when they'd first married. After living with Rachel for so long, he wasn't accustomed to someone so soft-spoken and obliging. Hannah, on the other hand…she challenged him as Rachel did.

"You appear quite occupied with your thoughts." Andrew stepped from the cabin. "May I venture a guess?"

"No." Joseph walked the trail to the barn. The nearby stream gurgled, but not loud enough to mute Andrew's chuckles.

"I am glad you brought her along."

"At least one of us is."

Andrew came alongside. "You would have preferred she had not come?"

"I'd prefer everyone besides us and the Reids to stay oblivious to the fact she's even here."

"And your marriage."

"Especially our marriage. Don't you think people will see it for exactly what it was? I made a bargain with the enemy for the sake of my life and land. While everyone else in this valley remains at risk. I'll be a traitor in their eyes." Joseph turned to his brother-in-law. "And you remember what happens when our *good neighbors* root out a traitor…or a spy."

Andrew drew his hand across his neck and the scar from the noose that had once wrapped it. "But surely they cannot feel threatened by you, someone who fought and bled at their side. They will understand once the situation is explained to them."

Joseph shook his head. "I'd like to hope so but would rather not risk it."

"What do you intend to do with your bride, then?"

"I honestly don't know." He continued on to the barn with Hunter. "Unless you have a sturdy cord."

"Or an empty smokehouse?"

If only that were an option, but Hannah would make him pay even more than his neighbors.

"She should count herself lucky," Andrew replied drolly. "At least she is not under threat of being shot."

Joseph glanced over his shoulder. A smile pulled at his mouth. "She's my wife. Not some British officer overstaying his welcome."

~*~

Hannah took a steaming loaf of bread from Rachel and set it on the table. Perhaps she needed to ask what Joseph enjoyed eating. He'd swallowed down the cornbread that morning, but it hadn't appeared an easy thing for him. Many of the meals she knew were learned from Mama and her people. What if none of them pleased him?

"Why don't you sit for a while?" Rachel said. "I appreciate your help, but I don't want to risk you hurting your arm."

"It's healing well enough."

Rachel set a second loaf beside the first and reached for the nearest chair. "Well, I think I shall sit, and I encourage you to join me." She stretched her legs out under the table as she reclined back. Her hands smoothed across her stomach. "I tire so easily lately."

Hannah sat. "Are you…?"

"I am quite sure of it now." Rachel sighed and nodded toward the two girls playing with a couple of wooden utensils and a bowl on the floor across the room. "I hadn't considered the possibility of another baby so soon, but Joseph's Martha wants to eat everything she sees us eating. She doesn't nurse as much as Sarah did at this age, and she already sleeps through the night."

No wonder the three children had become too much for her. Hannah had helped care for the younger children when Mama expected another. Perhaps she'd been too young when Samuel was born, but Miriam had been like a doll for five-year-old Hannah. She had run errands for Mama and helped tend the baby. A screech from the other side of the room saved Hannah from the ache in her heart.

Little Martha gripped Sarah's blonde locks.

Sarah let out another wail, her face turning scarlet.

Rachel moaned and pushed up.

Hannah waved her back. "Let me." With gentle pressure on the baby's hand, Hannah forced her to release the hair. Sarah jumped to her feet and ran to her mama, leaving Martha to Hannah's care. "That was unkind," she scolded as she rose with the baby. The wisps on Martha's head were dark, but her eyes were as blue as her father's.

"When she's weaned, I think it best for her to be with her proper family—with her father. And you."

Hannah's hold on the child slackened momentarily. This would be—was—her daughter.

"We'll take it slowly for everyone's sake," Rachel said.

Hannah swayed with the child on her hip as she returned to the table.

"And if you ever need anything, you have only to ask. We are sisters now, after all."

"Sisters." Hannah's heart thudded. Used to being surrounded by family, the last few months had introduced her to a peculiar sort of loneliness. She clung to the hope of finding Myles and Samuel, but to be part of a family again…to belong...

"Oh, and please don't say anything to Joseph or Andrew about me being with child."

"Your husband doesn't know, yet?"

"He worries far too much, as it is." Rachel gave a small smile. "I'll wait until after the fields are planted."

Hannah glanced down at the baby she held, her daughter through her marriage to Joseph. Perhaps even if Joseph never learned to care for her, she would find the love she needed through his children. Perhaps even in her own children…

Martha looked up at her with Joseph's studious eyes. While Hannah wasn't yet ready for the consummation of her marriage to the child's father, she did someday hope to experience every facet of motherhood. Even the painful ones. Mama had served as midwife for more than one woman after their return to her village, and Hannah had gleaned everything she could from what she'd seen and heard. What a wondrous process to be a part of—a perfect mingling of both agony and joy, the very heart of life. Perhaps when Rachel's time came, she would let Hannah attend her.

Or maybe, if Joseph ever decided their marriage was real…if he ever came to want her in that way…

Heavy footsteps just outside the cabin tightened Hannah's spine. With the baby on her hip, she helped Rachel finish setting the table. She ignored Joseph's presence. Even thinking about him warmed her cheeks. Was it wrong to want a real marriage someday? Was it wrong to hope her husband would grow to care for her?

Someone touched her arm, and she turned to Joseph's broad chest.

"I'll take Martha."

"Oh. Here." She passed his daughter to him and stepped back. The propped open door provided no relief from the overwhelming heat coursing through her. What had become of her resolve to never feel anything for this man? Not even a week and her defenses already crumbled.

Meanwhile, his defenses showed no sign of wear.

15

Hannah sat on the edge of the roughhewn bench. Silent. Invisible. Just as Joseph wanted her to be.

James stood with his little cousin at the edge of the clearing as they picked leaves from a low-hanging branch. James threw his handful at Sarah and darted away, making a beeline to where his pa visited with the Reids—Benjamin joined by his wife and three daughters. No sign of the son, Daniel, but he may not be a religious man.

Hannah wasn't even sure why *she* was there. Only that she hadn't wanted to be invisible anymore.

Joseph swept up his little boy and started toward the small grouping of benches, long planks laid over short lengths of logs. A handful of families already waited for the beginning of the meeting. She recognized some of the men who had driven her family from the valley. She should have listened to Joseph and stayed home. Maybe it wasn't too late. She could slip back to Rachel and Andrew's cabin and wait out the meeting. Wouldn't Joseph love that! She'd be giving him exactly what he wanted.

Bible in hand, Andrew kissed his wife and worked his way to the front. Despite the hint of a limp and his homespun clothes, his movements had grace to them. They, like his speech, seemed out of place in this wilderness.

"Can you take Martha?" Rachel asked coming

beside her.

Hannah opened her arms to the sleeping baby, unable to withhold a smile. The child stirred against her and then settled.

Rachel snatched up Sarah and planted the child on her lap.

Hannah's smile died a quick death. Joseph remained at the back. He waited until everyone else sat, and then slipped onto the last bench with the Reids beside Nora. And as far away from Hannah as he could position himself.

It doesn't matter.

Hannah shrugged the shawl off her shoulders, the warmth of the sleeping baby mingling with a new heat surging through her.

As the small congregation—no more than twenty in attendance—bowed their heads, Andrew began to pray over them and their time together.

Hannah glanced back one last time at her handsome husband, little James on his lap playing with a pocket watch. Sandy locks fell across Joseph's eyes, and his lips formed a straight line. He looked unhappy. No doubt she was on his mind. Perhaps he wished he hadn't been forced into marriage. He'd preserved his farm and his life, but lost his freedom to her.

An ache compressed her lungs. What if he'd had plans to marry Nora? She possessed a soft disposition like her sister. Unlike Hannah's temper and stubbornness. Hannah wasn't docile like the Reid girls.

Andrew opened his Bible and began speaking something of a certain Jew making a long journey, but Hannah knew nothing of Jerusalem or Jericho, and her mind continued to linger on the man behind her. Why was she letting Joseph affect her this way? She hadn't wanted this marriage either. She'd come to find her brothers and her search was not yet over. She couldn't get distracted.

No matter how blue her husband's eyes were.

Better to forget that he was her husband.

"Leaving him half dead."

Hannah focused on Andrew. Who was left half dead? The traveler?

"'And by chance there came down a certain priest that way: and when he saw him, he passed by on the other side. And likewise a Levite, when he was at the place, came and looked on him, and passed by on the other side.'" Andrew's gaze scanned the group, a gentleness present as he closed the Bible. "'But a certain Samaritan, as he journeyed, came where he was: and when he saw him, he had compassion on him, and went to him, and bound up his wounds, pouring in oil and wine, and set him on his own beast, and brought him to an inn, and took care of him.'"

Though much of the story remained a mystery, Andrew's voice held Hannah's attention.

"I have read this story dozens of times, and have tried to understand what Christ asked of the people he spoke with—what he asks of us. To be a neighbor. To do good to others no matter what your differences may be. The Samaritans and the Jews were not friendly to each other during the life of our Savior. You might even call them enemies."

The story began to make more sense now, and Hannah struggled to not look at the man who had once been a literal neighbor…and also an enemy.

"Never had I considered myself as the Jew who was left for dead by thieves," Andrew continued. "And yet, not four years ago, was I not left to that same fate? If not for the goodness of others, my enemies, I should have perished." He glanced at the closed Bible clasped in his hands. "However, that is not what I mean to speak of to you today. But forgiveness. Whether we play the part of a Jew, or a Samaritan, let us not remain as the priest or the Levite."

He continued on about the war surrounding them, the heartache many felt. And the anger. "One day this war will end, and it will be up to us whether to hold to old scars and hatreds, or to live again as neighbors."

Neighbors? Like the ones who had burned her home and taken her brothers? If forgiveness was what their God required, then she had no desire to be a Christian. And she obviously no longer belonged in this valley. Or with Joseph. Hannah didn't have to look to see him and Nora seated together. The image etched itself within her. Why had she even returned? She could have begun her search in Albany.

The last of Andrew's words only buzzed.

She sighed with relief when he finally concluded the meeting with a prayer, addressing his God as Father. Strange how he spoke with the Creator of All as though He were present. As though He cared.

While others returned to visiting or discussed what had been said, Martha wiggled in Hannah's arms. The child's mouth stretched with a yawn, and her eyelids batted open. As soon as she saw that Hannah held her, Martha began to cry.

"Here." Rachel took her and the wails stopped.

What had Hannah expected? That just because she'd married Joseph, she could become a part of his life? Obviously not what he, or his children wanted. So why was she here? "I'm going back to the cabin."

Rachel frowned but nodded, understanding in her eyes. "All right. We'll be along shortly."

Hannah turned away. She wouldn't correct the assumption, but it was Joseph's cabin she was returning to. She circled wide of the gathering and the curious gazes that followed her.

"Wait, aren't you one of Cunningham's half-breed girls?" A man barreled toward her.

Hannah tilted her chin higher and kept walking. She wouldn't let him see her fear.

"Why, except you being a girl, you're the image of that bloody Tory." He grabbed her arm, his grip biting her skin.

"Leave her be, Cyrus." Joseph pushed his son into Nora's arms and hurried to intercept.

"Why? What's she to you?" He released Hannah. "And what is she doing here? Unless her Pa and your brother-in-law used to be friends when they rode against us at Oriskany. Cunningham was there too, wasn't he?"

"My brother-in-law? You mean the man who has spent the past hour imparting God's word to us? The same who has ridden at our sides to defend this valley and our families?"

He ducked his head. "I'm not questioning Wyndham's loyalties. I'm wondering what this girl is doing back in the valley."

Hannah forced herself to face him. "I am looking for my brothers."

The man laughed. "You're wasting your time. If I heard right, that oldest one got a ball through the head for desertion not long after we sent him east."

"No." *Not Myles*. Her vision hazed. She couldn't breathe. The man had to be mistaken.

His raspy voice continued to grate her. "Probably wasn't much longer before that younger pup—"

Joseph's fist slammed into the man's face and he reeled back. "You shut your mouth, Acker."

The man touched the blood at the corner of his mouth, before glowering at Joseph. "Why should I? What's she to you, Garnet?"

Joseph's fist clenched and unclenched, as beads of sweat glistened from his temples. He resembled a young horse tied short and about to be saddled for the first time. Cornered.

He blurred behind a veil of moisture, and Hannah stumbled back a step. "I'm his wife." She spat the words as though they were vile. No doubt to Joseph, they were. He'd never say them—never claim her.

~*~

Joseph's feet were rutted into the ground, as Hannah darted past him to the woods. He should go after her and make sure she didn't get lost, even if she did know the area as well as he did, and—

"Your wife?" Cyrus Acker twisted a glare at him, but he wasn't the only one moving in with questions.

Even Benjamin looked on in shock.

"Is it true, Joseph?" Despite her question, Nora appeared the least surprised.

"Yes. As of six days ago."

Cyrus's eyes widened. "The day after the raid? After you disappeared without a word. Did you find her out there?"

"Something like that." He looked to the woods that had swallowed Hannah.

"Why, of course. She was with the raiders, wasn't

she? They're probably her kin. And she came back with them to find her brothers."

The truth tumbled out with alarming ease. And there was no way Joseph could deny any of it.

"But now you're married into their clan, aren't you? So you and your farm have nothing more to worry about."

Benjamin leaned into his cane. "Is that true, Joseph?"

Again words failed him. He knew his betrayal well enough.

Acker shoved Joseph's shoulder. "You took a little Tory squaw to protect yourself." A string of curses spewed like water from a kettle, with the same burning effect.

"What would you do if Otetiani and all his warriors showed up on your land with no warning? No chance to prepare yourself?" Joseph pushed back. "I had no choice other than see my family butchered."

"Like mine was?"

Exactly like that. Joseph had helped dig the graves.

"Except I was already committed to the cause," Acker said. "I spend my year in the army only to come home to find my wife dead along with our younger boy. Only one child remaining to me. For you to make a bargain with those heathens…" Acker swore again and rotated to where his son waited beside the youngest Reid girl. "You might as well be one of them now, Garnet."

Joseph stiffened. He stood in place as others followed Acker's lead and headed to their wagons and mounts, their silence condemning.

Even Benjamin said nothing.

"Give them time." Rachel set a hand on Joseph's

arm. "They'll not hold it against you."

"Why? Because they found a way to accept your British captain? That just makes this worse, can't you see? How can they trust any of us now?" He wasn't sure he trusted himself.

"Joseph..."

"I need to go home." And find Hannah. He could only pray their *neighbors* had listened to Andrew's sermon. But what about those not in attendance today? News like this would not stay whispered for long.

16

The ride home and a thorough curry of Hunter's sweat-dampened coat tempered Joseph's frustration. He still didn't understand why Hannah couldn't have held her tongue as he'd requested, but what was done was done. They would deal with the consequences as they came. He filled his lungs with the resolution to be patient and pushed into the cabin. All was silent and still. He'd taken his time with his return, and with caring for the horse—Hannah should have been home already.

Joseph crouched at the fireplace to poke dead logs. Charred, they crumbled at his prodding. Much like the cascade of emotions within him. Somehow the cabin felt even emptier than before Hannah's coming. "What am I doing?" He couldn't wait. He'd finish looking after the stock and if she wasn't back by then, he'd go search for her.

A forest could change a lot in a few years. Trees stretched taller and trails overgrew. Maybe she had gotten lost.

Unable to shove aside his doubts that Hannah could have found her way back if she wanted to, Joseph hurried with his chores. Not having a milk cow shaved off quite a lot of time, and he didn't bother searching out eggs. After throwing some feed to the chickens, he headed for the mare's pasture. As soon as he finished checking on her, he could saddle Hunter again and try to find Hannah's trail.

The sun lengthened over the pasture and rugs of emerald grass.

The mare walked the length of the fence, head down as though hunting for another morsel to taste, but her focus was not on the grass. Heavy breathing flared her nostrils, and she released an airy knicker.

Joseph slowed.

Her steps betrayed discomfort. She paused and gave her head a low shake.

"Is that foal coming tonight?" Joseph's voice sounded hollow against the backdrop of silence. He didn't enjoy the quiet anymore. Too empty.

"I think that is for certain."

Joseph pivoted, and his chest seized with relief.

Hannah sat not ten feet away against an old oak, her gaze steadfast on the mare. She tucked the hem of her gown down to hide her feet.

He cleared the tension from his throat. "Why didn't you fetch me?"

Hannah still refused to look at him. "You're not needed here."

By the mare…or by her?

Yes, the mare probably fared well enough without him, but he wouldn't mind being needed by someone. Maybe that added to the loneliness of late. He wasn't really needed here. Andrew wasn't a born or raised frontiersman, but he would make do with Rachel at his side. And they had the children.

Joseph frowned. Is that why he worked so hard on both farms? Not because he was needed…but because he wanted to feel needed? He rubbed one calloused palm over the other. What if Hannah was the only one who really did need him? To find her brothers. And then?

"Mind if I watch with you?"

She folded her arms and tucked her knees up. "It's your farm. Your mare."

Yes it was. He sat beside her and stretched out his legs. His hat bumped the tree and he plopped it to the ground. Arms folded to match hers, he settled in to wait.

Not only silence, but peace gradually settled between them. Or maybe just acceptance. He didn't dare ask her what brooded behind her pretty eyes. Probably what Cyrus Acker had said about Myles. His words had been cruel. Even if they were the least bit true.

The breeze teased the grass and high branches of the trees. Shadows continued to lengthen. As twilight darkened the fields, coolness seeped into the air.

Hannah shivered. She wore no shawl.

"Why don't you head to the cabin and get some rest?" Joseph suggested. She was probably plenty tired. He was.

She shook her head.

Arguing with her never got them anywhere, so he pulled his arms from his coat. "Then put this on."

For the first time since his arrival, Hannah glanced at him. "Then you'll be cold."

He dropped the coat onto her lap. He had enough worries to keep him warm.

Unmoving, Hannah stared at the coat. She prodded it with her finger, her face sad, and then slipped the sleeves on backwards.

Again silence filled the inches between them. Elsewhere, crickets sang and the breeze whispered.

The mare laid down and whinnied. A short time

later the foal made its appearance.

Joseph relaxed into the tree as the gangly filly struggled to her feet and became acquainted with her mother. Fascinated with the foal, Joseph hardly noticed Hannah slump against him. When he looked at her face, the moonlight revealed dark lashes on her cheeks. Poor thing was exhausted. He should get her to the cabin and put her to bed, but instead he sat there, watching her, enjoying her closeness, her touch. *Don't fool yourself.* She might need his help to find her brothers. But she didn't need him.

Joseph slipped his arms around and under her, but she hardly stirred. She moaned, but didn't open her eyes as he carried her to the cabin and laid her on the bed. He drew his coat from her arms and tucked the quilts to her chin. "Sleep well."

Good thing she was asleep, or she'd probably balk at that, too.

Back outside, he moved the new mother and foal to the barn for safekeeping in case the afterbirth attracted wolves or other predators. In the lamplight the filly's coat showed more chestnut than had initially been apparent.

Joseph smiled. What if he made a gift of her to Hannah? She'd always admired the sire. Perhaps the filly would cover some of his wrongs and give Hannah a reason to stay. Because more and more, he hoped she would.

~*~

Hannah lay still, not wanting to wake Joseph. He'd rolled over during the night and his arm now lay tight against hers. His breath heated her neck, his face tipped her way. She dared a glance, only to find his face inches from hers in the early morning glow. The open doorway gave very little light to study him, but that was for the best. Just the slope of his relaxed jaw and his parted lips threatened to be her undoing.

Hannah looked away. The quilt already held her on the edge of perspiring, she didn't need any more warmth rushing through her. Or a longing she could never fulfill.

Awaken him or not, she needed to move. Last night had been bad enough when she'd fallen asleep against his shoulder and Joseph had swept her up in his arms. Whether for the sake of her pride, weary limbs, or the feel of being held by him, she'd pretended to remain asleep, only to lay awake for a long while afterward.

Motions steady and slow, Hannah rolled away from him, breaking contact. She slipped her feet to the floor. Last night Joseph had only removed her moccasins. If she could keep from tripping on her hem, she'd soon escape this room. If only she could escape thoughts of him so easy.

Joseph gave a soft groan.

Hannah froze and glanced back.

No movement. His breathing again deepened.

She tiptoed out the door. After a drink of water, Hannah stepped into the hazed sun rising up beside the barn. Splashes of light spilled over ugly black marks strewn across the wall. A single word written in charcoal and ash.

"Joseph." Her voice squeaked. She looked toward the pasture where the mare had foaled. No sign of them. Or Hunter. She should go see whether they sheltered at the edge of the trees or along the barn, but instead she retreated. "Joseph."

Charcoal meant fire. Torches. Like the ones that had burned her family's home.

"Joseph!"

His stumbling footsteps hurried out. "What is it?"

A low growl merged with harsh words on Joseph's tongue. He pushed past her.

"What is it?" Hannah hurried after him. "Who did this?"

"I can very well guess who was involved." He rushed to the barn and brushed his hand over a long streak spearing downward. His palm came away black.

"What does it mean?"

He spun to her. "You know very well what this means. It means they could have just as easily rode in and burned down the barn or the cabin with us in it. It means—" He broke off. Understanding touched his eyes. "You don't know what it says, do you?"

Her head vibrated with her attempt to shake it. She had learned to speak Papa's language better than Mama's, but knew nothing of reading or writing.

"*Tory.*" Joseph stared at his blackened palm and then wiped it on the leg of his breeches. "It says *Tory.*"

17

"Let me help you."

Joseph shook his head, breathing too hard to form a proper refusal. This was his problem and he'd fix it. He lowered one pail to the ground and splashed the other against the barn wall. The black lines ran with the water. The cursed word faded. But not quite into oblivion. Even fifteen pails of water couldn't wash it from his mind.

Tory.

They'd accused him of being a traitor.

Jaw clenched until it hurt, he emptied the next pail.

Sixteen.

Hannah watched on, her eyes wide, mouth drawn tight.

He made four more trips to the well before he was too tired not to be satisfied. Joseph dropped the empty pails to the ground. One rolled against the wall. Any gratification of erasing the word was lost in the worry flipping his stomach. He'd been branded a Tory. His family was no longer safe. He thanked God only charcoal had been used, but the warning was clear. Nothing kept them from using flames next time.

"When I'm finished with chores, I'm riding down to talk to Andrew and Rachel. Stay in the cabin and load my musket."

Hannah had her arms hugged across her stomach.

Perhaps she felt as sick as he. Such a little thing. The need to protect her reared within him as it had when Cyrus Acker started talking about her brothers. "Just in case. I won't be gone long."

"Joseph…"

"Just stay put, as I said." Maybe he should take her along, but he needed to think clear, and that was becoming increasingly difficult with her around.

Her head tipped forward. "Do you want me to fix you some breakfast?"

Joseph almost laughed. He probably wouldn't be able to force food down if he wanted to. "I don't have time for that. Just go on into the cabin, and for once, don't argue with me." He had enough on his mind.

~*~

He wouldn't be gone long. Hannah had no time to delay, or to second guess her decision. She had to leave now.

Head spinning, she took up a small satchel and pushed in the remaining cornmeal cake from the morning before. She would leave her buckskin leggings behind—they would only get her into more trouble. Though cumbersome, she'd wear one of Fannie's gowns with the shawl to ward off the chill that still hung during the evenings. She needed nothing else. She'd already taken enough from Joseph.

Stepping from the cabin, Hannah glanced upward and blinked at the brightness of the sun. What if the Great Creator whom Mama had taught her of was the same as the God Andrew spoke of and Joseph prayed to? What if one could call upon His name and beg His mercy? Would He help?

Though she'd intended to bypass the barn, Hannah couldn't deny the pull of the new foal. She hadn't seen it in the light of day.

The mare nickered as Hannah stepped inside. She left the door open to light the stall where the spry filly stood on long legs. *"Skennen'kó:wa kenh ontiatenro'shón:a?" How are you, my friends?* She crawled into the pen and cornered the filly so she could stroke the shiny chestnut coat. So like Hunter's. "You'll grow as beautiful as your sire, won't you? You have his spirit, as well. I can see it already." Hannah crouched low and pressed her forehead to the warm, silky neck. "I wish I didn't have to go."

But she did. And neither wishes nor prayers changed that. She needed to know for sure if Myles had really been executed so brutally, and whether or not Samuel had somehow survived. And she needed to give Joseph back his name. She'd not been braced for how deeply the word 'Tory' would wound him. But it had. She'd seen it in his face, and his determination to clean away every last smudge of black from the wall.

Even a week ago she would have been glad. She would have told him he deserved to know how she and her family had felt to be so despised by their neighbors. Instead, she only wanted to spare him that pain. She wanted to keep him safe.

Something he would never be so long as she remained.

~*~

Joseph swung from Hunter and charged to the Wyndham cabin. The ride from home had only etched the image of the charred letters into his mind all the more. They taunted. After years of fighting at their sides, losing Pa, and even some of his own blood, how could his neighbors so quickly turn against him?

"What are you doing here?" Rachel jerked upright in Ma's rocking chair set by the fireplace.

Martha started to cry.

A fine greeting. He was in the mood to skip niceties anyway. "Where's Andrew?"

"Out in the south field." She resumed rocking and Martha quieted.

Joseph glanced around. The cabin seemed strangely empty. "Where are the children?"

"After you left, the Reids took James home with them for the night, and Sarah's still sleeping. Did Hannah arrive home all right?"

"Yes, fine." He turned to go.

"Then what is wrong?"

"Acker's stirring up trouble." He'd spare her the details. "I need to talk to Andrew." Because they needed to do something about it before someone got hurt, and Joseph was too angry to think straight—something Andrew was capable of in any situation. Well, *almost* any.

"What kind of trouble?"

Joseph hardly heard Rachel's question as he jogged out and across the yard to the foot bridge. The stream wound through the property, separating them from acres of fertile land they'd cleared to the south. He didn't have far to go before Andrew's lone form came into view, sack over his shoulders. Planting more corn. His arm rose and fell with each handful of seed he spread.

"What, do you not trust me to sow a single furrow without supervision?" Andrew's eyes twinkled with humor.

"You have planted half the field already, so obviously…" Joseph's witty response crumbled by the wayside. "I have much more pressing things on my mind."

Andrew frowned. "What happened?"

"Tory. They wrote it in charcoal across the barn while we slept last night."

"Cyrus Acker, or others?"

"Not sure. From what I could tell, there were four or five horses."

"So others are involved now. Probably his boy, Levi. And Kastner with his oldest. They usually stick pretty close." Andrew pulled the sack off over his head. "If we start with Kastner, it will not take us too long to ride to Acker's farm after."

"You agree we should confront them, then?" Joseph was surprised, but definitely in the mood for confrontations. On his terms.

"I suggest we call on our neighbors and put out some fires."

Joseph cracked a smile. "No starting any?"

Andrew shook his head, no amusement apparent. "Let us hope no one feels it should come to that again."

Again.

A chill clenched Joseph's spine. Four years ago he'd been detained in Fort Schuyler under suspect of harboring a British spy. A mob of their neighbors had terrorized Rachel and left their barn in ashes. How well he remembered that feeling of being gutted. He'd built the barn with Pa, dead not quite two months. The barn he'd constructed in its place was no more than a shed in comparison, but what of his cabin? And his wife?

Hannah. She wasn't safe there alone. His muscles

surged with the need to hurry. "We'll pause at home first." She'd probably laugh at his concern. It was the middle of the day. For some reason mobs preferred the cover of dark.

Joseph volunteered to saddle Andrew's gelding while he informed Rachel of their plans. Better he do it as Joseph was not in the frame of mind to answer any of his sister's questions.

Both animals and riders wore a sheen of sweat by the time they reached the Garnet homestead.

"You can wait here." Joseph forced himself to walk the short distance separating him from the cabin. No one else was here and nothing appeared out of the ordinary. He was overreacting. It was broad daylight, for goodness sakes. He tried the latch and the door swung open with ease. He'd make sure she barred it when he left again. "Hannah?"

No answer.

His boots echoed against the floor as he moved to the bedroom.

No sign of her.

Anger and worry tugged at him from separate directions. Why did she never listen to him? Or had something happened? He twisted back to the main room. No sign of a struggle. The musket remained over the door. Fool girl!

Hunter whinnied in the yard and the mare returned the call. Of course. Hannah wouldn't be in the house with a new foal in the barn.

"Is everything all right?" Andrew questioned as Joseph stepped from the cabin.

Joseph pushed out a laugh. "Of course." He'd just forgotten that Hannah wasn't like Fannie. He could see her now, relaxed against the corner of the stall, a smile curving her lips as she watched the filly. Or maybe she'd be introducing herself to the foal.

As he stepped through the door, he smiled. Maybe now would be a good time to tell her the filly was hers to keep. He'd bribe her to stay in the cabin when he was gone.

But the mare stood over the foal, chickens pecked the ground, and not a person in sight.

"Hannah?"

Where was she?

He wandered to the stall, and then back out into the blinding sunlight. The garden sat barren. As did the closest pastures and fields.

"Hannah?"

"You cannot find her?"

Joseph scratched his fingers through his hair and replaced his hat. He began to search the ground for prints, any clue to where she had gone. She had visited the foal at some point this morning. But then what? Her trail, as far as he could tell, led east…toward the Cunningham homestead.

"I think I know where she went." He mounted Hunter and reined toward the road. No use breaking a trail through the forest when it wasn't much farther to go around.

Joseph almost didn't recognize the place. He'd only returned to the Cunninghams' homestead once since Hannah's family had left. Four years ago. After Oriskany. He swallowed back a new wave of nausea.

"Hannah?"

No sign of her anywhere. But she had been there. After some searching, he found tracks leading toward the river. He quickened his pace, letting Andrew follow slower with the horses. From there the tracks turned toward home. But his mistake was evident now. Old and set in mud. Several days at least. This is where she had come after leaving that first day. She'd washed in the river and returned sopping wet, her hair loose and streaming water down her back, her eyes wide and questioning. How had he not recognized her?

Unless he hadn't wanted to.

"Do not tell me you have lost her."

"I never had her."The words where too apt, and stung. "These tracks are old. I followed the wrong ones. We have to go back."

"Back to where?"

The ones that led from the barn had been fresh. He was sure of that. So back to what remained of the Cunningham cabin. She'd already been here once. Had she hoped to find something more? Or to say goodbye? The thought struck him like a rod across his midsection. Why would she leave?

Too many reasons.

He needed to find her new tracks.

"You do not think straight when it comes to this woman, do you?" Andrew asked. "You used to be good at this."

"It's not as though she's dependent on a broom or dragging her feet."

Andrew frowned at the memory of his predicament. "She is most fortunate."

"And she already has a fair head start." Joseph had wasted valuable time following false leads, something he should have recognized right away.

"You think she does not intend to return?"

"No." There had been something in her expression when he'd told her to stay put. She hadn't intended to.

With news that Myles might already be dead—possibly Samuel too—she wouldn't wait any longer. Joseph groaned. "What am I to do?"

"Go after her, of course. You cannot let her travel all the way to Albany and perhaps farther on foot and with no provisions. You promised to assist her. And she is your wife."

"I know that." He didn't need reminding. "But how can I leave with the fields only half sown? And the animals? How can I leave with my home under threat?" What about his children? Indecision threatened to rip him in two. "How can I leave?" But with Hannah out there… "How can I stay?"

Andrew dismounted and faced him. "First, answer me truthfully. If you were to follow her, would it be because of Henry Cunningham? Or because of Hannah?"

Joseph dropped his gaze to his dirt ridden boots, the same boots he had worn when marching along with eight hundred other men—local militia and soldiers under General Nicholas Herkimer—to bring relief to Fort Schuyler, twenty miles upriver and under siege by the British. They had only made it halfway.

Oriskany.

Why did both father and daughter share the same eyes?

"Truthfully… I don't know."

18

Hannah wove around trees and scampered over logs, heart in her throat. The temptation to turn back grew with the distance put between her and the Garnet farm. Perhaps she never should have left. Setting off on her own had been the right thing to do, the brave thing to do, but she felt anything but brave as the sun began it's descent. Lost. Scared. Overwhelmed with the task of finding the truth of Myles and Samuel's fates. Fearful of what that truth might be. Not brave. "What am I doing?"

She should have at least taken time for better provisions. The cornbread would last her little more than a couple of days, and that was if she only nibbled. Despite feeling ill with uncertainty, trying to put as much distance as possible between her and Joseph set fire to her appetite. Willpower would be required not to inhale all her food when she stopped for the night.

Willpower was already in full use to not turn back.

Following along the river did not make for the smoothest of terrain or directness of route, but she didn't dare wander far from it for fear she would lose her way completely. She had never been much farther east, but the Mohawk River would lead to the Hudson River, and on to Albany. That much she knew.

Fabric ripped and tugged Hannah to a halt. She glanced at her torn hem, snagged on the jagged stub of a broken branch. She ripped it away. What had she been thinking wearing heavy skirts? The crackling of twigs and dry leaves made her pulse race. Something moved through the forest. Not toward her, but paralleling her trail.

And, of course, she'd left to wander through the wilderness without any form of weapon. Joseph left his musket in the cabin. Why hadn't she taken it? Or a knife? Or even an old pistol? She'd let Joseph Garnet under her skin and had thrown any common sense to the wayside. If she died out here after being mauled by a bear or gobbled by a wolf, it would all be his fault.

Not that he'll ever know what happened to me. Which brought no peace of mind.

She kept walking, not daring to stop even as dusk lowered its haze over the forest. Not only had she left without a weapon, but also without means to start a fire and no more protection than the woolen shawl to ward off the growing chill as the sun fell away. She had no choice but to keep moving.

Or go back.

Joseph *had* promised to help her. If he was a man with any honor, nothing should affect that.

Hannah's feet faltered and she glanced back. She was tired and the comfort of a real bed beckoned. A real bed that Joseph warmed.

But if she went back, Joseph would see how utterly weak she was.

She stood at an impasse, eyes watering.

The rush of branches being brushed aside and trod underfoot broke through the stillness of the woods. Then all fell quiet. The birds ceased their evening serenade.

The sudden silence of the forest only encouraged the loud thudding within her chest. Hannah crouched low and felt the ground for something she could use as a club or spear, but never looked away from the dark shadows and looming trees where the noise emanated. Hairs bristled on her arms. Something stood there, just out of sight, watching her. She sensed it.

Hannah wrapped her fingers around a broken length of branch. Her fingertips met on the other side, but barely. She tried to bring it up, but it dragged with unexpected weight—the thing was still attached to half a tree!

Something moved toward her. A dark shadow.

She dropped her would-be weapon and crept backward, not wanting to remove her gaze from what approached. She could make out nothing in the looming shadows, but her imagination did not lack vivid details. She hated the woods at night. Had always hated them.

Pain ripped into her ankle, and she leapt away from the thorny vine. In the wrong direction. The briars scratched up her legs, soft linen undergarments providing little protection. A scream broke from her as she fell into the thicket. Pinpricks of fire bit into her backside.

~*~

Joseph dropped Hunter's reins and charged in the direction of the scream. It sounded close. Another scream vaulted him over a thick log. This shriek held less fear and more agony.

"Hannah?" It was hard to see anything in the gathering darkness.

She answered with a squeak of pain and a moan.

"Where are you?" He couldn't be far now.

"Right..." She gasped sharply. "Here." Buried in the middle of a tangle of new and old blackberries canes, she sat, hem of her gown to her knees, bloodied palms extended. "Help," she squeaked.

Joseph stomped down the nearest vines with his boots and reached past her extended hands to her wrists. Her eyes clamped closed as he hoisted her upward. "Are you all right?"

"Fine," she muttered, but didn't pull away.

Relief made his head light. "What got into you, running off without telling me? I have enough troubles without needing to ride out after you."

Her body trembled, and she tried to pull away.

Joseph tightened his hold. "I should haul you back to the cabin and lock you up again until planting's done, as we agreed."

She shoved away, wincing as she did so. "Go back to your fields and forget about our agreement. I don't need you."

"I definitely got that impression when I arrived." He let the sarcasm roll, still reeling from what her screams had done to his insides. Much too affected.

They pinned each other with their glares.

Hannah's taut jaw drew a nice line, and her lips pursed with a determined pout. As pretty as her eyes looked with the last hint of daylight swimming in them, it was hard not to lower his gaze. Especially with how close he still held her. His heart rate refused to slow. But then, only inches, and he could taste the warmth of her lips.

Would that be so wrong? She was his wife.

Her face tipped up, shortening the distance he needed to cross. Her gaze shifted to his mouth. Did she share his thoughts, his curiosity? Would it be hard to fall in love again? Would she fill the gap that Fannie's death left? Would she learn to love him in return, leaving them free to explore every aspect of this marriage?

Or would even hoping for such be a sin?

A lie?

The truth of her father's death wedged between them.

Joseph broke his hold. "I should start a fire before it gets too dark." He turned, not wanting to see the confusion in her eyes turn to hurt. The low light of a campfire would hopefully hide anything he felt. One thing he'd learned from his marriage to Fannie was how nice it was to be loved by a woman, and to have her faithfully by his side. Watching Fannie carry and then give birth to his children had swept him with such an overwhelming sense of wonder and love. For a short moment he'd let himself hope that feeling would again be possible. The loss of that hope tunneled a larger hole in his center.

He would not forget himself again.

Protect her. Help her. But he could not let himself love Hannah Cunningham...Garnet.

~*~

Wrapped in the large shawl, Hannah huddled near the flickering orange and red flames, trying to glean what little heat the new fire offered. Not that the warmth did much for the stinging of her hands and ankles. She tried to examine her scarlet streaked palms. If she'd known Joseph was so near, she would have continued screaming and not tried to pull herself out of the blackberry briar.

Thankfully, Joseph came prepared. Flint and steel, bedrolls, food—almost as though he had suspected it would take longer to find her. Or he planned to go with her. So hopeful of the latter, Hannah was afraid to ask which.

"Here." Joseph set the last log into place, and then reached for the leather canteen behind him. "Hold out your hands."

She did as directed, and a stream of cool water trickled over her palms.

Joseph braced her wrist and turned her palm to the firelight. "A couple of the thorns are still imbedded." He reached for one, but with far too much pressure to the rest of her hand.

Hannah flinched her hand away.

"I'm sorry." He stood. "I'm not any good at this."

"Your nails are worn flat. I'll probably have better luck." The tiny slivers were almost impossible to see in the firelight. She picked the thorns from her hands as best she could.

Joseph stood by with a strip of cloth for each palm. Though not perfectly gentle, his attempts to wrap her hands without causing any more pain seemed earnest.

"Thank you." She'd be wrong not to express gratitude. "Can I use more water?"

"As much as you want." He motioned in the direction of the river. "We have an endless supply only yards away."

She tried not to think of his close proximity as she bared her torn ankles.

Without a word, Joseph tucked her hem around her knees and slipped the moccasins from her feet. Then he took up the canteen again.

"Umm." As with tending to her wounded arm, he

appeared unaffected by her bare skin.

"What's wrong?" He looked at her as though he honestly didn't know. His hand warmed her knee.

"Nothing." Other than the heat he stirred within her.

He didn't look away.

"Umm, I was going to say that I while I appreciate you coming after me, I can't go back with you. I can…"

His hand slid down the back of her calf, and her mind spiraled out of control. Hannah forced her thoughts off his hands and their ministrations. "I will no longer delay finding my brothers." The sensation of Joseph's nearness faded into the background with thoughts of Myles and what had been said. What if he was dead?

"We're not going back." Joseph poured the water across her ankle.

We? "What of your fields and family?" And the threat from his neighbors?

"I promised I would help you."

Her heart skipped. With hope. With questioning. "After the planting, you said."

"Plans change." He grunted. "Besides, there isn't much left. Andrew will manage."

So engrossed in his proclamation, Hannah hardly felt the pressure of his fingers as he pulled a thorn from her leg. "Because of…" She couldn't think of a single reason that would compel him to leave everything behind for her sake. Unless it was to be rid of her. Perhaps he only sought to redeem himself in the eyes of the community. If she were gone…

"Because I promised."

And because she'd refused to wait. Little did he know that was more for his sake than her own. He probably suspected hearing of Myles's possible execution drove her. And it did. It just wasn't the only catalyst. "Do you think what that man said was true? About Myles?"

Joseph stared at her ankle as though searching for any more offending thorns, but his focus had turned inward. Probably trying to think of the kindest way to remind her how outspoken her brother could be, and how passionate he had been about her father's loyalties. Almost six years fighting for an army he'd despised? Myles wouldn't have made it. He wouldn't have stayed. And if he had been caught trying to desert…

She clamped her eyes closed. "Never mind. You don't need to say anything."

He patted her knee. "Don't give up so easily." The tenderness in Joseph's voice drew her eyes open. His mouth showed a thin smile.

Strange to think how strongly the urge to kiss him had been only minutes ago. He'd looked down at her with such gentleness, his lips parting…

"Acker was trying to upset you. You can't trust what he said."

She let the air seep from her lungs. "I'm not sure who or what to trust, what to hope for, anymore."

"Hope in the God who created them, that He preserved them. And trust that I will do everything within my power to help you find both your brothers."

19

Joseph set another branch on the fire. He'd woken throughout the night to keep the flame alive for Hannah's sake. The night had taken on a chill a single blanket couldn't dispel. Even now, as dawn crept over the horizon and filtered its light through the trees, the temperature felt as though it continued to drop. Hopefully, the sun would rise warm before they needed to start their journey.

He settled back with a blanket draped over his shoulders. He'd given up trying to sleep—he'd only managed a few hours through the night. His mind ran rampant. Would Andrew be able to handle the farms on his own, especially with Rachel busy with the children and worn down by another pregnancy? Would Cyrus Acker and his friends leave well enough alone while he was away, or would he return to ashes? And what of Hannah? What would she do when she discovered her brothers' fates? Even if Samuel had survived by God's grace, Joseph didn't hold the same hope for Myles.

"You don't look very happy." Hannah watched him.

Joseph's frown deepened. "I'm naturally a bear in the mornings. Best to ignore me."

"I shall do that." A smile toyed at her lips.

He shed the blanket and reached for the packs. "We'll eat something and then be on our way." He heated water in the tin mug he'd brought along. Though he'd not thought to bring coffee grounds or tea, a hot drink would warm her more than the cheese and bread Rachel sent. They ate quickly and loaded the saddle and packs back onto Hunter. Joseph insisted she ride while he led the horse back to the road. They'd make better time without breaking new trail along the river.

"You didn't know Myles very well, did you?"

Joseph glanced over his shoulder. Her thoughts had likely been on her brother all morning—the reason behind her bleak expression.

"I always sneaked over to your farm to see the horses. But he kept more to himself. Him and whatever piece of wood he whittled away at."

That, Joseph remembered.

"He made all sorts of things. Tops and other toys for Samuel and Miriam. Spoons for Mama. He even made a comb for my hair once. Saw Rachel's and modeled it after that."

Silence settled for a short time, and Joseph wasn't sure whether to feel regret or relief.

"Do you mind me talking?"

He shook his head. He liked the sound of her voice. And so far the subject was harmless enough.

"I know Mama's language well enough, but it's not what we spoke growing up in the valley. She gave it up for Papa. Her home, her people. Until he was gone. Everything changed after he was killed."

Joseph stiffened. Time to redirect the conversation. "What was it like, returning to live with your mother's people?"

"Hard, at first. I didn't know the language well enough. And all the customs. It became better before the end, but then the fighting came too near. There was no place to go. The land around the Great Lakes had little food and new shelters needed to be built. Too many came. Other clans gathered there, as well. The British made little effort to help."

Nothing surprising there. "The British never help. Why do you think we want them all to go home to England and leave us be?"

"All except your brother-in-law?"

"He's not a soldier anymore."

"And you never were one?"

Joseph tensed. "What do you mean?"

"You've fought. But I gather you never joined the Continental Army."

A terseness in her words sounded warning bells in his head. "No, I did not."

"And why is that, if this war is so important to you? Or are you simply content to let others fight your battles?"

Like her brothers. No wonder her eyes smoldered down at him.

"My battles have always been close to home."

"Like next door."

"I don't mean it like that." And yet that's where the war had taken him. Maybe he couldn't be held responsible for anything that had happened to her brothers. But he was far from innocent of her family's hardships.

~*~

Hannah bit her tongue. It was wrong of her to aim her frustrations at him. He was helping her. Still an apology was too much to scrape from her throat with so much emotion brewing inside. It was hard enough to admit she owed him one.

Not much more was said. They paused only briefly at midday, and then pressed on. Most of the time Joseph walked ahead, leaving her to stare at the back of his head. And admire his strong, steady pace. If she were wise, she'd stop admiring him at all, but that was easier said than done. The other option was to ask him exactly what he planned for their marriage...but that was easier left as a thought.

Joseph muttered something under his breath and pulled Hunter to a stop.

Hannah leaned forward. "What's wrong?"

"Move back so I can get on." He motioned her to slide behind the saddle. "Take a look at those clouds forming over the eastern horizon."

She maneuvered over the bedrolls and glanced at the sky.

The horizon wore an unnatural shadow under high reaching cotton. A thunderstorm.

He swung up in front of her. "I'd rather find shelter before those clouds reach overhead."

Hunter lurched forward into a lope, and Hannah latched onto Joseph's coat. Ignoring the pinch of her almost healed wound and the sting of her palms, Hannah wrapped Joseph with her arms. "What is the next settlement?" They'd passed what remained of the Frankfort settlement about an hour ago.

"Last time I rode this way not much remained between here and Fort Herkimer. The German Flats used to be a large settlement, but Brant burned most of those homesteads a couple of years ago."

Hannah loosened her hold. She'd heard about Brant's campaign. Otetiani and his warriors had ridden with him and the British that fall. Their success hadn't meant anything to her until now.

"You aren't related to Brant too, I hope?"

"No." Not directly, at least. From the bite in Joseph's tone, she gathered he'd never speak to her again if she had any close connection to the Mohawk chief who had led most of the raids against this valley.

"Good."

Nothing more passed between them for the next few minutes. Not that there was much space between them for anything to pass. Hannah let her head relax against his back and closed her eyes. Though she didn't fully understand why Joseph followed her, she was grateful. Perhaps he was more like his father than she had supposed. And perhaps their marriage was not so unwanted after all. Up until yesterday she hadn't imagined he'd ever feel anything toward her. Then he pulled her from the briers.

Perhaps one day he would learn to care for her.

Perhaps with a little encouragement, he'd learn faster.

Joseph slowed Hunter as the trees thinned and a stone wall came into view. Beyond the stones, logs formed a taller fortification. The gates were propped open, and Joseph directed Hunter through.

Hannah peered around his shoulder at the men watching their approach, and what appeared to be a church in the center of the yard. Limestone walls rose with a tower at the front of the church, and a small cannon on a swivel nestled on top.

Thunder rumbled in the distance.

"I suggest we stop here for the remainder of the day. We'll find somewhere to stay, and then I'll see who I can track down to ask about your brothers."

Joseph dropped to the ground then reached for her. "Though let's suggest they volunteered for their service." He lifted her down. "Folks will be more willing to help us if it's assumed your brothers are Patriots."

His perfect logic chafed her pride, but the important thing was to find Myles and Samuel. She turned back to the horse to pull her shawl from where she had stuffed it between the saddle and bedrolls. She tugged on the corner but it didn't come.

"Let me help." Joseph reached past her.

She gave a harder yank. "I'm fine." A caught thread popped free and her arm flew back to slam against Joseph's face.

"Ouch!" He shuffled back and grabbed his nose. Blood ran between his fingers.

Her jaw fell open and all words fled. Hannah grabbed the handkerchief that peeked from his coat pocket and thrust at him.

Joseph groaned as he dammed the blood with the cloth. "I'm only trying to help. Was my suggestion really so offensive?"

"I didn't mean to hit you this time."

"This time?" After another minute, he sniffed and started to clean the scarlet from his hands. "I find it hard to believe you do anything by accident."

She opened her mouth to argue, but the corners of Joseph's lips twitched. His chest shook. Hannah nudged his arm. "Are you laughing?"

"Why would I laugh at having my nose broken?" But his smile was less contained now and his eyes twinkled.

"That's what I'm trying to understand."

The bleeding slowed, and Joseph gingerly

prodded his nose.

"Do you really think it's broken?"

"No. You were unsuccessful this time."

"But I wasn't trying to—"

He laughed and glanced to the man who stood back, waiting for an opening. Joseph tied Hunter to the hitching post.

"Good day." The slender man wore his hair lose to his shoulders and a coat too large. He eyed the show of blood at Joseph's nose. "Are you all right, sir?"

"Fine. Just a little *accident*."

"Oh." He glanced at Hannah but only briefly. "What brings you to Fort Herkimer, Mr…?"

"Garnet. And we're just passing through. On our way to Albany."

"Can't blame you, sir. This backcountry has become unfit for civilized man. Especially with a family."

Hannah almost smiled at the sudden tic in Joseph's jaw. He thrust his bloody handkerchief back into his pocket. "Oh, we aren't leaving. Just looking for my wife's brothers. Joined the army a while back and haven't heard anything from them in a long time. You know how women get on to worrying."

Now Hannah's jaw tightened. As though she didn't have cause to fear for her brothers.

The man chuckled.

Thunder rumbled.

"You know of a place we can wait out that storm coming in?" Joseph asked.

"Of course. We've waited out more than just bad weather in here." He motioned over his shoulder. "Those buildings over there are the Army's, the ones here trade supplies, but that row opposite were built for holing up in during the Indian raids. Nothing fancy, but if you're not done with this valley then you'll find nothing to complain about."

"Appreciate it." Joseph spoke with the man a few minutes more and arranged for Hunter's care in the nearby stable before they made their way across the compound to the indicated shacks.

"Will you tell me what you found so amusing back there?" Hannah asked.

Joseph chuckled again. "You hate not knowing, don't you?"

Not anymore than she hated that question.

"I think that was the first time you've apologized for hitting me."

Hannah saw no humor in that. "I told you it was an accident." Unlike every other time.

"As did the expression on your face." He opened the door to one of the tiny cabins. Rudimentary, but adequate, with a small fireplace and bed.

Hannah stared at the single cot hugging one wall. Half the size of the bed they had shared in the Garnet cabin. They could both fit, but with no room to spare.

Joseph brushed by her with the saddle and dropped it in the corner with the packs.

She turned to him, the quickening of her pulse making words difficult. "Joseph."

"Umm?" He tossed their bedrolls on the cot.

"Wh—what would you like me to do?"

"Sit tight while I see if I can find anything more substantial to eat than what I brought."

Her stomach pinched at the thought of food. Their midday meal had been brief and already seemed forever ago.

Joseph splashed some water from the canteen on

his face and cleaned the blood from his hands, before flashing her a smile. "I'll be back."

Hannah wished she felt more certain of that. Maybe he'd stick with her for now, but as soon as they found Myles or Samuel, what would keep him from walking away and not looking back? Hannah sank to the cot and pulled her feet up. What would it take to win that man's affections? Fannie Reid had somehow managed it.

Fannie Reid with her chestnut curls and fair complexion. Not to mention her docile nature. The perfect wife for a man like Joseph Garnet.

~*~

"Thank you for your time, sir." Joseph shook the officer's hand. "I hadn't expected you would know of them, but felt it best to ask all the same." He glanced out the open door at the torrents of rain turning the ground into thick mud. A long, wet walk to let Hannah know they still had no clues.

"You should ask Colonel Willett. He was just given command of the Mohawk Valley. He might point you in the right direction."

"Marinus Willett?" The man had served directly under Colonel Peter Gansevoort when it had been decided a certain British captain could remain in the valley. He'd even been present at Rachel and Andrew's wedding.

"Aye."

"Good to know. Where would I find him?"

"He's made Fort Rensselaer his headquarters, so you don't have far to go."

Not far at all. Less than a day's ride. "Thank you."

He had something more hopeful to tell Hannah now. Maybe she'd forgive him for speaking with the army without her. Collar pulled tight round his neck, and hat set low, Joseph plunged into the deluge. He dodged through the mud across the yard. As he passed the church, he couldn't help but wonder about the nearby gravestones. He'd been told General Herkimer had made it back this far before he'd died.

Joseph changed course.

None of the graves belonged to the general, but a larger stone stood apart from the rest. Not a grave, but a tribute to the man he sought.

General Nicholas Herkimer 1728-1777.

Joseph straightened and raised his right hand to his head in a salute. Hannah was wrong. He hadn't needed to leave home to fight in this war, even at the side of some of the greatest officers the American cause knew.

The slosh of footsteps warned him of someone's approach, and he glanced over his shoulder.

"What are you doing out here?" Hannah clutched the shawl under her chin, but the rain appeared to have already penetrated it.

He removed his hat—no longer caring for the water pouring down on them—and motioned with it to the memorial. "I served under General Herkimer once. He'd gathered the local militias on his way to break the British's siege at Fort Schuyler—you probably know it better as Fort Stanwix."

She nodded. "What happened?"

Joseph's hand sagged to his side.

Hannah stepped closer. "You never made it that far, did you?" She said it as though she already knew the answer—knew what had happened. Perhaps she did.

"No. We made it about halfway when we were ambushed."

"By the British?" She sniffed and swatted at the drops of rain dripping from the tip of her nose. "Or by Loyalists?"

"Everyone was there." But mostly the Tories and Iroquois.

"You're talking about Oriskany, aren't you?" Her large eyes moved to look at the nearby graves. She didn't even know that her father had one.

And he couldn't tell her.

"Please, Joseph, I want to know what happened that day."

He let the air out of his burning lungs and filled them afresh before summoning his voice. As much as he didn't want to, he would return one last time. For her. "There were over eight hundred of us. It had rained a little that morning." He glanced heavenward. "Though not as torrential as this. Finally, the sun came out." But it had still been hard to breathe with the heavy humidity. "We had less than ten miles to go before we reached the fort." And faced the British. He'd felt a strange sort of anticipation as they'd started the last leg of their journey.

"Pa and I marched together along with others from the area. I remember watching the men in front of us file down into the ravine. I'd wished that they'd hurry." He closed his eyes, and the memories sharpened. The thick foliage surrounding them. The first shots cracking the stillness of the woods. "Then they started to fall. Some by arrow. Some by ball. Some by tomahawk."

Like Pa.

"That's how it began?"

Joseph glanced to her and nodded. When he spoke again, his voice rasped on the back of his throat. "General Herkimer took a ball to his knee right away. But that didn't stop him. Propped up against a tree, he shouted for us to attack, to keep fighting, to protect ourselves. We tried to keep together and took shelter in the trees. With a partner you had time to reload before the enemy could get close enough to raise your scalp. I was with Pa for the first while, but somehow we got separated. I found Daniel Reid with his arm already opened by a tomahawk. I tried to hold everyone back long enough for him to get the bleeding staunched."

Joseph's head spun even now at the memory of blood. Everywhere. Daniel had just regained his feet when Joseph saw Pa again. In time to witness the fatal blow of a tomahawk.

Even the memory almost made Joseph lose his footing. And his mind.

After a while there had been no time to load the muskets. Sabers and knives became their best defense. Joseph had only his long hunting knife left when he came face to face with Henry Cunningham—a face he knew too well. Someone to hold responsible for the insanity surrounding him. Someone who wanted to kill Joseph as much as he had wanted to kill them.

Their grapple had been brief. Joseph had survived. And then, when the Tories had finally withdrawn, he'd spent the next half hour retching into the bushes.

"Joseph?"

Hannah's voice broke through the blackness swallowing him, but he couldn't look at her. Couldn't draw his gaze away from the stone darkened with moisture. When he'd gone back to the ravine a few days later to find Andrew Wyndham's scarlet coat, most of the corpses had remained. Including Henry Cunningham's. Joseph had done his best to scrape a shallow grave for the man who had been his neighbor. The man whose young daughter had always fascinated him with her flashing eyes and obsession with Pa's horses.

"Joseph?"

Where had he left off his tale? He couldn't let her guess how greatly he'd been affected. "We lost almost half our men. Most of us headed home. Herkimer was taken back down river this far and died within a few days."

Hannah braced his arm. "Are you all right?"

All right? Joseph looked at his hands. They trembled. No. He was far from all right. Especially as he turned to the woman who stood beside him. She searched his face with such innocence, and something more. He wasn't sure what, but for some reason he feared it—feared to know what she hid behind those lovely eyes.

He pulled away. A faulty step back. Was he more afraid of her secrets…or the ones he kept from himself? Like what he was beginning to feel for this woman.

20

"I'm sorry. I never should have asked you to remember that." Hannah wasn't sure what he had remembered, but she'd seen enough torment written on his face to understand why he couldn't seem to voice it. Joseph didn't need to tell her anything more for his agony to crack her heart open. It bled for him.

He combed his wet hair with his fingers and pushed his hat back onto his head. "You need to get out of this rain before you catch your death."

And he wouldn't? Joseph had stood out here longer. But his eyes hadn't focused on her yet. He still hadn't completely returned from wherever she'd sent him.

Hannah remained mute as she followed his determined stride to the cold shack where they'd left their things. Not much more than four walls and a roof. No lamp, but she took a minute to dig out Joseph's flint and steel and light a fire.

Joseph didn't move from where he stood near the door, the muscles in his jaw rigid.

"Come." She took his hat and set it on the saddle with her soaked shawl, and then drew the coat from his arms.

He watched her now, a ridge forming on his brow.

"Your shirt is wet too. You won't get warm with it on."

Gaze still on her, he tugged on the single button

securing his collar. "You're just as soaked as I."

And yet at the moment she didn't feel cold at all, not as she touched the ties of the simple gown. They were married, and it was not wrong to remove the wet frock, but still… "Turn your back."

The corner of his lip extended slightly, and he rotated away. "Then wrap up in one of those blankets before you chill."

She started loosening the thin cloth ties binding the bodice to her, but her hands faltered as Joseph raised his arms over his head, his shirt following their motion. She'd seen him without his shirt in the confines of his cabin, but never had she been so affected by those broad shoulders and tapered waist.

He found a peg near the door to hang his shirt to dry. "Are you finished?"

"No." Her voice squeaked, and she deepened it. "Not yet." Almost normal.

Joseph rubbed his arms. "I could use one of those blankets."

"Oh." He was probably freezing. And she was still modest. Hannah grabbed one of the quilts and draped it over his shoulders.

"Thank you." He took the corners and pulled the blanket around this torso.

She still couldn't move.

Joseph glanced at her. "You're still in your wet gown."

And he still had a strand of hair plastered to his brow releasing droplets down his cheek. Eyes like a clear day stared into hers. And then looked away. He stepped past her and reached for one of the bedrolls to unravel it. With his own blanket hooked over his arms, he raised the new one to form a wall and block his view of her. "Go ahead."

Though he stood closer now, it was somehow easier to undress without seeing him. She quickly loosened her ties and slipped from the gown. The shift was moist, but she left it on and grabbed the last blanket from the bed.

Across the room she found another peg and hung up her gown. More warmth enveloped her shoulders and body as Joseph wrapped the other quilt around her.

"Thank you."

"You are most welcome." Again his mouth stretched but this time with a downward turn. "I forgot to ask how your hands and ankles feel."

"They're fine." The deeper cuts still stung a little, but not enough to distract her from him. Did he have any idea how his closeness twisted her in knots?

Concern marked his expression and kept his eyes soft. At least, she wanted to believe it was concern she saw. Perhaps he hadn't yet recovered from the memories of battle.

"What about your arm? Does it hurt?" Joseph's hand settled above where the ball had ripped her flesh.

"Not much." Only a scab remained. She'd hardly thought of it today. But there had been so much else to think about.

Like Joseph Garnet.

Her husband.

Hannah's pulse hammered. She gave him a quick smile and retreated. "You haven't told me anything yet. Any word of my brothers?"

"Oh." Joseph's chest expanded, and he straightened the blanket around his arms. "They knew nothing, but Colonel Willett, who has taken command of the area, has set Fort Rensselaer as his headquarters. As soon as this rain stops, we'll continue down river and ask if he or anyone has records of your brothers. If not, I still believe Albany is our best course."

Hannah nodded and tried not to be disappointed. She hadn't expected to hear anything yet. But hopefully soon.

"Try not to worry about them right now."

Not easily done. Hannah sat on the thin straw mattress, and Joseph moved to do the same. There wasn't anywhere else.

"Nothing we can do right now but pray this storm passes." He spoke of prayer as though it were the natural thing to do.

"I don't know how to pray." And she didn't know who to pray to. The Great Creator? Joseph's God?

Under his studious gaze, she cinched the blankets tighter around her. Those blue eyes were much too penetrating.

"Can I show you?"

Hannah forced her shoulder into a shrug. It couldn't harm anything.

"Here." Joseph took her hands. Then frowned. "Does this hurt?"

"No." Hardly at all.

"Good." His head bowed.

The rain pelted the roof above them, filling in the lull of his words.

"Dear Lord. We come before Thee as Thy children…"

Hannah couldn't close her eyes or look away as he continued, his voice rumbling, his words contrite. He asked for her wounds to continue healing. Then he spoke of her brothers by name. Asking for God's mercy to protect them wherever they were. "Help us find them."

"Lord…" Joseph paused for so long Hannah almost wondered if he were finished, but he never opened his eyes. His hold on her hands strengthened, and she fought to contain a wince. "Lord, I acknowledge that all things—all Thy creations—are in Thy hands. *We* are in Thy hands." His head dropped a degree lower and he sniffed. "In Jesus's name…amen."

Joseph's lashes flickered. He stared at their hands, not letting go. His thumb smoothed over her knuckles only marred by a few thin red lines. He swallowed hard.

"You didn't pray for the storm to pass," she whispered, not really wanting to break whatever trance held him.

He smiled a little. "The crops need the moisture."

Always a farmer. Which made his sacrifice all the more pronounced. He'd left before all his fields had been planted. For her.

"Thank you."

Joseph nodded. "I only wish my faith were stronger."

After hearing him pray with such earnestness, as though speaking to Someone there with them, Hannah could not imagine how a soul could have more faith. Unless she misunderstood. "Stronger?"

~*~

Joseph released her—something much more difficult than it should be—and dragged both hands over his face. If only he could hide there. Pressure built behind his eyes and he pressed two fingers along the arch of his brows. If he *were* stronger, he could pretend to not be breaking inside. But returning to Oriskany, even though just in his mind, had scraped him raw. Especially being here with Hannah. How could her presence both smooth a balm over the wound Fannie had left, and rip the hole wider?

Joseph pushed to his feet and started pacing. Not that the small shack afforded him much distance. The blanket sagged off his shoulders, and he jerked it back up.

"Joseph, what's wrong?" Hannah sounded afraid.

Had he done that to her? He forced himself to face her. And immediately regretted the action. She looked too vulnerable sitting there wrapped in blankets, her moist stockings peeking from beneath, her braid all but undone. The need to protect her overwhelmed him. And he would protect her. From himself. Not remembering what he had planned to say to her, Joseph turned to where he'd hung his drenched shirt and discarded the blanket. The shirt felt like ice as it met his skin, but he suppressed a shiver and donned his coat as well.

"Where are you going?"

He didn't look back this time. "To hunt down more firewood. And maybe a kettle." Hopefully the by time he got back he'd be able to think clearer and have gained more willpower. Because it would be too easy to throw logic aside for a taste of her lips. Maybe he'd find some more blankets, as well. Lying beside her with not so much as an inch between them would only borrow trouble.

21

Joseph loaded Hunter, trying not to look to where Hannah waited. After four days of rain, she hadn't seemed at all happy when he'd suggested they not leave for one more day to let the roads dry. And attend church. Not that it had been a proper sermon—or at least what he'd counted as one since listening to Andrew preach—but it was nice to have an actual church building. Perhaps someday they would build one in their part of the valley.

He swung into the saddle and extended his hand.

Hannah didn't look at him as she placed her hand in his and her foot in the stirrup. He pulled her up behind him and the bedrolls and nudged his horse forward. Mud still adorned the ruts of the road, but they would have been a lot worse the day before.

Hannah kept a light hold on his coat, her mouth sealed. She'd been rather quiet the last few days—ever since standing with him in the rain—but he couldn't blame her. He hadn't really encouraged dialogue. Their quarters were too intimate and the sound of her voice too harmonic.

"Hunter's well rested, so we should make good time this morning even with the two of us riding." The silence was getting to him, and now that they were in the wide open, there was less reason to stifle conversation. "We should be there shortly after midday." Even if he walked part of the way to spare

Hunter.

"Good."

They rode in silence for the next mile or so, and Joseph couldn't think of a way to break it. Probably best to focus on finding her brothers. He didn't want to ponder his secrets or what they would do to her. He didn't want to think about her pa and the pure hate in his eyes as he had thrust his bayonet toward Joseph's head—hate Joseph knew had been mirrored in his own eyes. He couldn't bear the thought of seeing it in Hannah's too. Not anymore.

Hunter lunged sideways over a muddy rut to the grass beyond, and Hannah's hold strengthened around Joseph's waist. He wanted to lay his hand over hers, keep her there. But he was no longer sure there would be a way to keep her at all.

They rode a ways farther before Hannah spoke. "Do you think Myles and Samuel were kept close? Or would they have been sent to fight in one of the other colonies?"

"I don't imagine they would have been sent too far." New York had its fair share of battles. Not that Joseph knew how the rest of the country fared. They heard very little of what happened outside the Mohawk valley.

"Then perhaps Fort Rensselaer may have reports of them." Her voice rang sharp with artificial hope.

"If not Fort Rensselaer, I'm sure we'll find something between there and Albany."

The conversation lapsed for several minutes, but the rush of the nearby river kept them company.

Hannah released a sigh before speaking again. "Do you think my brothers will ever be accepted back into the settlement? Maybe it's foolish of me to ask, after what Acker and them wrote on your barn, but Myles and Samuel have been fighting on your side for most of this war. Won't that count for something?"

"I'd think it would." But many clung to the past too tightly. Even he struggled with that.

"I think Myles would settle back in the valley if he was allowed."

And if Acker's rumor about his death wasn't true.

"I remember he used to be quite taken with one of the Reid girls." As soon as Hannah said it, her hands dropped from Joseph's waist to the saddle.

He could guess why. "Myles and Fannie were about the same age, weren't they?"

Joseph sensed her nod. "But Fannie was always in love with you."

So he'd been told. He'd been too busy with the war and crops to see her as anything more than Rachel's friend and Daniel's little sister.

"When did you finally notice her?" It was as though Hannah read the direction of his thoughts, but she sounded sad as she asked.

He gave the question some thought. "Around the same time Rachel was falling in love with her British soldier, and Daniel was asking my permission to court her."

"Daniel Reid?"

He nodded.

"I always pictured them marrying."

So had Joseph, but the Lord had other plans. Joseph frowned and was grateful that Hannah couldn't see his face. Would he have noticed Fannie at that time if Rachel hadn't been on the brink of marriage? Daniel had his own cabin, and soon Joseph would have been alone. But there was Fannie with her pretty smile. The choice had been easy and logical. Love hadn't come for a while. It had crept up on him so slowly, he hadn't known what it was. Enjoying her company on a cold winter evening, listening to her talk about plans and dreams, watching her work alongside him.

The first time she'd placed his hand on her stomach to feel the new life growing within, a life he had helped create. That first birthing, her ma chasing him out of the cabin, and his heart pleading that all would go well. Hearing her suffer. The glow on her tired face as she'd passed his son to him. He'd begun to understand love. And that love had grown. Still, Joseph hadn't known how much he'd loved her until her life was slipping away. A piece of him also slipped away.

"What ever happened to Daniel?"

What? What did Daniel have to do with anything? What had they been talking about? Joseph dredged through their conversation, his heart echoing in his ears. Somehow it still beat despite the ache piercing it. Oh, yes. Rachel and Daniel. And what had happened. He cleared the thickness from his voice. "After Rachel and Andrew married, Daniel rode to Albany and joined the Army. That was almost four years ago. Last we heard was from one of the Carolinas. He wrote that he planned on coming home to help with planting this spring, but we've seen nothing of him." There was a lot of war between the Carolinas and New York.

Joseph's thoughts did not stay long on Daniel. He was too busy contemplating the irony of his life. He'd chosen a good woman to be his wife, but had taken too long to learn to love her. Now he'd been compelled into a marriage with a woman he could easily fall in love with—and that was the one thing he couldn't do.

~*~

Hannah stared at Joseph's back as he again slipped into the silence of his own thoughts. Not surprising. She'd reminded him of his dear wife. No doubt he had many lovely memories to recall. So much better than the present and thinking about the woman he'd shackled himself to. She'd been nothing but trouble. She would never hope to compare, or steal even a part of Joseph's heart from his beloved Fannie. He'd made that perfectly clear over the past few days. One moment on the brink of intimacy, and he'd withdrawn. He preferred a rainstorm to being close to her.

"I'm sorry for your loss." Sorry that she was such a miserable substitute.

Joseph glanced back at her, his expression curious, and then nodded. He'd seemed a step behind this whole conversation.

Don't think about Fannie.

Joseph was doing enough of that for both of them.

Hannah bit back a groan. She hadn't seen Fannie in years, and yet she was completely jealous of her, and the hold she had on Joseph's affections. Hannah didn't need his whole heart, but was it wrong to want her husband to feel something for her?

The silence was desired this time, and she let it wedge itself between them along with the bed rolls fastened to the back of the saddle. If only she could keep her heart safely on her side.

Only a few more minutes passed before Joseph dismounted and handed her the reins. "I'll walk for a while so Hunter doesn't have to work so hard."

Hannah scooted over the bedrolls and into the

saddle. Hunter pawed the ground as he waited, still obviously fresh and eager to move. Joseph was probably the one who needed a rest…from being so near her.

Is this what their marriage meant to him? He'd discharge his duty to her while keeping his distance.

Joseph started walking and Hannah nudged the horse to keep pace.

"What happens when we do find Myles and Samuel?" she asked. Did he plan to hand the responsibility for her over to them? Or did he expect her to return with him? And then what?

Joseph blew out his breath. "Let's decide that when we find them."

His easy response cut. "I know my brothers will have their own decisions to make, but…" *Do you want me?* Hannah couldn't ask that question for fear that she already knew the answer.

Joseph stopped, and she pulled Hunter up alongside him.

"But?" His eyes searched hers. "What do you want?"

How dare he turn her question on her? What she wanted was a husband who would let himself love her like Pa had loved Mama. She wanted four walls and a family. She wanted… Her heart thudded with the realization of exactly what she wanted. He stood before her with his hat pushed up on his brow and his blue eyes questioning. She wanted his heart. Not just the shell Fannie had left.

Hunter shifted his weight, reminding her that she sat astride one of the most beautiful and powerful animals she'd ever seen. She ached to spur him forward, to fly across the distance between her and possible answers about her brothers…and to put some distance between her and Joseph until she could clear her mind.

~*~

Joseph winced as a large clod of mud that had been molded to the underside of a hoof struck his shoulder. Smaller pieces pelleted him as Hunter dug earth and sprinted away. Obviously he'd said something wrong. And yet, he couldn't resist a smile. That woman was like a spring storm, showering him with life, while crashing with lightning and thunder—never letting him be certain quite what to expect.

He took two steps before again coming to a halt. His blood flowed through him, the breeze touched his face, and the sun warmed his neck and shoulders. He felt more alive than he had since Fannie's death. The effect Hannah had on him. A grin stretched his mouth and he lengthened his stride. Who could have guessed her riding off in a flare of temper could leave him so amused? Though he still hadn't figured out what caused the spark. She'd been asking about their plans after her brothers were found. He honestly wasn't sure. But he had asked what she'd wanted—a question most women appreciated. Hannah had not reacted as expected. She hadn't even answered him. Why?

Again his feet faltered. He'd lived with Rachel and had been married to Fannie long enough to know when a woman refused to answer a question it was because she wanted him to already know the answer. As usual, he'd failed. Joseph replayed their conversation, focusing on the end until his head ached. Each time, he came up with the same result.

"What have I done?"

All this time he'd been worried about Oriskany. He'd convinced himself to keep his distance and not make plans for a future because Hannah would never feel anything for him if she knew the truth. But he'd never told her the truth. She had no reason to protect her heart.

He glanced heavenward. "Oh, Lord, how could I have been so careless?" In order to protect himself, he'd convinced himself that her ignorance was for her own good. But he'd seen the vulnerability in her eyes when she'd looked at him. He wasn't completely blind.

Just daft.

Hannah was falling in love with him.

Joseph hiked along the trail, grateful for some time to think and make plans. He had two options. He could force himself to forget about Oriskany, give her his heart and pray she never discovered the truth. After they found her brothers, they could return home and start a new life together. James and Martha would have a mother and he'd have his family.

He smiled at the thought of waking up beside her and days filled with never knowing what she would say or do next. Watching her with the horses she loved. Holding her in his arms as they fell asleep at the end of each day. All he had to do was forget the worst day of his life, one that still haunted him in his dreams.

Or he could tell Hannah that he killed her father and let her hate him.

He drilled a thumb into his temple. Couldn't quite press the ache away. All too soon he came over a rise to see Hannah standing beside Hunter with a shy smile, eyes shaded with lowered lashes. His heart whacked against his ribs.

"Hunter got away from me for a moment."

"He can be quite spirited. Maybe that's why you two get along so well."

A becoming pink rose to her cheeks, and she made a face.

Joseph stifled a laugh he only half felt. He still hadn't made a decision, but the longer they stood here, the more the first option beckoned. "I needed to stretch my legs anyway."

"Seems you and Hunter have plenty in common, as well."

He paused face-to-face with her. What would she do if he took her in his arms now and kissed her as he'd wanted to five days ago?

What would she do if he told her everything?

"We should pause for few minutes and then head on to the fort." He reached for the canteen, his throat suddenly parched.

"How much farther do we have to go?"

Joseph glanced toward the river. He hadn't been paying attention to their progress or location. "We're probably close to half way. Why? Are you thinking of riding off without me again?"

Her mouth opened with a reply, but instead of saying anything, she shook her head. Her smile became demure—a word he'd never imagined associating with her. "Of course not."

22

Hannah clamped her tongue between her teeth until it hurt to keep herself from arguing with Joseph about accompanying him to speak with the officers of Fort Rensselaer. She had come to the conclusion that if she wanted him, she would have to start fighting for him—instead of with him. She'd never steal him from memories of Fannie unless she became what he wanted in a woman. Quiet. Reflective. Obedient. Feminine. That's what she remembered of Fannie Reid. Obviously they had been the traits that had won Joseph's heart.

"I shan't be long," he said as he turned away and left her standing with Hunter just inside the gates.

She had the mind to take the horse on another run and find a release for the frustration and anxiety spiking through her. But the poor animal, as magnificent and powerful as he was, had already spent most of the day on the trail and probably preferred a good currying and some oats. She'd try to focus on that instead.

Hannah only made it halfway across the compound when she saw Joseph exiting Colonel Willett's office with a stocky man without uniform. Joseph did not appear pleased. She reversed course, raising her brows in question as she met them.

"Seems Colonel Willett and his officers rode out on patrol this morning. We might have to sit tight for a couple of days."

"This morning?" So if they had ridden out after the storm and not stayed over in Fort Herkimer for the Sabbath, they would have arrived in time. She struggled to keep her gaze relaxed and not shoot daggers in Joseph's direction.

"And I'm afraid there's not much for accommodations in the fort for you and the missus," the man stated. "Not with the army headquartering here. But if you cross the river and ride northwest a couple hours, there's a real nice tavern that will put you up."

Hannah shook her head and was grateful when Joseph agreed. "I think we'll stay close so we'll know when they return."

"As you see fit. I can probably find you a tent that's not in use. Way the weather's been, hate for you and the lady to get caught out in any rain."

And yet Hannah had no regrets from the last time the heavens had opened on them. For a brief moment, Joseph had been hers.

"We'd appreciate that." Joseph took Hunter's reins and followed to a shed near some stables.

The man slipped inside for a moment before returning with a canvas roll, stakes and three poles. "Just bring it back before you leave."

"Appreciate it," Joseph said.

The man nodded and moved on.

Joseph turned to Hannah and indicated the dusty tent. "Up to giving me a hand with this?"

She reached for the poles and smiled. "Of course."

He gave her a strange look. Maybe he sensed the explosion she wanted to give voice to at the thought of waiting two more days.

They found a relatively flat area outside of the fort and Joseph unrolled the canvas.

"Isn't this…?" Hannah clamped her mouth closed.

"What's wrong?"

They were too close to the fort for her liking. And too out in the open—she would have preferred nearer some trees—but she smiled. "Nothing."

He raised a brow before smoothing out the canvas and locating the four corners of the base. "All right. Let's put the stakes in the corners. I'll push them down with my boot."

"But what about the ties at the doorway?" They were unfastened, making it hard to tell if the tent was truly squared. It was not much different from one her mother had traded for once they were forced from their village and longhouse.

"We'll worry about that after. Better it's open anyway while we slide the ridge pole into place and stand her up."

Hannah nodded and handed him a stake. Wasn't worth contradicting him, and perhaps the door would line up well enough.

Soon the stakes were driven into the soft earth and Joseph placed the ridge pole, and then pushed the leg poles into place on either end, standing the tent upright.

Hannah clamped hard on her bottom lip at sight of the wide gap hanging between the door flaps. The tent wasn't quite squared, and the door wouldn't fasten properly unless they took the tent down and started fresh.

Joseph huffed out a breath and glanced to her. "No gloating that you were right?"

With a quick shake of her head, she turned and

moved around the tent to the back leg pole so he couldn't see how hard it was to keep her smirk contained. It was even harder not to wonder if winning Joseph's affections was worth this torture. How long would she be able to contain herself?

~*~

Joseph reined in Hunter as he neared the river. Across the rushing water, swollen from the spring rains, Fort Rensselaer sat peaceful, only a few funnels of smoke rising from cooking fires. The tent he shared with Hannah was barely visible.

He felt his shoulders slump. Something was wrong with Hannah. Joseph wasn't sure what, but for the last two days she'd been far too sweet. Complacent even. If that were possible. What worried him most was the tick in her cheek now and again, though she appeared to be smiling. Or the slight flare of her nostrils when she'd agreed to let him ride to some of the nearby outposts and see if he could discover anything more, while she remained behind to watch for the return of Colonel Willett.

Hannah's eyes were another thing all together, and he began to question if he had ever seen affection in them. Which gave him more time before making a decision on how to proceed, but made him worry she might be capable of taking his life if she ever found out the truth.

Still, he missed her.

Joseph was about to nudge Hunter forward to catch the ferry across the river when the rush of hooves pulled his attention to the north. Trail weary animals and men came into view, most of them in uniform. The army had returned.

Joseph started in their direction, approaching the officers from the side. Colonel Willett's profile was easily recognized with his prominent nose and sharp features. Joseph recognized others as well, but was not as familiar with their names. He pulled Hunter alongside and saluted. "Colonel Willett, I wonder if I might beg a moment of your time. I'm looking for someone."

The colonel paused along with some of his officers, but waved the rest of the troop past, ordering them to continue on to the fort. "Who are you?"

"Joseph Garnet. I'm from farther up river, but met you briefly at Fort Schuyler several years back."

"And what is it you want? My men and I are weary so please be brief."

"Of course, sir. I am looking for two family members who joined the army almost six years ago."

"And they still serve?"

"That's what I'm trying to find out, sir. Their names are Myles and Samuel Cunningham. The first would be in his early twenties and the younger, not more than seventeen."

Willard's eyes widened. "How long ago did they begin their service, did you say?"

"A little less than six years ago."

One of the other officers, a lieutenant, cleared his throat. "I think I might know something of the boys you seek. They didn't come to us voluntarily, though, did they?"

Joseph shook his head, not sure whether to be relieved for some news, or fear that he might be running out of time with Hannah. "No, they didn't."

The lieutenant smiled, but his lips were barely

visible. "Their father was a Tory, I believe?"

"Yes, he was." Joseph could sense the demeanor of the men around him change.

"And how are they your relations?" Colonel Willett questioned.

"I recently married their sister." He held up a hand. "But no, I have little in common with her Pa."

The lieutenant nodded. He glanced at his commanding officer and the others who remained. "They were among a group of boys sent from Tory homes after their fathers left to fight for the British. We were supposed to make soldiers out of the willing ones, and put the rest to work with fortifications." He looked back at Joseph. "I remember the Cunninghams, because they were put under my command. I was a sergeant at the time, and the eldest did nothing but give me trouble."

Joseph's mouth went dry. Why couldn't Myles have swallowed his pride and done what was asked of him? Joseph didn't want to ask his next question. "What happened to them?"

"The younger one worked fine. He was a good lad. After a while they transferred him to a unit to fetch and carry for one of the generals. Farther east. We wouldn't have those records here."

"And the elder?" Joseph couldn't quite work up enough moisture for a swallow.

The lieutenant's jaw tightened, and he glanced down. "He's dead."

Acker had told the truth. Joseph couldn't manage any sense of surprise, but he still felt as though someone had booted him in the stomach. Poor Hannah. "Executed for desertion?"

"That's right. We had him hauling logs at Fort

Dayton. One night he slipped away. I went after him myself."

"And killed him yourself?"

A single nod. "I brought him back, and that was the order given. I did my duty."

It was Joseph's turn to nod, but he still couldn't swallow the bitter taste rising at the back of his throat. "I understand. Thank you for the information."

Joseph took his leave and followed the army across the river. They headed into the fort, while he veered toward the tent and the young woman standing at the door, hands working feverishly to bind her braid to the back of her head.

"Joseph, they're back. We can go and ask them what they know." Her excitement made his stomach coil. It was left for him to confirm the fears she had no doubt battled since Acker's pronouncement concerning Myles. He didn't know how to do it—didn't know how to break her heart.

"Please don't tell me we should wait, Joseph. Who knows what might take them away again. Or when."

"We don't have to wait." He swung from the saddle and dropped to the ground, but his knees barely held him.

Hannah hurried to his side and took Hunter's reins. "Then—"

"I already spoke with them." He faced her. Sweat moistened his hairline.

"You did?" She wet her lips, her eyes lighting. "What did they say? Do they have records they can check? Does anyone remember—?"

"Yes. Someone remembered," he swallowed, "your brothers."

The mix of hope and dread in her eyes speared

him through. How could he do this to her? How could he deal her another blow with so little hope to cling to? Maybe if they had found Samuel alive and well, she would be able to cope with Myles's loss. But he couldn't even give her that much.

Pain bit his arm through his sleeve as her fingernails dug in. "Tell me everything that was said?" She probably had no idea how tightly she gripped him.

"Um, one of the officers said your brothers…had been sent farther east." The plural of brothers jabbed his conscience, but he had to protect her from this. Just until they found Samuel.

Oh, Lord, please let him still be alive.

Joseph motioned to the tent to distract her from his face. "I don't think we should wait any longer. Why don't we pack up now and see how far we can go before sunset."

She stared. "That's it? They're not here, keep looking?" Her eyes glistened and her chin quivered. "They don't even know what regiment, or what city, or anything?"

"It was a long time ago and back at Fort Dayton by the sounds of it. But we'll keep looking." He braced her shoulders, and she slumped against his chest. The secrets he kept weighted his arms as he slipped them around her and held her. He wanted to protect her, but the task was impossible. "We'll keep looking. I promise you I will find him…them. I'll find your brothers." Only one's fate remained unknown.

23

Joseph lifted Hannah down from the saddle, and then fastened the reins to the hitching post outside a two-story inn. Civilization. At least more than Joseph had seen since his family traveled west eight years earlier. Despite the war, Albany had grown into a fair sized city.

Wide-eyed, Hannah stared across the busy street at the brick and stone buildings towering over any cabin or long house she'd probably ever lived in. Had she ever seen a city this big? He set his hand to the small of her back and guided her toward the door of the Huntsman Inn. Best to have a meal and a few hours of repose before they resumed their search.

Being mid-afternoon, most of the tables on the main floor of the inn sat empty. He directed Hannah to one and nodded for her to sit. "You rest while I see about a room."

She made no reply, but he hadn't expected one. The closer they had come to Albany, the less she'd spoken. But then, the journey that should have taken them no more than two days, had stretched itself across a little more than a week. They stopped at every outpost between Fort Rensselaer and Albany, not wanting to miss any clue to her brothers' whereabouts—Samuel's whereabouts.

"What can I do for you, sir?" a lean man asked as he approached, his hands wiping across his apron.

"You're the innkeeper?"

"I am. Nickolas Barstow at your service." The corners of his eyes expanded with a fan of creases as he smiled. "Is it a meal you desire, or lodging?"

"Both." Joseph glanced back at Hannah who sat at the table, hands clasped. "For myself and my wife. And I have a horse in need of feed and stabling."

"Of course."

Joseph worked his pouch open and fished for the last of his coins. "Will this be enough?"

Mr. Barstow rolled the coins over in his palm. "For one night and…I suppose I can give you two meals for it. But nothing more. No ale."

He didn't need any. But they would need more than one night's lodging. Hannah was already worn thin from days of travel, waiting, and nights under the stars. The nights and days had warmed now that June was well upon them, but he wanted to give her a comfortable bed for as long as he could manage it. He emptied the pouch into his palm.

"What is this worth?" Joseph held Pa's pocket watch up by the chain for the man to see. "It's high quality gold." Given to Pa by Grandfather Garnet before he'd died back in Boston. The year before they'd headed west.

"May I see it?"

Joseph handed him the piece, not letting himself think about the sacrifice. Or that he should pass it to little James when he was grown. It was just an object. Not worth risking Hannah's health.

"This is a fine piece. Very fine. It's been in your family for some time?" He sighed. "How long are you looking to stay?"

"Hopefully only a few days." Long enough to

uncover Samuel's path.

The man took a moment to look Joseph over, and then glanced at Hannah. "You two have come a far ways, haven't you?"

They did appear quite trail-worn. "From up the Mohawk Valley a ways."

"Aye, we've seen quite a few come through from thereabout with all the Indian raids."

Joseph recognized the assumption and bristled at it. "Except we have no plans to abandon our land. We won't be staying away long."

Barstow nodded toward Hannah. "Your bride has a look about her. She's got some Iroquois in her, don't she?"

Joseph stiffened. "Would you prefer we take our business elsewhere?"

"'Course not." He popped the watch open and then closed it again. "You are welcome as long as needed and when you leave, I shall give you whatever is left owing for the timepiece. If you wish, you can ask around to make sure I give you a fair price."

"I could trade it elsewhere, and bring you the funds if you prefer."

"No." He tapped the cover of the watch and handed it back to Joseph. Along with the coins. "War is not a good time to gather pounds. But gold—and a fine crafted piece such as this—its worth will not be diminished, no matter who the final battle falls to."

Joseph slipped the heirloom back into his pouch and returned to the table and two watchful eyes. Hannah didn't have to say anything for him to know her questions.

"We'll stay here as long as we need. I thought perhaps we could wait until morning before—"

"I don't want to wait." Her defiant tone made him want to smile. She'd been far too withdrawn and contained the last while.

He feigned a frown. "Are you sure? I could use a good night's sleep before we go interrogating every army official in the city."

"Then you can rest, and I'll go myself."

"I don't know if I trust you not to ride off and leave me here."

"You can't." Some of the sparkle returned to her eyes, and she pushed to her feet.

Joseph grabbed her hand. "Don't you think we should at least wait until we've eaten something first?"

"Oh." The chair squeaked as she dropped back into her seat. "I suppose we should." She tipped her shoulder toward her ear. "For your sake."

He grinned. "Thank you." Then he looked at her hand, still in his. He didn't want to let go. But a woman, probably Barstow's wife, approached with two steaming bowls and a round loaf of bread on a tray. He released Hannah and lowered into the nearest chair.

"Stew's heavy from warming most the day, but it'll fill you."

They thanked her and ate their meal. Joseph watched Hannah's hands. He still wished he hadn't needed to let go. "I'm glad you are feeling better."

"Feeling better?"

"You haven't been yourself." For a while now. Ever since she'd bolted away on Hunter, pelting him with mud. He'd missed the sparks she usually sent flying when she'd talked to him.

"I suppose I've merely been…anxious. About finding my brothers." But something in her tone suggested she hid another reason for her mood. She gave a brief smile. "But now we're here. Farther than I probably would have made it on my own. And so much closer to answers. Thank you."

Her praise warmed him more than the stew on a hot June day. "I just hope we find…them." And hoped he found the words to tell her about Myles when the time came.

She looked at him with a strange but studious expression. "I really mean it, Joseph. Thank you. I've misjudged you so many times. But everything you've sacrificed to help me." Her gaze fell to the pouch tied to his belt. "I don't know how to ever repay you."

"You don't have to. I made a promise." A promise to protect her and to cherish her as her husband. A promise made before God and man.

"And yet, I don't even have the means to replace the window I broke." She stared into her stew and started eating again.

Joseph lost all interest in satisfying his stomach. *I made a promise.* And because of it, Hannah was his responsibility. He'd taken that upon himself and no one else was capable of removing it from him. Her father was dead as was her older brother. The younger, if alive by some miracle, was still a lad and would not have the means of caring for his sister. Joseph had no choice but to forget about Oriskany and give himself to her fully.

The weight of his dilemma lifted from his shoulders, offering liberty. And relief.

This wasn't just for his own good, to protect himself. It was what was required to keep her safe and see that she had everything she needed. A home. Family. And a husband who loved her.

~*~

Hannah hugged herself and fought the surge of hopelessness and frustration. They'd located army headquarters, but found no one there with access to the records. They were told to return tomorrow—an eternity from now.

Joseph's arm brushed hers and she glanced at him. He walked alongside her, leading Hunter. What was he doing here with her? She'd taken him from home for too long. His poor children probably wondered if they would ever see him again. And his farm. How would Andrew and Rachel manage everything? How could Joseph walk along as though her concerns were the only ones that mattered to him?

He stopped so abruptly, she stepped past and had to turn around to see him staring in the window of a milliners shop—according to the sign. He hefted his pouch. "Let's step in here for a moment."

Hannah had no idea what a milliner even was, so she simply followed. Displays of ribbon, thread and beautiful fabrics greeted them with too much cheer. She trailed Joseph toward the back, puzzled. What use had they of any of this?

Joseph continued to the woman who hovered over an older lady, assisting to add ornaments to a hat. "Do you have any gowns already made?"

The woman turned and frowned at Joseph. Her gaze narrowed with distaste. "That depends who the gown is for. Her measurements."

He stepped aside, removing Hannah's shield. Both ladies cringed. Heat rushed to Hannah's face, but she couldn't blame them for their horror. Compared with the fine gowns they wore, hers was nothing more than a rag, and a tattered one at that. The blackberry briers had shredded the hem, and miles of muddy roads coated the skirt with shades of brown and grey.

"Um, I might have something one of my regular patrons was not satisfied with." The woman excused herself and slipped through an open doorway at the back of the room. In moments she returned, folds of dark green draped over her arms. Not the loveliest color, but the material felt sturdy and the dark shade would wear well for travel and farm work.

Joseph took the gown and held it up to Hannah. "What do you think?"

The size appeared about right, though the hem would need to be brought up. Crisscrossed ties at the bodice would make up for any discrepancy in the waistline. But what more would this cost Joseph? "Are you sure?"

"That one you're wearing was already threadbare before we left. It won't hold up to much more use."

Hannah had no argument, so she nodded. "Whatever you feel best."

She joined Hunter outside while Joseph finished his purchases.

When they returned to the inn, Joseph handed her the parcel. "I requested before we left that water be sent up to our room so you can bathe." He scratched his hand across the back of his neck as he half-smiled. "I'll take my time with Hunter."

For the second time she had no argument for him and simply nodded before slipping away. Perhaps her attempts at being more like Fannie were beginning to take hold, despite her earlier failings.

Upstairs, a large tub—not large enough to

immerse herself in, but big enough to clean herself properly—waited half full. One pot of boiling water added to the top made the water a wonderful lukewarm. Hannah washed quickly, but made sure her hair was rinsed well before brushing it out. She'd let her tresses hang loose so they could start to dry before she braided them. She put on the shift wrapped with the gown and washed her old undergarments. She was cinching the ties of the bodice when a tapping came at the door.

"Hannah?" Joseph's voice.

Her pulse raced as though she were again sprinting away on Hunter. "Come in."

Joseph surveyed the room as he entered and dropped the cocked hat to the bed. His studious gaze settled on her. "Did you find everything you need?"

"Yes." *Thank you.* The last two words didn't quite make it past her lips.

Joseph had not been idle. He appeared bathed as well, and two weeks' worth of whiskers had been scraped from his face leaving the angles of his jaw smooth. But nothing held her in place as firmly as the intensity in his eyes, their complete focus on her.

He took a step nearer. "They've started serving dinner. If we want anything, we should go down."

"I am quite famished." In truth, her appetite had fled at the sight of him. Her stomach felt suddenly unsteady, and her fingers fumbled with the ends of her bodice ties in an attempt to form a bow.

Joseph took another step, and her lungs tightened around the breath she'd just taken.

"There's something I've wanted to speak to you of," he said.

"What is that?" Her voice rang a pitch higher than

it should.

His blue eyes smiled along with his mouth. "Promises made."

Hannah's breath hitched as Joseph's fingers slid up her arm to her elbow, and then higher still, across her shoulder. What promises did he speak of? The ones he had made? Or hers?

To be his wife.

Warmth caressed her jaw, his mouth making a crusade of its own. To her ear. How was this possible? That he wanted her? Dared she hope that was what this meant? She didn't move least he change his mind.

"Hannah."

She tipped her face toward his. Joseph's blue eyes searched hers as he cupped the side of her face. She let herself lean into the embrace. He loved her. Even if only a little. Why else would he hold her like this?

Unless he had simply thought of a way in which she could repay him.

Joseph ducked his head and touched her mouth. First with his finger. Then with his lips. No movement, just their mouths touching, lingering on the brink of something more.

A shiver moved through her. She'd never wanted anything so much, and feared it so greatly. The moment seemed to balance on one question that remained unanswered.

Did he love her?

Pressure built upon her mouth, and she realized he was kissing her. Soft at first, but then with an increasing neediness. Or longing? She couldn't be sure which, but a huge chasm divided the two. What if she were only a memory of Fannie?

Joseph, please…

How could she fight against something she craved so dearly?

One of his hands slipped to the bow she had just tied and he pulled the ends free. His kiss paused as he looked at her face. He froze, his gaze never wavering though the light of moments earlier slowly faded away. He cleared his throat and stepped back. "We should go down to dinner." Without another word, he collected his hat and moved to the door.

Hannah gasped for a breath, but it wouldn't come. All her attempts to emulate Fannie, and to what end? So that Joseph could lose himself in a memory? Reality was not so kind to him. She'd seen it in his eyes when he'd looked at her and saw her as she was. No, she could never be Fannie. And what good was his love if it wasn't for her?

24

Joseph stared at the streak of dim blue stretching from the window and across the blackened ceiling. The path of light extended almost to the far wall before it came to an abrupt end. Darkness continued in its place. How like Hannah that light was, bursting through the sorrow and loneliness that had enshrouded him. He didn't want to face the darkness again.

He rolled on his side. The floor felt even harder with her in the bed only feet from him. But instead of helping himself to a side of the bed like he would have done in the past, he laid out a quilt for himself on the floor, the fear he had seen in her eyes hours earlier reining him like the jerk of an iron bit.

Why would she fear him? Didn't she see how much he cared for her, that he only wanted to make her happy? To hold her and love her? He smothered a groan in his hands. What had he done? Her youth and inexperience was her virtue. He'd frightened her. If he wanted her heart, he would have to proceed slowly and gently.

He couldn't afford to lose Hannah now.

Eyes closed, Joseph let himself recall the feel of her in his arms, the softening of her lips against his. A short moment when she had returned his kiss. He clung to that as he fell asleep.

In the morning, he awoke to find Hannah already dressed and ready to leave. He covered a yawn and climbed to his feet. "I'll meet you downstairs if you wish," he said as he returned the quilt and pillow to the bed she'd already made up.

She gave a curt nod and left.

He pressed the heels of his palms into his eyes. He didn't understand the sudden ice in her eyes when she looked at him. She was no longer afraid. She was angry.

By the time he made it downstairs, Hannah pushed her plate aside and stood from the table. "You sit and eat your breakfast. I have plans of my own today. You've done too much for me already."

"What?"

"I'll make some inquiries on my own. You needn't bother yourself." She turned to go.

"It's the reason I rode, mostly walked, over a hundred miles, and now you are concerned about me *bothering* myself?"

She rotated to him and leaned in. "Well, I'm sorry to have dragged you all this way." Though whispered, her words cut.

"Hannah, why are you angry with me?" He kept his voice low and led her toward the stairway, away from the curious stares and listening ears of others in the room. "Is this about last night? Because I kissed you?"

"Of course not." But her voice rose the way it always did when he had her upset. "I merely don't want you to trouble yourself on my account." She spun and broke from his grasp.

Joseph let her go this time. If she wanted to search on her own, so be it. There were other places he could ask about Samuel. Yesterday Joseph had gleaned from their brief exchange at the local headquarters in Albany that the 1st New York Regiment had rejoined the Northern Department days ago. They camped only miles from the city. Maybe if he found a lead to her brother's whereabouts, Hannah would forgive him for his crime. He was obviously guilty of something.

Joseph declined breakfast and hurried to the stable to ready Hunter. A few hours later he'd found the encampment where he was shuffled from one officer to another until he stood in the front of a captain's tent. He hoped the burly man would have some answers—or at least point him in the right direction.

Joseph barely explained his purpose when he was waved away.

"I have no time for this."

And yet this is what Joseph had sacrificed weeks for. "You do not even recognize the name?"

The captain laughed out loud. "How could you expect me to remember one boy from the thousands I've led over the last half-decade?"

"But you have records."

"Of course, but they are for army use only and I see no uniform on you. Never mind rank or office. Have you even served in our army or for our cause?"

"Not in the army, but I—"

"We are in the middle of a war, and I have little time for a man who does not value our freedom as I do."

Joseph gritted his teeth. "I had no need to go out to find the war. It came to me—onto my land, stealing my family. I have fought the British and the Tories with as much determination as any of your soldiers in their uniforms."

The officer shook his head and turned on his heel, leaving Joseph to his indignation. Did the man have any idea what they had faced in the Mohawk Valley between raiders and British advances? Joseph snatched Hunter's reins and swung aboard. First Hannah, and now arrogant captains.

Joseph headed back toward the inn. He should check to see if Hannah had returned. Gradually he relaxed into Hunter's gait, though he scanned the faces of those he passed. How did they see him? A backwoods farmer? A man who only worried about protecting his own land instead of taking the offensive against the British? A fool?

A dark-haired lady and a man passed him in a light wagon, and Joseph jerked back on the reins and pulled Hunter's head around. The man had a very familiar look about him. But it couldn't be.

Could it?

He brought Hunter alongside the wagon, riding up far enough to make out the man's face. "I dare not trust my eyes."

Daniel Reid twisted in his seat, and confirmed the truth of his identity.

"Heard you were on your way back, but never dreamt of meeting you way out here," Joseph said with a grin.

Daniel laughed in disbelief. "Joseph? What are *you* doing here?" He glanced at the young woman beside him, who watched with her pale eyes and pursed brow. "This is one of my oldest friends. And my brother-in-law. Married to my sister Fannie."

Joseph frowned. Did Daniel not know?

"We are on our way home," Daniel continued, turning again to Joseph. "I had hoped to return before spring planting, but..." A smile stretched across his face. "But first I should introduce you to Mrs. Lydia

Reid."

Joseph cocked his head. "Reid?"

"My wife."

He took a little longer in his assessment of the woman. She was lovely, her complexion much like Fannie's had been, but there was something different about her. Perhaps the fine cut of her gown, very different from the more practical ones worn by woman on the frontier. Her gloved hands. Her demure smile.

"I am very pleased to know you after everything Daniel has told me." She spoke with a definite tone—a very cultured one.

"You as well?" He eyed Daniel. "You were supposed to be off fighting the British. When did you have time to find a wife?"

"By miracle I found time for both, but that is a long story, and we are in the middle of the road. Where are you bound?"

"To the Huntsman Inn just up the way. And you?"

"We've just arrived and have not settled on a place to stay yet, so let me turn around and I shall follow you."

"Splendid." Joseph inwardly cringed as he remembered the news he had to break to Daniel, news that was not right to speak in the middle of the street. "I have much to tell you."

"And I am famished for word of my family."

Joseph rode ahead, working out in his mind how he would inform Daniel of his sister's death. *Oh Lord, please don't let Hannah have returned yet.* Perhaps they could send Lydia in to make herself comfortable while they cared for the horses. That would give Joseph a moment to explain everything that had happened and why he had come to Albany.

He remained with Hunter as Daniel helped his wife down from their wagon. She gave a little moan, and Daniel steadied her. "How do you feel?"

"I will be fine as soon as I can lay down for a little while. And eat something."

Joseph stepped near. "Are you unwell?"

Red touched her cheeks. "I—"

"She is with child," Daniel said, pleasure displacing much of the concern of moments before. "The reason I did not make it home any earlier. She was quite ill at the beginning so we stayed on with her kin in Virginia until she felt well enough to travel. We've come a far piece over the last few days."

Joseph extended his hand and clasped Daniel's. "Congratulations. To you both." He quickly tied off Hunter's reins. "Let's get her inside and settled before we worry about anything else."

Like the horses. Like the bearing of bad news.

They made it as far as the door when Mr. Barstow swung it wide. "Oh, Mr. Garnet, I thought I heard your voice. Your wife just returned and was inquiring for you."

Daniel pivoted. "Fannie's here? And the children?"

Joseph opened his mouth to speak, but Hannah stood just inside the doorway.

"Oh," said the innkeeper, "There she is."

~*~

Hannah spied Joseph through the door and stepped that direction. Her search had been fruitless, and she was anxious to know if he had any success. She'd put aside her hurt and even her heart for the sake of her brothers.

The innkeeper mumbled something and the color drained from under Joseph's tanned skin. But perhaps that had something to do with the young couple standing with him. The man looked somewhat familiar, but he faced Joseph.

Her next step faltered. She did know those dark waves and broad shoulders. And she recognized the coal-like gaze he turned toward her.

"Where is she?" He scanned the room.

"Daniel…" Joseph's voice crackled. He mumbled something Hannah couldn't quite make out.

"But he said—"

"Don't worry about what he said. Not yet. First we need to talk."

"But…" Daniel looked from Hannah to Joseph, and back again. "She looks familiar."

"Of course I do." Hannah pressed a tight smile. "We were once neighbors."

"Cunningham? The Tory's daughter?"

She bit her tongue so hard it hurt. She shouldn't say anything, but he spat her family's name as if it tasted foul. And Joseph stood there mute. "You do remember. But that would no longer be correct." She raised her chin and refused to look at Joseph, his widening eyes, the look of horror. "But my name is Garnet now."

Hannah didn't wait for her words to take effect. Gathering her skirts so she wouldn't trip over her hem, she lengthened her stride to the stairs. She would grant Joseph enough mercy to not make him explain himself in front of her. She didn't want to hear his excuses anyway.

She waited in their room, seated on the edge of the

bed, half wondering if he simply wouldn't return. How could she blame him if he didn't? After everything he'd done for her, she'd given nothing in return. Only frustration. She'd fought him. Argued with him. Refused him. And shamed him…merely by her existence in his life.

With the lowering of the sun in the window, shadows lengthened across the room before the door cracked open and Joseph stepped in.

Hannah flopped back on the bed and stared at up at the ceiling. It would have been easier if he'd left her here.

"Why are you angry with me? Or…I don't know. I don't know what you are thinking. Or feeling. I'm trying to help you. I'm trying to…" He blew out a breath.

"I'm sorry. I shouldn't have said anything. And I'm sorry." Tears singed her eyes and she blinked them back.

"Is that what you think? That I didn't want Daniel to know that you are my wife? That I'm ashamed?"

Hannah hugged herself. Hearing her fears voiced by him only made them sound worse.

"The only thing I struggled to tell Daniel, was that his *sister* is dead. How do you look a man in the eyes and tell something like that?" Joseph slumped against the wall beside the door and drew his hat from his head. "How do you tell anyone that?"

"I'm sorry. I did not think..." She hadn't thought any of this through.

He sighed. "It doesn't matter anymore. He knows. I told him about Fannie. I told him about us. I told him about your brothers. I even asked for his help."

She pushed up on her elbows. "I don't want his

help."

Joseph's blue eyes hardened. "Well, I think we need it. At least he has some credibility with the army. The farther east we come, the less they want to talk to me."

They hadn't much wanted to make time for her either. "Fine."

"Good."

"Anything else?"

"No." He straightened and looked as though he might leave, but didn't. "I mean, yes. I'd like to know what you want from me."

"What do you mean?"

Joseph raised his hands and took a step closer. "I asked you a question once, and I'd like an answer. We were talking about what would happen after we found your brothers. I asked what you wanted." Another step. "What do you want?"

He was much too close now, almost to the bed.

"After growing up with Rachel and being married to Fannie, I figured I understood women well enough. But I can't figure you."

She wasn't sure about herself either. She'd never felt such a swirl of feelings.

Joseph stepped back. "Are you coming down to dinner?"

"I'm not hungry." At least she had an answer for that.

"Well I'm starved." He stalked away. The door echoed his departure.

Hannah flopped back on the bed. She'd been wrong to tell Daniel, not giving Joseph time to explain. What right did she have to call herself Joseph's wife, when she did not act like a wife? A man had the right to sleep in his bed and lay with his wife. To kiss her. To hold her. And isn't that what she wanted, too?

Maybe Joseph didn't love her yet, but how would he ever learn to if she kept him at arm's length?

25

The hard chair made Joseph's backside ache, and not more than an inch of yellowy wax remained of the candle in the center of the table, but he still had no desire to move. Instead, he watched the flame flicker while he listened to the conversation and laughter from the only other table that hadn't lost its occupants. The three men seated there had not been stingy with their consumption of ale.

Maybe that's what he needed.

Joseph shook his head. Pa hadn't agreed with men losing themselves in a jug or bottle. A man kept his head clear and did not cower from his problems.

Pa's life had probably never been as complicated as his.

Joseph pressed his fingers into his temples and massaged the ache growing there. Life with Fannie had been simple. She kept the house, cooked the meals, and minded the baby while he worked the land and kept it safe. In the evening, light conversation about daily happenings and playing with little James had given life a feeling of completeness. And then he lay beside his wife in the bed they shared.

"You look like a man with a lot on his mind." Daniel lowered into the chair across from him.

"Just trying to figure out what I'm doing out here."

"Your explanation to me made sense."

Joseph leaned his elbows on the table. "Made sense to me once, too. But sometimes I wonder if I am doing any good. If everything would have been better off if I'd stayed where I belong. Rachel and Andrew have the children and two farms to look after."

"I am sure they are fine. Not that I know Andrew well." He smiled tightly. "But Rachel has always been independent and resourceful, and I can't believe she would give her heart to a man who couldn't keep pace beside her."

Joseph contained his grimace. Daniel had once done everything within his power to win Rachel's heart, only to concede defeat and retreat for three-and-a-half years. And yet, it had not been difficult to see the way Daniel looked at his wife. He loved her very much. Even more so than he had once cared for Rachel.

"Besides, I can't imagine them not having any record here for the Cunningham boys. And as I said, I shall help. Lydia needs a rest before we continue up the valley. Myles and Samuel, right? Shouldn't be too hard to find them."

"Actually, there is only one left to find. Myles was shot for desertion. Cyrus Acker told us before we left and it was confirmed at Fort Rensselaer."

Daniel glanced up as Mr. Barstow approached with a jug. "No. Thank you." He looked back at Joseph. "I am sorry to say that doesn't surprise me much. That boy was too proud. Like his father. But Samuel. He struck me as someone who liked to please people, keep everyone happy. He'll probably have fared well enough as long as he wasn't killed in battle. He was young enough they might have kept him for messages and fetching and carrying for officers."

"That's my hope." For Hannah's sake.

"You might have to travel as far as New York to find him, though."

"Isn't the city still held by the British?"

"Yes. But from what I hear, General Washington's been eying it up for a large offensive with the French. Personally, I'd like to see them go south. The British are pulling most of their troops into Virginia."

After so long focusing on their little corner of the war, it was hard to grasp the full magnitude of the fight.

"And Joseph, about Fannie." Sorrow showed in Daniel's dark eyes. "I was real pleased when Mama wrote that you two had married. You have always been a true friend, despite my faults. Despite all the trouble I caused. What I am trying to say is I have no doubts that you were a good husband to my sister. But I hope that you find happiness with Hannah, as well. You deserve it."

Joseph cleared the sudden thickness from his throat. "Thank you, Daniel." He lowered his voice. "Though I must admit I expected it to bother you more that her Pa was a Loyalist?"

Daniel chuckled and glanced at the stairs. "Lydia's father and I would not have agreed upon politics either, and that's not even the half of it. But, as I said, that makes for a long story, and I should get back to my wife before she wonders what became of me and the water she requested." He grinned. "I shall see you in the morning."

Joseph nodded and watched him go. He pushed to his feet. He needed sleep before they renewed their search, and he wouldn't get any down here.

A lamp lit the room, revealing Hannah in the bed, sitting, blankets drawn up, shoulders bare except for the hair that spilled over her smooth skin. The image was enough to make his knees weak, and he dropped into a chair to pull off his boots.

"I thought you'd be asleep."

"Thought? Or hoped?"

He wouldn't answer. If she was asleep, he might have stolen a part of the bed and been comfortable through the night. But with her sitting there with her solemn gaze, he'd be better off on the floor. Joseph moved to the bed and took one of the pillows.

"Don't sleep on the floor again." She spoke so softly Joseph almost didn't hear her.

He took up a quilt as well. "I don't mind." Though he definitely wasn't looking forward to it.

"Do not lie. What sane man would want to sleep on a hard floor when he had a soft bed two feet away? One he paid good money for."

Joseph couldn't argue with that. He dropped the pillow back beside her and pulled his shirt over his head. Trying not to look at her, he laid in bed, faced up. His pulse sped at her closeness as she lowered beside him and touched his arm.

"I'm sorry," she whispered.

"You already apologized. It's forgiven."

"Then why won't you look at me?"

He turned on his side. And swallowed hard. The low light was soft across the gentle contours of her face, and he ached to trace them with his fingers. Or his lips. Her lips had a slight purse to them, but he couldn't read her expression.

"What do *you* want?" Her voice wavered. Her gaze never left his.

Joseph didn't dare voice what he wanted right now. Didn't know how to put it into words. But she was close enough…

He pressed his mouth to hers. A brief kiss. Nothing more. But she touched his face, and then slid her fingers through his hair to the back of his scalp. Her lips made a slow reply, drawing desire through him. He wrapped his arm over her and sidled her closer. Was this her answer? Did she want him, too?

Their kiss continued and his need for her grew. To hold her. To have her.

His wife.

She stiffened.

Joseph didn't have to see her fear to recognize it. He released her and dropped onto his back. "I'm sorry."

For a moment he could only hear Hannah's breathing. She sighed. "Why? What are you sorry for?"

"I'm frightening you." He looked over to see her gaze steady on him.

Hannah pushed up on her elbow. "Is that…is that why you left the last time you kissed me?"

He nodded.

"Only a little." Her mouth softened. Almost a smile.

Joseph couldn't resist touching her face. He laid her down and gave her a single kiss. Then, he slid his arm under her—his shoulder would act as a pillow. With her head tucked against his and her hand resting on his chest, Joseph closed his eyes and relaxed into the bed. This was all he needed right now. To hold her and let the emptiness in his soul be filled.

~*~

Hannah leaned against the doorframe and tapped

out a rhythm on the scarred wood. Why had she not insisted on accompanying them? As much as Daniel's presence made her nervous, Joseph was right that he had the contacts with the Continental Army that they needed. If only there was something she could do while she waited.

"Pardon me, I am afraid our husbands failed to introduce us yesterday."

Hannah turned. The woman she'd seen only briefly stood behind her. "You're married to Daniel Reid?" Hannah never would have imagined such a lady with a man like Daniel—who had so many rough edges.

"I am. Lydia Reid." She smiled, but something else lingered behind her blue-green eyes. "Did you know him well? Mr. Reid, I mean."

"Well enough." As well as she had wanted to at the time. "But my family left the valley at the beginning of the war."

"I can understand that."

"Why, because my father was a Tory?" Hannah folded her arms and looked back at the street. Where were those men?

"Do not think I mean to judge or criticize your family. Such would make me a true hypocrite."

Hannah glanced back. "You were a Loyalist? Or your family?"

Lydia gave a subtle nod. "And perhaps I still do not understand the drive behind men like Daniel—"

"And Joseph."

"To give up anything and everything for this country and their freedom." She smiled again. "*Our* freedom. But I will no longer stand in the way of something wanted so dearly." Her hand smoothed over the slight swell of her stomach. "Perhaps it will be worth whatever the cost for future generations."

"How far are you along?"

A blush rose to the lady's cheeks. "Almost four months. And already so weary of feeling ill and uncomfortable."

But how wondrous would it be to carry the child of the man you loved?

"I just pray everything will be well." Lydia looked at her with a sudden intensity. "Hannah…may I call you Hannah? I know we are hardly acquainted, but if I understand correctly, we shall soon be neighbors."

"I suppose we will." She could not imagine not returning with Joseph now. "And of course, you may call me Hannah."

"Thank you." Lydia took a breath. "I hesitate to press Daniel because of his determination to go home and confidence that all will be fine, but what is there for midwife or doctor in the valley? I know I cannot do this on my own."

Hannah's heart softened toward this woman who also carried so many fears. "Daniel's mother has birthed five children. I am sure she knows what to do." Hannah wished her own mother were alive and in the valley. Not only had she given birth to four children, but she had assisted many women after they'd returned to her people. She had seemed to know everything about birthing.

"Daniel said something similar, but…"

"He's a man." Hannah finished for her.

They both chuckled.

"Will you and Mr. Garnet return to the valley soon?" Lydia asked. "After you find your brother?"

"My brothers." She emphasized the *s*. "And yes." *I*

do hope so.

"Oh, I am sorry. Daniel told me you had one younger brother to find. I did not realize two were missing."

"My older brother, as well."

A strange look passed Lydia's face. Confusion. Or concern? "I will add both brothers to my prayers."

"Thank you." Something Hannah wished she could do as well. But even after Joseph's brief lesson, she wasn't prepared to address a God she didn't know.

Lydia looked at the streets and Hannah followed. She saw Hunter first, Joseph astride, and hurried out to meet them. Daniel rode beside. She didn't wait for either to dismount. "Anything?"

Joseph swung down and fastened Hunter's reins to a rail. He took her arm. "Come inside and let us catch our breath."

"Why. You're talking fine as it is. Tell me, Joseph."

He chuckled and led her inside to a table.

Fine. She sat down and crossed her arms. *But please hurry.*

He pulled a chair beside hers and turned it to face her.

Oh, please don't have bad news. But there was something in his eyes that fed hope.

"Daniel found one of his old commanders and made some inquiries. We don't know anything yet, but they said to return in the morning and he will tell us anything they've been able to discover."

More waiting. "Tomorrow?" Always tomorrow. Always another day.

Daniel lowered into a chair across from them. "If Samuel is to be found, we will find him, Hannah."

She snapped her head up. "Not just Samuel.

Myles, too."

Daniel's brow furled. He looked at Joseph. "You never told her?"

Hannah's heart thudded before plummeting to her stomach. "Told me what?" *No. Please no.*

Joseph's mouth opened and froze. The color drained from his face.

No. Not Myles. "What Acker said was true?" She felt something crack open in her, but stiffened her spine and found her voice. "When? How long have you known?"

"Fort Rensselaer. They told me at Fort Rensselaer."

Well over a week—almost two. He'd lied to her.

"Hannah, I didn't want to say anything until…"

He was still talking, but she could no longer hear him over the rush in her ears. Her focus, her sanity, everything was slipping away. She shoved away from the table and rushed to the stairs. It was true. Myles was dead. Killed for wanting nothing to do with the Patriot cause.

~*~

Joseph shoved to his feet, but a hand gripped his sleeve.

"Give her some time," Daniel said.

Time? To face this alone? She had no one, not even God to cry to. He couldn't leave her alone. He pulled away and followed up the stairs. The door slammed ahead of him. He steeled himself and took hold of the latch. "Lord, help me comfort her." He stepped in the room.

Hannah spun to face him, tears on her cheeks. "Go away."

I cannot do that. "Hannah, I'm—"

"Sorry? That you lied to me? Over and over, making me believe there was a chance he was still alive. Making me believe either of them are alive. Do you know about Samuel? Is he dead too and you're just dragging me along? Why? What do you want from me?"

"Hannah." Joseph tried to touch her arm, but she struck his hand away.

"Don't touch me." More tears rolled from her lower lashes. "Don't ever come near me again. In fact, what are you even doing here? Get out. Leave. Go back to your farm and your family. You don't owe me anything, not your promises, not your presence." She grabbed his saddlebags from the floor by the bed and tossed them at him.

They thudded to the floor, and he stepped over them. "Hannah, I'm not going anywhere." He caught her arms.

She jerked back, but he held her fast. Until her foot slammed into his shin. He swallowed the pain with a grunt and tried to reclaim her arms. He missed one, and her knuckles plowed into his face.

He tasted blood.

"What sort of devils shoot boys for not wanting to fight?"

"Hannah..."

"And if you'd been there, you would have sat on your horse and watched, wouldn't you have? You wouldn't have done anything. You never did anything!" She screamed the last words at him and struck again. Both fists pummeled his chest.

Joseph pulled her tight. "Hannah."

She tried to shove away, but he wouldn't let her. If

he let her go now, she'd never let him in again. She'd lock him out and face this battle alone.

"I hate you!"

She struggled against his hold, but he only tightened it and tucked his head against hers.

"I hate..." The word died with a sob. She trembled in his arms, her fight failing. Tears tickled his neck.

Joseph didn't dare speak, even to soothe. So he simply held her as she wailed. And then cried. And then sobbed. She sagged into him, and slowly they sank to the floor together. Still, he held her. Rocking gently as he would one of his children.

Shadows lengthened across the room and her eyes dried. Still they didn't move. Or speak. Joseph stroked her hair. How gladly he would bear her pain for her, to keep her safe from it. To protect her. He pressed his mouth to the top of her head and took a jagged breath. Still his lungs ached. No, not his lungs. His heart. Ached with emotions he'd felt before for another woman, emotions he felt no weaker now. Not just attraction, not just a need to protect, but something that stirred the very depths of his soul.

26

Hannah leaned into Joseph, eyes closed against more tears as he cradled her with a tenderness she'd never imagined any man possessing—especially not Joseph Garnet. In the darkness of approaching night, the room around them vanished away. His heart thudded in her ear, matching the rhythm of her own. His hands, though calloused, gently stroked her hair away from her face.

Gradually her eyes dried, though the open wound in her heart remained. As did thoughts of Myles. He didn't deserve death, and definitely not an execution. She could picture him on the ground, leaning against the cabin or under a tree, knees bent up, knife in hand as he whittled away at whatever piece of wood he'd chosen to bring back to life.

The agony rippled through her with another sob, though she had no more tears.

"Shhh." Joseph's breath warmed the top of her head. He stood and pulled Hannah with him, never releasing his hold on her as he lifted her into his arms and set her on the bed. He got in beside her. "Try to sleep."

"I can't." When she closed her eyes she saw passionate, determined, stubborn Myles. Had he begged for his life when the soldiers discovered him trying to leave, or had he simply glowered at them with those almost black eyes he'd inherited from

Mama? Had they hurt him too, or killed him immediately?

"You have to have faith that Samuel is still out there, and that we'll find him."

Faith? In what? The brutalities of war? She didn't have anywhere to put her faith. If only she knew a Great Creator, or Loving Father to grant her some sort of hope. The hope Joseph must have had to be able to leave his family to help her search. The hope Lydia Reid held that despite her fears she would follow her husband into the wilderness.

Hannah rotated in Joseph's embrace to face him. "Do you really believe your God hears prayers?"

For a moment he said nothing, then a nod. "I do."

"Will you help me pray?"

He kissed her hairline and took one of her hands in his. The other remained around her. "Dear Lord…" He waited.

"Dear Lord." She closed her eyes and tipped her head forward until it met Joseph's.

"Tell Him what's in your heart."

Her heart? She didn't want to look that deep. Too much pain resided within. More than she could bear by herself. "Help me."

Joseph gripped her hand, but said nothing.

She turned her plea to one she couldn't see or feel. "Help me, God. Please. Will you take everyone from me? Myles…I wanted to see him again, to see what manner of man he'd become, to see Pa in him, to…" *have family again.* "I—I don't want him to be dead." *I don't want to lose everyone I love.* "All my hope lies with Samuel. That he's somewhere alive. Oh, Lord, please leave him alive. I need him." *I need him, God. And I need Joseph. I didn't realize how greatly until now, but God, I wouldn't have been able to survive this without him here with me. Let me keep him forever this way.* "Bring Samuel back to me." *And let me keep Joseph.*

When Hannah said nothing more, Joseph squeezed her hand. "Lord, this *we* pray, in Jesus's name."

Neither of them spoke more. Gradually Joseph's hold relaxed and his breathing deepened. She stared at the shadows on his face. She had never expected this gentleness from him. This patience. Her heart swelled, but not just with feeling for him. Hope was also there. Almost like a tender embrace from within, and the whisper that Someone she had never known, or spoken to until tonight, loved her.

~*~

Numb tingles shot pain up and down Joseph's arm, but Hannah lay so peacefully in the light of day. He'd woken a while ago, but other than the pain in his arm from the pressure of her head, he was quite content to watch her sleep. Besides, she needed the rest. She'd tossed and turned beside him most of the night.

He reached out with his free hand and brushed the dark strands of hair from her cheek. "Lord, please hear her prayer. Protect Samuel and help us find him." *Even if You don't hear my prayer, hear hers.* Joseph smoothed his thumb over her eyebrow, following the curve. It was impossible to ignore his own desires. "But if my prayers are heard…I want her, Lord. I want to find her brother and take her home. I want my children at home with us." His lungs burned and he forced a breath. "I want a family again."

Hannah stirred, releasing a soft sigh as she rolled toward him. He slid his arm deeper so her head came onto his shoulder, then stretched his arm and worked feeling back into his hand. Relaxed, Joseph smiled at the thought of a future together. And never a dull moment. He'd do his best to make her happy, while she kept him on his toes with her sharp wit and fiery temper. Once in a while he might even provoke her, just enough to watch her flair. She was real pretty when angry.

A tapping at the door broke through his daydream. Hannah moaned, but her eyes remained closed. Joseph quickly extracted himself from under her and hurried to answer the door before they woke her. Thankfully, he was still fully clothed.

He cracked the door open to Daniel's curious gaze and half-smile.

"So you did survive. I had my doubts when you didn't meet me this morning."

Joseph stepped into the hall and pulled the door closed. Downstairs bustled with activity. "How late is it?"

"Almost midday. So I decided to go without you. Figured things had gone very poorly last night and she'd murdered you, or things went very well and you wouldn't want to be disturbed." Daniel grinned. "By the looks of you, I'd guess closer to the first."

Joseph waved him off and combed his hair down with his fingers. "Did you find out anything?"

"I did. I could have waited, but what I have could help smooth yesterday's blunder. The most recent record of Samuel Cunningham was four months ago. He was transferred to the second infantry unit of the Third New York Regiment."

"So he is alive." Joseph felt his own grin pulling now.

"As of four months ago, but I don't think that unit has seen much battle in that time. As I said last night, General Washington is making plans, but nothing has been decided. And I don't think anything will be for a little while. Not until Lieutenant General Rochambeau, the French commander, reaches General Washington just north of New York. From the information I've gleaned, you'd do best to head toward White Plains."

"White Plains?" A five or six day's journey down the Hudson. But now with some hope that they would find what they sought. Samuel Cunningham was probably alive and there was a possible end in sight. Then they could go home.

"I reckon that's the end of my usefulness here, but we should be back in the valley soon. Is there anything I can do for you there?"

Joseph leaned against the wall, wishing he didn't have to wait to return. He'd never even had a chance to say goodbye to James. Maybe his son wouldn't remember him by the time he made it back. "Check on Rachel and the children. Tell them what you know. And that I will come home as soon as I am able."

"Of course."

"The cabin's empty. It might only be for a few weeks, but feel free to make use of it if you wish."

"Thank you," Daniel said. "And I'll see if Rachel and her husband need any help with the farms."

"I'd appreciate that." Joseph extended his hand. "More than I can say."

Daniel gripped his hand and pulled him into an embrace. "I hope you don't mind that I still consider you my brother."

"On the contrary. I'm grateful." His brother and friend. What a blessing Daniel's return proved to be.

"Forgive me for my next question, but Hannah doesn't know about what happened between you and her father at Oriskany, does she?"

Joseph shook his head and sighed. "Only you and Andrew know."

"Probably better that way."

"I hope so." But doubts nagged.

"You saved my life that day. And your own. You're not at fault for his death."

"How can it not be my fault?" Joseph questioned. "I killed him with my own hands."

The door creaked open behind him, and he pivoted.

Hannah wrapped a shawl over her shoulders as she stepped out, sleep still in her eyes. "I heard you talking."

He could only stare. How much had she heard? Surely she didn't realize the topic of their conversation or her hands would be at his throat.

"I was informing Joseph what I discovered about Samuel," Daniel replied smoothly. He quickly explained everything he'd already reported.

As soon as Daniel finished, Hannah turned back to Joseph, her eyes bright. "When do we leave?"

"As soon as you wish."

"Then let's not wait. I don't want to wait."

"I'll settle with the innkeeper and let him know we shall depart after we've eaten something."

She gripped his hand and gave a wobbly smile. "Thank you."

The two words kneed him in the gut. Forgetting Oriskany was not as easily done as he'd hoped.

27

"How can it not be my fault? I killed him with my own hands."

Who? Who had Joseph killed?

Far too often in the past week, Hannah had sifted the question through her mind. At first she had told herself he could have been talking about an animal. A hog? A cow? But she knew better. No animal could evoke such horror as she'd sensed in his voice and expression when she'd appeared. No, Joseph had spoken of a man.

The steady plod of Hunter's hooves on the hard packed road merged with the steady hush of the Hudson River. Hannah rested her hands on the pommel of the saddle, watching Joseph and his long strides. The colonies had been at war with themselves and Britain for well over a half decade—longer here in New England. Of course he'd killed men. He wouldn't have survived this long if he hadn't been willing to protect himself and his family.

But this wasn't just anyone. Daniel must have also known the man.

"Whoa, boy." Joseph paused as they neared a stream. He glanced to her. "That sun is plenty hot today. Would you like a drink?"

"Please." Summer had fully arrived in New York, and while nights were much more comfortable, days were not.

Joseph helped her down, handed her the canteen, and then walked with Hunter to the edge of the stream. "What you need is something to keep the sun off your head."

"That would be nice." The warm water flowed from the canteen over her parched throat. When her thirst was quenched, she joined him and handed the canteen back.

After taking a drink, Joseph tied it onto the saddle. With a half-smile, he pulled his cocked hat from his head and plopped it on hers. "There you go."

Fitting large, the hat tipped to one side. Hannah straightened the front point so it lined up with her nose and smiled. "It's still pretty warm under here."

"But it suits you. Looks as though you are ready to take the reins of this family. Didn't you tell me Mohawk people are ruled by their women?"

She took the hat and set it back on his head. "But they still let men be their chiefs."

"So the woman let the men pretend they are in charge?"

"Precisely."

"I appreciate that." A smile stretched across his face, but didn't reach farther. Not to his eyes. "I shall try to remember who to heed."

"See that you do." He could start by telling her what he and Daniel had talked about the morning they'd left Albany—what had returned the haunted look to Joseph's eyes. The same look he'd worn after he'd told her about Oriskany in the graveyard at Fort Herkimer.

He gently squeezed her arm and then helped her back onto the horse. Again they faced due south and

Hannah forced her thoughts to her brother. The closer they came to their destination, the more torturous each mile became. Still pausing to question the location of the Third New York Regiment at every Continental outpost, their journey had taken longer than it should, but soon they would reach White Plains.

Nervous excitement fluttered through her. Almost six years since she'd seen Samuel. Would she even recognize him? How tall had he grown? How much had the war changed the sweet boy she'd loved?

Hannah leaned forward in the saddle. "How much farther now?"

"Should arrive sometime tomorrow morning." He smiled at her. "Not much farther now."

They traveled a ways more before pausing to eat, and then resumed their journey. Hannah joined Joseph walking for a while, her legs needing to stretch. And it was nice walking beside him. She got him talking about his Pa and the first years in the valley. Life before, when he had lived with his family on a farm outside of Boston. What had made them leave everything behind to start a new life along the Mohawk?

"It was my fault," Joseph said with a grunt as though a confession of a crime.

"Your fault?"

"I was restless. Everyone seemed to be heading west, deeper into the frontier and wilderness. Meanwhile, everything back here in the east—all the land already tamed—was quite boring to me."

Hannah raised her brows at him. "Now you are starting to remind me of my pa." She had never taken Joseph Garnet as an adventurer. His land and farm seemed all that mattered to him. "What changed?"

He readjusted his hat. "I was seventeen when Pa decided it was better to follow me then lose me. I really believe he would have preferred to stay if he wasn't so certain I'd leave. Anyway, I was young and full of big ideas about life—" his shoulders slumped as though under a heavy weight. "—before I learned the true cost of life. And taming land."

She felt his sorrow. Shared it. "I wonder if my pa ever learned that. If he ever realized what adventure cost."

They walked for a while longer, no one speaking.

The sun arched downward, making its way west—its way home.

"We should probably find a place to make camp," Joseph finally said.

Hannah looked to the southern horizon. "Do we have to? If we're so close?"

"We'd have to walk half the night to get there before dawn. What good will that do us? We'd still have to take time to sleep sometime."

She bumped him with her shoulder. "Maybe you would."

"I don't know what you're talking about." Joseph nudged her in return. "You're usually snoring long after I get up in the morning."

Hannah fought the urge to bump him harder. "If you hear snoring, then you're obviously not awake yet."

"Ha." He turned as though he wanted to make another retort, but it broke into a real laugh. "I think I might have to concede that one."

"You are learning to be wise like your pa."

Joseph's blue eyes softened. "I hope so."

Hannah felt herself tip toward him. Her gaze fell

to his mouth. She missed his kisses. Wouldn't it be within her rights as his wife to steal one now? She brushed her fingertips along his sleeve. "And I'm learning to not fear every adventure…more like my pa."

Joseph set his hand over hers, but he now looked sad. "You are a lot more like your pa than you might realize."

"What do you mean?"

"What sort of girl rides with a raiding party, prepared to travel across New England, farther perhaps, on her own? You would not have stopped, even if I hadn't come along. You would have found a way to find your brothers. And not let anything stop you."

Hannah wasn't so sure anymore. She couldn't imagine coming this far without Joseph. "That makes me like my pa?"

"Yes. Yes, it does. That and your eyes. You have his eyes."

"You say it as though you remember his eyes."

Joseph looked away momentarily. "Your mother's were not so light, were they?"

She chuckled. "No. No they were not."

Joseph shuffled his boots against the ground. "Your pa meant a lot to you, didn't he? You loved him?"

"Of course. He was my papa. I never liked when he'd go away, trapping, or to fight for the British, but only because I missed him." She squeezed Joseph's hand. "And I think, if not for this war, for your differences in political views, you might have found much you do have in common." What would Pa have thought of his son-in-law?

She couldn't imagine him not liking this wonderful man.

~*~

Joseph patted Hannah's hand and motioned to the south. "Why don't we go a little farther tonight?" He needed to move again, to put some distance between himself and their conversation.

"All right." Hannah watched him much too closely.

He ignored the trickle of sweat down his brow and snugged his hat lower. Hunter followed his lead, as did Hannah.

"It really angers you that my pa sided with the British, doesn't it?" She maintained pace beside him.

Joseph kept walking. Thankfully, she still had no idea what really tore him. "We don't need to talk about it."

"Maybe we should."

No, we shouldn't. A conversation about allegiances breeched dangerous territory.

"Joseph…" Hannah stopped.

"What?"

"I don't share Pa's loyalties. Not to the British. You know that, don't you? My loyalties have always been to my family."

Joseph turned back. He couldn't help himself. "I understand that."

"Then don't look at me like Daniel did. Don't think of me as the Tory's daughter. I may not understand your cause, or why separating from Britain is so important to you, but I am a Patriot's wife now. And…and I don't want to think about the past anymore. This war will end. I want to think about the future."

He reached out his hand, and she took it. "Me, too." But how long would they succeed in burying the past? Like smoke on a battlefield, it seemed to linger long after the last shot was fired. Haunting.

Her gentle smile faltered as she looked past him. She let go of his hand. "Are those…?"

Thin chimneys of pale smoke rose above the treed horizon to the southeast. "Campfires."

"There are so many."

And more appearing every few seconds. It had to be an army, perhaps a full regiment. But whose?

"What if that's them? What if Samuel is there?"

"It's a possibility." Or it could be the British. New York City was still a British stronghold, and they weren't far from there.

"Then let's not wait. They are not far off."

Only a mile or so. No distance at all. But dark would nearly be upon them by then. "Maybe we should wait."

She spun to him. "Why?"

"We don't know who they are."

"What does it matter? If it's the British we tell them we are Loyalists. You can let me do the talking. And if they are Continental, then maybe we can find Samuel."

Joseph still hesitated, but arguing with her would do little good, so he nodded. "Very well. But mount up. I want to get close enough to see what we're getting into before we lose the light."

28

The woods gave way to a large clearing along another stream. Men, most in uniform, swarmed among a patchwork of tents and campfires. The odor of horse and sweat hung on the air.

"Who goes there?"

Hannah braced against Joseph as he slowed Hunter but continued toward the camp and the guard who had spoken.

"My name is Joseph Garnet from the Mohawk Valley. And this is my wife. We're looking for someone."

"Who?"

The guard took Hunter's bridle and Joseph swung down. "A Samuel Cunningham. He's a soldier in the New York Third Regiment."

"This is part of the Third. But I don't know that name." He smiled up at Hannah for too long, making her want to squirm.

"Do you know every name in the Third?" She gave what she hoped was a pointed look.

The guard laughed. "Definitely not."

"Then who do we talk to?" Joseph countered.

The guard stepped back and looked Joseph up and down. "Lieutenant Jones is over there by the fire. You might ask him."

"Thank you." Joseph stepped around the guard and moved in the indicated direction, leaving Hannah with the reins. She hit the ground and caught up before he reached the campfire and the officer standing near.

She nudged Joseph with her shoulder. "It's *my* brother we are looking for."

"What? Who are you looking for," the lieutenant asked before Joseph could make his reply. "Who are you?"

They again explained their purpose and the lieutenant shook his head. "Not a name I am familiar with. Colonel Hardy is camped up the creek that-a-ways with his headquarters. He might point you in the right direction." He narrowed his eyes at Joseph. "Where have you served? You look familiar."

Joseph stiffened beside Hannah, but his voice remained unaffected. "Mostly up along the Mohawk. Thank you for your help." He nodded and pulled Hannah along, taking a wide circle around the preparations for night as it descended upon them.

So many faces. Hannah searched them, trying to imagine what her little brother looked like now. What if she walked right by him? Would she recognize him, or would he be a complete stranger?

Even more men bustled around what looked to be the colonel's headquarters. Joseph hung back as though looking for the best opening. How could he appear so calm—something that completely eluded her?

She couldn't stand here so close to answers. So close to Samuel.

"Excuse me." Hannah pulled away and darted to the door of the large tent where several officers talked. "Excuse me, who is Colonel Hardy?"

"I am he." A middle aged man drew off his hat. "But I haven't time for…" He peered at her. "What do you want, miss…?"

She wouldn't waste precious moments with introductions. "I'm looking for my brother, Samuel Cunningham. I was led to believe he might be under your command." *Lord, please let it be so!*

One of the other officers stepped to intercept her, his head shaking. "Miss, as Colonel Hardy said, we don't have time for—"

"It's Mrs." Joseph stepped close behind her and set a hand to her arm. "All we ask is for a few minutes of your time. He is either here, or he is not."

"And who are you?" a third officer asked.

"Joseph Garnet. We're from the Mohawk Valley."

All the men eyed him as though unsure whether to brush him aside or not. "Who have you served under?"

"I've ridden with General Herkimer. Before his death. For a short time I rode under Colonel Gansevoort, as well."

"Colonel Gansevoort had command of Fort Schuyler for a time, did he not?"

"Yes, sir."

"And Herkimer. Nicolaus Herkimer?"

"Yes, sir."

Colonel Hardy looked to his junior officers. "General Herkimer led a force into one of the bloodiest battles we've known in this war. Lost half his men in an ambush. Over four hundred."

"I was at Oriskany with him." Joseph's voice rumbled.

The colonel's expression took on a new respect. "Step into my tent for a minute." Inside, he pushed a pipe into his mouth and lit it. "You said you are looking for Samuel Cunningham, I believe?"

Hannah's heart skipped. He spoke as though he

knew the name. "Yes. He is my brother."

The colonel gave a small smile. "Interesting."

"Why do you say that?" Joseph asked. Both his hands supported her shoulders now.

"Because I've read the original reports on Private Cunningham. He was the son a Loyalist."

He did know Samuel! "Yes. And I was the daughter of one. Please, where is my brother now?"

The colonel looked from Hannah to Joseph and back again. "Here."

A sharp intake of breath didn't keep her head from spinning, or from that same air being released as a sob. "Here?" Samuel was alive? She'd found him? Perhaps a loving God did indeed exist.

"Yes. He's served under me for a few months now. A fine soldier."

Hannah clenched her teeth to keep control of the sudden surge of emotion that threatened to break from her. She leaned into Joseph and soaked up his strength. Samuel was alive, and she'd found him. How could she make herself believe it?

"Can we see him?" Joseph asked, speaking her heart.

"Yes. I shall send someone for him. Wait here."

Colonel Hardy left, and Hannah twisted to Joseph. She had so much she wanted to say, to thank him for helping her, to tell him how unbelievable this all was, but words collided in her head before they could be birthed.

Joseph wrapped her in an embrace, making it easy to close her eyes and let warmth roll to her cheeks while they waited another eternity.

Oh, where was Samuel?

The tent door swooshed behind her. "I was told to

report to..." The voice was deep—so much like Myles's. But Myles was dead. "Excuse me, mister. I must have misunderstood."

"Samuel?" Hannah pivoted to the lanky youth nearly as tall as Joseph. Dark hair hung over his brow, obscuring, along with the shadows of night, his familiar features, but she still knew him. "Samuel."

His mouth hung open. "Hannah?"

She nodded and threw herself at him with a squeal.

He staggered back a step and gripped her hard. Almost as hard as she held him. "What are you doing here?" he asked.

"I came to find you."

"Where's Mama?"

Hannah gripped him tighter. All she had left. "Not now. I can't tell you right now." She wanted to hold on to this moment. This feeling of perfect happiness.

~*~

The hundreds of tents sat silent, and the campfires had died hours ago.

Joseph had chosen a site for their bedrolls not far from the colonel's headquarters, not far from where they had visited with Samuel long into the night.

Hannah slept in the blue haze of approaching dawn. She'd taken a while to fall asleep after hours spent with her brother, swapping news and stories, but she'd slept soundly since. As far as she was concerned, they had succeeded. She'd found Samuel and would never have to be separated from him again. Reality was not so kind.

Joseph had not thought beyond finding her

brother, either, but the boy was still a levied soldier. He wasn't free to walk away.

Joseph clenched his jaw against a yawn but his eyes still watered. He'd hardly slept thinking about today—about what he would say to Colonel Hardy, what arguments he could make. *Oh, Lord, help me. Please give me success. For Hannah's sake.*

Instead of feeling peace, uncertainty drove Joseph to his feet. He moved to the dead coals and dug for any hint of life. In the very heart of the largest charred log, he found a tiny glow of red. Just like his faith had always been. Small. On the verge of fading. But still there.

He found some kindling and blew softly. With some coaxing the ember grew and then flickered into a flame. A few minutes later he added a small log to the kindling and watched the blaze spread.

If only his trust in God's plan for his life were so easy to stoke.

"What is Thy plan, Lord?" *Or do you even have one for me?*

Footsteps preceded Samuel's voice. "You are awake early."

Joseph nodded. "You, too."

"Didn't sleep much last night." Samuel pulled up a short length of stump next to Joseph's. "Thinking too much."

"Me, too."

"What have you been thinking about?"

Easy enough to summarize. "Your sister."

"Hannah will be all right. She has you. And I'm glad for that."

"She has me, but I don't think she will be able to walk away without you." And chance losing him all over again. The war was far from over.

"I doubt there will be much choice in the matter." The young man rested his elbows on his knees and dropped his head forward. "I sometimes wonder if there will ever be a way out. I hardly remember home and family anymore. Seeing Hannah…" Samuel craned his neck to look at his sister's sleeping form tucked in her bedroll. "Seems more like a dream. Maybe that is why I was afraid to sleep. Didn't want to wake up and find out I had imagined her."

Joseph tried not to consider what it would be like to never see his children again, or Rachel and Andrew. To never go home. To go years without knowing if they had survived. No word. No hope.

"Thank you for this much." Samuel grinned at him, but it couldn't mask his pain. Or his fear.

"She would have found you with or without me," Joseph said.

"Maybe. Hannah is strong. Always has been. But finding me is only half of what she's had to go through. Learning about what happened to Myles. That wouldn't have been easy for her. And leaving here…"

"Nothing is written in stone yet." Joseph tossed another log on the fire. He couldn't let Hannah suffer another loss. "We'll speak with the colonel. He seems a good man."

"Aye, he is. But…" Samuel shrugged and looked to the dancing flames. "I guess we shall see."

The sun worked into the sky and another soldier set a pot over the fire to brew some coffee.

Hannah tossed a few times before waking. She came to the fire with a smile on her face. A genuine one. What Joseph wouldn't give to keep it there. "Good morning, you two." She stooped behind Samuel and wrapped her arms around him before pressing a kiss to the side of his head. "How could you let me sleep? Have you been here long?"

"No." Samuel stood and hugged her properly. "Can't stay long, either. I have to report to my lieutenant for duty this morning. And I think we have some drills later today. I don't know when I'll have more time. But I will find some. I promise."

Hannah remained speechless as her brother kissed her cheek and saluted a farewell to Joseph. As soon as Samuel was out of sight, she turned. "They can't keep him any longer."

Joseph cupped her hands in his. "We might not have much choice in that."

She jerked away. "No. They've already taken too many years. They can't have more. They can't have his life."

"Hannah." He braced her shoulders.

She shrugged away.

Joseph held up his hands. "Losing our tempers and making demands will not help Samuel. We will talk with Colonel Hardy. But we need to reason with him."

She nodded stiffly. "All right."

They both looked at Colonel Hardy's tent. There was no sign that he'd woken yet. They would have to be patient.

For a couple hours they waited, Hannah looking like a cannon with its fuse burning into oblivion.

Finally, the colonel emerged from his tent fully dressed and with several officers.

Hannah beat Joseph across the camp. "Colonel."

"Yes, Mrs. Garnet?"

"I need to speak with you."

"I imagine you feel as though you need to, but I can save you the effort. You have had your reunion with your brother, but that is all. We need him."

"Need him? He's still a boy!"

Joseph touched her arm with a downward stroke. "Easy," he whispered.

Hannah took a breath, and Joseph stepped forward. "With due respect, sir, he has already given you six years."

The colonel's eyes sharpened. "He has not given *me* anything. That service was to his country. Just as mine has been." He folded his arms tight against his chest. "How long have you given, Mr. Garnet?"

Joseph opened his mouth, ready with an answer.

"You said yesterday that you rode with Colonel Gansevoort and General Herkimer," Colonel Hardy continued. "You did not serve under them, though, did you?"

"No, I didn't, but that does not mean I haven't fought for this country or sacrificed for our freedom."

"Our freedom? Or *yours,* Mr. Garnet? Tell me truthfully, how far from your farm have the battles been that you've fought?"

Oriskany was ten miles.

Fort Schuyler wasn't much farther.

Always on the defense. Stopping the British and Tories from coming near his home and land. Never in attack to push the British from the colonies. He had never been a part of the larger war. Like Daniel. Like Samuel.

"I thought as much," the colonel said. "I have already reported my numbers to General Washington, Mr. Garnet. He has asked for more men, not less. We are on the cusp of a great offensive. As we speak, General Washington makes plans with the French. So while I understand your desires to protect your family, I have orders, and I have men I am both accountable for and to. Good day."

Joseph stood helpless as the colonel moved away with his officers. Hannah looked back and forth between him and them. "That's it?"

"Hannah, I..." How could he explain what bound him now? He didn't even understand it himself.

"Joseph, please tell me there is some way we can save my brother. You heard him, didn't you? They're marching into another battle. They're sticking him in front of the British for target practice!" She pinched her lips together, and her eyes watered. "I cannot lose him, too. Not after seeing him again. I won't let go. I don't care what it takes. I want my brother."

Numbness spread through Joseph as he opened his arms and Hannah stepped in. She trembled as she cried. And all he could do was hold her. What else did he have to give?

But himself.

Every muscle in his body tightened at the turn of his thoughts. *Is this what you had in mind from the start, Lord?*

29

Hannah wrapped her arms against her abdomen and the nausea within. "I do not care what it takes. I refuse to lose Samuel again."

Hunter gave a low knicker and nudged her with his nose.

She stepped to him and hugged his neck. "I've never been so frightened." Not for a while, anyway. Not since being slammed to the ground by a frontiersman who didn't want his horse stolen. Who could have suspected how dependent she would have grown on that man? Her hope rested with him now—him and his God.

She glanced heavenward.

Hunter leaned his head in, an itch to scratch.

"I found my brother and he's alive. Was that God's work?" She rubbed the horse's sleek summer coat, tawny in the sun. "And if He could do that for me, could He not also find a way to set Samuel free?"

Joseph always closed his eyes and tipped his head forward in prayer, so she did the same. "Dear Lord," that was how Joseph addressed Him. But Andrew had also called Him *Father*. Hannah liked that image. Her father had loved his children. She'd like to think God did, as well. "Please, Father, give me my brother back. Don't let them take him from me again." She leaned her forehead into Hunter's strong neck. "Please."

"Hannah?"

She steeled herself and turned to Samuel and his wide grin—the one she'd always loved. Wonder and worry both struggled within her, making her ill.

"I just came from Colonel Hardy." He held up two sheets of parchment.

"What are those?"

Her brother's eyes glistened. "One is my discharge." He sniffed, and a tear rolled free. "It says I am free to go."

Hannah's lungs seized. She couldn't breathe. Her chest trembled with the attempt. *Thank you, Lord!* She threw her arms around Samuel and held tight. She didn't have to let go. "I don't understand. How did Joseph convince the colonel?"

"I wasn't told. But he is still speaking with Colonel Hardy. Joseph said he'll come shortly. As soon as he's finished."

Hannah pulled back to look up at her brother, and the papers in his hands rustled. "What does the other one say?"

"That one, Joseph insisted on. The colonel read it to me himself." Samuel beamed. "It is a letter that says I have served honorably in the Continental Army and am due all the rights and respect as a vitrine of such." He held it so she could see. "His signature is here, and this is his seal. My past and what papa did are no longer tied to me."

"Then you can come back to the valley with us. You can have whatever life you wish."

"Which is only what he deserves," Joseph said.

Hannah looked past Samuel to where he stood. She let go and raced across the short distance between them. "Thank you, Joseph!" She flung her arms around him and pressed her lips to his. *I love you!*

He captured her against him, not just with his embrace, but with the caress of his mouth, moving as though to speak to her soul. Hannah replied. She loved this man more than she'd thought possible. She loved his sparring, his teasing, his warmth, his gentleness. She loved how he held her when she needed to be held, despite her. She loved his strength. She loved his love for the land. And for his family. And she loved that in this moment, she couldn't doubt that he loved her, too.

Ever so slowly, Joseph pulled away. Still, his hands cupped her face. He tipped his head against hers and filled his lungs. "I need to speak with you."

She sank her fingers into his hair. "Samuel already told me. I just don't understand how you did it. The colonel was so set when we spoke to him last. He said he couldn't afford to give up a good soldier."

"He can't." Joseph braced her shoulders.

"But…?"

"I told him I'd take Samuel's place."

"Oh, Joseph, no." *Not that.* Everything spun back out of control. "You can't do it. What about your land? What about your family—your children. James and Martha need you." *I need you.*

"They have Rachel and Andrew, grandparents, and even Daniel and his wife. They don't need me. The land, the cabin—between Andrew and Daniel, seed will still get planted in the spring and harvested in the autumn."

She searched Joseph's face, and saw the torture within. "What about me?"

"You have Samuel. He's a man now. He will take care of you." His arms fell against his sides. "You'll be fine without me."

"But I won't." Her hands lowered to the nape of his neck. She wasn't sure if she should kiss him or shake him. Didn't he know she couldn't walk away from him, either? "You're my husband, Joseph. You're my husband and…and I love you." *So very, very much.*

He blinked rapidly as though surprised. And then straightened away from her. "You can't."

"What do you mean I can't? After all you have done for me and everything…" *we've shared. Weeks of travel. Kisses. Nights only inches apart.* "Wives are supposed to love their husbands."

Joseph swallowed hard and shook his head. "That was a mistake. If there had been any other way to keep my family safe, I wouldn't have let you marry me." He took her wrists and held her away from him. "If you knew the truth…if you knew the truth, you would have encouraged Otetiani to take my scalp and burn down everything I'd ever built."

Hannah fell back a step. "How can you say that? How can you even suggest—"

"I killed him," Joseph whispered.

Him? The same him from his conversation with Daniel?

"I should have told you before now. Maybe that day at Fort Herkimer when you asked about Oriskany. I should have told you then."

Hannah stared. Another step back. She didn't need to hear any more. She already knew. And it wrung her. "Oriskany? Papa?"

Joseph glanced to where Samuel stood. "You need to hear it, too. You don't owe me anything. Your pa and I fought at Oriskany four years ago. And I killed him." Joseph wiped a hand down his face and closed his eyes. "I killed him."

No. Anything but that. And yet she couldn't doubt it. He'd told her before. In his silence. The pained look in his eyes. He'd confessed over and over and she'd never listened. Hannah clasped her palm over her mouth as though she could somehow contain the agony ripping through her and what had moments ago been overwhelming love for this man. How could she feel that now? What was she supposed to feel?

What did he feel?

Hannah waved her unsteady hand at him. "I don't understand. Why all of this? Is that why you came with me? Is that why you made your promises? It was never about me, was it?"

"Of course it was about you." He released his breath. "You were my neighbor."

~*~

Joseph braced himself as Hannah fled into the woods. He couldn't go after her and hold her until everything was all right again. That was no longer his place. He walked to Hunter before facing Samuel. "The horse is Hannah's now." Joseph had forgotten all about the foal he'd wanted to give her. Now it didn't matter. She could keep the sire. "He's already seen enough of this war."

"Haven't we all?"

Joseph wanted to agree, but it seemed premature. His life was no longer his own, and he was about to march into whatever offensive General Washington decided upon. He was a soldier of the Continental Army and would obey whatever orders he was given. For once he would look beyond himself and his family and fight for his country.

"I think you are wrong." Samuel remained in place.

"About what?" Joseph had been wrong plenty of times, but everything seemed pretty straightforward in this instance.

"That we should blame you for Pa's death. Hannah might struggle for a while, but she does love you. Any fool can see that. And how can a man be held responsible for what happens in the thick of battle? Unless you purposefully sought him out with the intent to murder him."

Joseph shook his head. "But that doesn't mean I didn't feel justified in what I did." He pushed the memory from his mind and patted Hunter's neck. They had been through a lot together and somehow survived. Now he would continue on alone.

"Can I ask you one question?"

"Go ahead." Joseph steeled himself.

"When you fought my pa, if you hadn't killed him, would he have killed you?"

Very likely, but..."That doesn't change anything." He crouched by the saddle and packs to find anything he might need. His pistol. Powder horn. What else? It was hard to care.

"How does that not change anything?" Samuel stepped to him and extended a hand. "I don't blame you for Pa's death. And I am grateful for what you've done for me." His eyes glistened as he gripped Joseph's hand with both of his. "I will always think of you as the brother you are to me now. Thank you. Thank you for my freedom."

Joseph stood dumfounded as the boy embraced him, and he was helpless not to reciprocate. Giving up his own freedom was suddenly worth it, and more so.

He'd given Hannah back her brother and with the funds he still had from the sale of Pa's timepiece, they could make do while they made plans. Hunter would take them wherever they needed to go.

Warmth filled Joseph, along with gratitude to a watchful God above. Perhaps the Lord never did answer his prayers, but how often had He used Joseph as an answer to someone else's? Like a wounded British officer left among the dead? Or a girl in search of her brothers? That was enough for Joseph. Whether or not he survived whatever waited for him and the rest of the Continental Army.

30

Hannah leaned against the window ledge and peered down at the street below. Albany had begun to show the first signs of autumn—farmers' wagons loaded with corn and other vegetables, the tinges of yellow and reds in the leaves, the days growing shorter. Three months since they'd left Joseph behind. Three months of feeling ripped in two.

Footsteps sounded up the stairs of the Huntsman Inn and Hannah pushed away from the window. Samuel didn't need to find her brooding here again. But the footsteps continued past to one of the other rooms, leaving her alone a little longer. She returned to the window and looked out in time to see Samuel duck inside the front door. Better to go downstairs and meet him for supper—save him the hike up the stairs to fetch her. The work he'd found harvesting with a local farmer usually left him exhausted.

Hannah straightened the green skirt of the gown Joseph had bought her and started down the stairs.

Samuel met her at the base. "I was on my way up to meet you."

"I thought I'd save you the effort. Mrs. Barstow prefers when you wash up down here anyway, to save her from hauling water upstairs." She followed him to the washbasin and pitcher waiting on a stand beside the door to the kitchen. Mrs. Barstow always kept the water fresh for their guests. "How was your day?"

"Good." He splashed water on his face and across

the back of his neck, and then washed his hands.

Hannah held out a linen towel for him to dry on. "You like farming, don't you?" He seemed so content and pleased when he returned no matter how long the day.

"I do. It's…" His face momentarily vanished behind the towel. When he set the towel aside, it was as though he'd wiped away any pleasure from his youthful features. "It's peaceful."

She squeezed his arm. He hadn't spoken much to her about his time in the army—only places he'd been, people he'd met, and what he'd learned from some of the good men he'd served with. Never about the battles, the gore, or the death.

They sat down at their usual table, and Mr. Barstow brought their meal. Samuel remained quiet, only halfheartedly acknowledging her meager attempts at conversation.

"Are you feeling unwell?" she finally asked.

"I'm fine." Samuel ripped off some bread and shoved it into his mouth, but didn't look at her.

"Did something happen today?"

His gaze briefly lifted to hers. "I overheard news of Washington's army."

Joseph.

Her hand gave an involuntary tremble, and she set the spoon on the table beside her bowl. "What have you heard?"

Samuel glanced around at several other occupied tables before whispering, "They are marching through Virginia."

"Virginia?" That made no sense. Up until now it was believed Washington's army lingered just outside of New York City, preparing for an offensive.

"Seems they left a decoy for the British."

Hannah sank against the hard back of her chair. The stew's wonderful aroma now turned her stomach. The war was taking Joseph farther and farther from where he belonged. From his farm. And his family.

From me.

She forced the thought from her mind. Joseph's place was not with her. Never would be. "Where is their destination?"

"From what I understand, a city along the coast. Yorktown. The British have brought their main forces up from the Carolinas."

"How many?"

Samuel's focus shifted to his food. "Reports are varied."

"How many?"

He sighed and dropped the bread back to the table. "Somewhere between six and ten thousand."

Ten thousand? She could not even imagine that number. "How many does General Washington have?"

"The General only has three thousand or so with him. But the French have a substantial army, as well. They aren't facing the British alone." He reached across for her hand.

"But there will be a battle." And it would not be a small one. Men would die. Joseph might die.

"You're worried about him, aren't you?"

She picked up her spoon and started eating again despite her lack of appetite. The heavy gravy hit her stomach like a stone.

"You know, it should be me marching against Yorktown."

"No. You should have never been in this war."

"Hannah, all of us are in this war. It surrounds us.

It doesn't matter anymore what happened back in the valley; none of us escaped. We can't escape it now. Least of all you."

"I don't understand you. We're safe here." At least for now.

"Your heart is somewhere between here and Yorktown. Isn't it? Maybe four years ago you would have preferred Joseph die so Pa could survive. But what about now? You don't want him dead."

"Of course I don't. But that is hardly relevant." As was this conversation. She stood and headed for the stairs. She returned to their room and the window to wait for Samuel's footsteps. Minutes passed before she heard them.

The door opened and then tapped shut. "Pa made his choices," Samuel said. "Stop making yourself pay for them."

Hannah hugged herself. The earlier hustle and bustled on the streets had begun to wane with the day. "You make no sense."

He moved to her. "Pa left us to fight for the British. That was his choice. He died fighting for the British. His choice. Myles, Mama, little Miriam. They didn't escape the consequences of—"

Hannah spun. "You can't blame Papa for what happened to them."

Samuel held up his hands. "I loved Papa, too, Hannah. But surely you've asked yourself what would have happened to us if he had stayed. I'll tell you what would have happened. Whether we left the valley or remained, we wouldn't have been separated. As a family, we would have been stronger." Dark locks fell across his forehead with the shake of his head. "I spent the last six years paying for being the son of a Tory.

Don't do the same."

"I am not—"

"It is true, isn't it, that Joseph Garnet is your husband?"

"Yes, but…" She had no argument for that.

"And you love him?"

Her heart throbbed. "I…"

"Do not let Pa take that from you, too."

"Samuel…" Hannah turned back to the window and the world moving forward as though there wasn't a war raging just over the southern horizon. In Virginia.

"It is not a sin to love him."

"Not a betrayal?" How could it not be?

"Joseph didn't kill Pa. The war killed him." Samuel stood beside her and wrapped an arm over her shoulders. "But Joseph did give himself for my freedom—and possibly my life."

"I know." Another reason for how torn she felt. But loving and forgiving wasn't her only fear. Joseph had made it clear that he hadn't wanted to marry her—only to atone for taking Pa. He'd been kind to her, and he'd held her and kissed her as though he might actually care. But Rachel had been right about him. He didn't like to be alone. The reason he'd married Fannie. The reason he'd held her.

"Have you thought much on what we will do once harvest is over and I have no more work here?"

Hannah had been trying hard not to think about the future. Her heart called her to return to Joseph's precious valley, but how could she? He didn't care for her as a wife. Only a *neighbor*.

Oh, how she hated that word.

But not as much as she hated not knowing what

Joseph really felt for her.

~*~

To think he'd once coveted adventure.

Now he just wanted to go home.

Joseph's feet still ached from marching over four hundred miles, though they'd reached their destination two weeks past. In the hazy morning light, Yorktown sat on the horizon, the York River and silhouettes of ships—both British and French—its backdrop. How long before they made the city theirs? How many lives would it cost?

Joseph massaged the muscles of his shoulders, stiff from digging a four-foot-deep trench in pouring rain several nights ago. At least the cover of darkness and pelting rain had shielded them from the British, one thousand yards away behind their fortifications. Safely out of musket range. Not very many casualties yet.

"Men…"

Joseph snapped his attention back to Colonel Hardy.

"I should have no need to explain to you the importance of Yorktown's surrender, how great a blow it would be to the British. But first we must to reach beyond their fortifications. I am to select my best men to join Lieutenant Colonel Hamilton and others under his command in the advance against one of the southern redoubts."

Joseph stiffened. The French had made an attempt on a redoubt when they'd first arrived. And failed. The British were well dug in to their remaining redoubts, with mounds of earth and tall spikes impeding any offensive.

"You are whom I have chosen. Lieutenant Abrams will accompany you to where you are to report."

Joseph cinched his hat down a little lower as he glanced to the dozen or so men standing with him. Seasoned soldiers.

"Garnet."

"Yes, sir?"

Colonel Hardly motioned him to follow to the door of his tent. "I have yet to see you in battle, but only half of General Herkimer's men survived Oriskany, and I am not unaware of what Brant and his Mohawk chiefs have wrought upon your valley. I believe it is men like you who will win this war for us."

Joseph remained silent. He wasn't sure which was more important to him now. To win a war…or return to his family.

"If the redoubts fall to us, the city will follow, and the tide of the war will shift in our favor." The colonel gave a slight nod. "Perhaps then we might be able to do without so many men."

Joseph swallowed hard and returned his nod. He dared not take the colonel's words to heart. First, he had to survive. And even then there were no promises.

Being dismissed, Joseph followed the others to Lieutenant Colonel Hamilton's camp farther to the south. Again they waited as men were gathered and then given their orders. Redoubt ten was theirs—the one closest to the river—while the French provided both a diversion and attacked redoubt nine.

"You will not load your muskets," Hamilton informed them. "Bayonets only or you risk shooting each other."

It was explained that with the south side of the redoubt protected by a steep slope to the river, they would attack from three sides, plowing through whatever fortifications awaited them on those walls of earth while dozens of guns rained balls down on them.

A trickle of sweat maneuvered down Joseph's spine. How many times could a man cheat death? Tonight others would commence construction of another trench only three-hundred-and-fifty yards from the fortifications surrounding Yorktown. Why could that have not been the task given him?

They positioned themselves, readied their muskets, and then watched as the sun made its slow arch over them until at long last it reached the western horizon.

"Are you ready, men?"

They nodded to their commander.

Joseph touched his hand to the bayonet attached to his musket, making certain it was secure.

"Hard and fast, men," Hamilton continued. "And I remind you, cold steel only. We must take this redoubt. The French depend on us as greatly as we do on them. If we fail…" His gaze swept over them. "We cannot fail, men."

Joseph glanced at the glow in the west where the sun had last resided. Darkness was soon upon them. No more waiting.

Continue Your care over my family, Lord. And Hannah. Though he doubted he would ever see her again. Even if by some miracle he survived the night.

A miracle.

Joseph closed his eyes. If he could ask for one miracle, what would it be?

To see my children again.

And my wife.

But God knew what was best. Joseph saw that

now. He would trust in the Lord's plan for him.

My life is Thine.

Joseph watched as Hamilton continued to organize his troops, placing the men with axes, nicknamed miners, at the front. They would need to hack a path through the abatis, sharpened stakes buried into the face of the earth and pointed outwards, making the redoubt resemble a ridiculously large porcupine.

The world eclipsed into darkness.

"All right, men. Let's go."

They rose silently from the trenches and followed their commander over the open terrain, but only a short ways before the signal was given to lay down.

Joseph flattened himself to the ground with the others. Spiny grass prickled his face. It was already halfway through October—five months since he'd ridden away from his family to find Hannah. Were they finished with harvest at home? Was there enough food? How difficult would the winter be?

All sat silent in the lines behind them as the first of the stars appeared on the horizon. The world and every man lay braced for the signal to charge. Too much time for introspection, something he'd done with each mile he'd marched. If he did survive this, he needed to go home and be a better father to his children—more like his own pa—spend more time with them. He should spend more time in the Bible, too. He'd probably never know it as well as his Scripture-spouting brother-in-law, but he could pick the book up more than once a week. Maybe he'd…

A cannon boomed behind them. Then a second in quick succession. And a third.

"Rochambeau." The word muffled along the line,

sounding more like "rush 'em boy" than a French name.

The signal to go.

Joseph lurched to his feet with the other soldiers and sprinted across the open distance to the British and their guns, the only sound the rush of their feet on the ground. Yard over yard they raced against the time they had before the British noticed them.

Then the pop of musket fire began. Men began to drop.

Joseph kept his focus steadfast on the wall of earth and the spikes rising from it. A little farther and they would be there. He pushed harder. Until his feet dropped out from under him. He slammed against rutted dirt out of sight of the redoubt. A fist sized stone dug into his shoulder. Joseph groaned and rolled to his knees, musket still in hand. Pain radiated down his arm. No wonder men were vanishing from sight. Holes big enough to bury an ox littered the area—a gift from their own artillery's large shells.

Not giving himself time to catch his breath to consider what he raced toward, Joseph scrambled up over the edge and rejoined the attack. The leading wave of miners had just reached the first of the abatis.

The men with axes made quick work of the wood spikes obstructing their path, and the infantry pressed forward. Joseph followed the flow of men through the low trench, over the mound of dirt and into the hornet's nest of redcoats.

Beside him a man cried out and grabbed his face.

"God, save us." If not their earthly tabernacles, then their spirits as they returned to Him.

A blur of red spun Joseph back to the battle, and he sliced his bayonet toward a British soldier, catching

him in the arm. The man screamed out as he dropped to his knees. Joseph cracked the back of his musket against the side of the redcoat's head. The man sagged to the ground and another lunged to take his place.
The popping of muskets barely registered above the fray—and the pain searing the side of Joseph's torso.

A flash of light registered in his brain, and it was difficult to refocus on the scarlet clad soldier yanking his musket from his hands.

His own bayonet slashed towards his head, more like a memory than the reality he faced. Joseph ducked and thrust his shoulder into the man's gut. Together they fell. Fire tore at the wound in his side, but he seemed detached from even that. They rolled, the air pressed from his lungs. Hate darkened the eyes above him, but this this time Joseph didn't feel that either. He didn't hate this British soldier. He wanted only his life. And his freedom. And his family.

Joseph grabbed for his musket and wrested it from the man, shoving him back. They regained their footing about the same time, but now Joseph held the weapon. He could only see terror now in the eyes of the redcoat as he staggered back.

"Please."

For a moment the world seemed to sigh. The firing had stopped in the immediate area. The redoubt was theirs.

Joseph glanced down at the torn fabric of his coat, soaking up the blood.

A graze.

Keeping his bayonet and empty musket trained on his prisoner, Joseph pressed his hand over the gash in his side and forced his lungs to expand. Perhaps the Lord was not finished with him, after all.

31

The thin layer of snow crunched under Joseph's boots, and he breathed into his hands. Every day the temperatures dropped a little more. But every day also brought him that much closer to home. He broke into a jog as he passed the old Cunningham homestead. Not just to warm his blood, but to put behind him that last mile.

One mile and he'd finally be home.

A stitch formed in Joseph's side, forcing him to slow. He couldn't seem to take a proper breath. The Lord had preserved his life, and shortly after the surrender of Yorktown and over seven thousand British troops, he'd been released from his obligation to the army. His journey to Virginia and back had worn the soles of his boots thin, and they leaked moisture from the snow, but that hardly mattered now. He'd thaw his feet when he held his son and daughter.

A pang hit his chest. He would give anything to hold Hannah again, too.

Joseph stepped off the main trail onto the path leading to his farm and stopped. The cabin sat silent and peaceful as did the barn and pastures. The fields showed short stubble prickling up through the blankets of white. The mare and foal looked to him briefly before lowering their heads back to the pile of hay laid out for them. The filly was almost as tall as her mother, favoring Hunter's height. Her winter coat was not much darker then her sire's, as well. She would be a beautiful horse. Joseph would have liked Hannah to see her. They would have made a wonderful match.

But Hannah was gone and had the best horse he had to offer.

Joseph moved to the cabin, but his hand paused on the latch. Fresh prints in the snow suggested Daniel still lived here with his wife. He knocked. And waited.

No shuffle of feet. No open door. Nothing.

A billow of white showed on the air as he puffed out a breath and turned back to the expanse of his farm. Everything appeared well kept. The silo was probably full. The animals appeared content. Joseph pulled his pack and bedroll from his back, dropped them against the door and started to the barn. Understanding dogged his steps. He might have been missed, but he wasn't needed.

Despite his fingers being stiff with cold, Joseph hurried to bridle and saddle his mare. The filly whinnied loudly as he rode back to the trail, but he wasn't about to walk all the way to Rachel's and Andrew's if he had the choice. Not after already coming hundreds of miles.

Joseph encouraged the mare to a gallop in an attempt to escape his thoughts and the cold that settled through him, but reaching the second farm only confirmed what he knew. Fields were bare, their fruits stored away, and large stacks of firewood lined the wall of the cabin. He should be grateful, and thank God that his family had everything they needed for a comfortable winter, but instead he wondered if they even felt his absence.

"Whoa."

The mare whinnied as he tied her to the hitching

post beside the barn. An answer came from inside. The barn door swung open and Andrew stepped out with a pitchfork over his shoulder. "Excuse me, sir, who…"

Joseph grinned. "Has it been so long since you've seen me in a full beard?"

The pitchfork fell and Andrew grabbed him in an embrace. "It has been too long since I have seen you." He pulled back but gripped Joseph's shoulders. "We have worried from hearing nothing of you for this many months."

"It has been a while, hasn't it?"

Andrew clapped him on the back. "But what are we doing out here? You are probably frozen and starved, and I know a few people sitting in that cabin who will never forgive me if I delay you any longer." He hurried to shut up the barn. "I was about to hitch the wagon, but I see no purpose for that now. Not yet."

"Where were you going?" Joseph asked, but Andrew had already broken into a jog across the yard. He followed. The generous billows from the chimney suggested warmth and his family waited.

Andrew beat him to the door but didn't enter. Just grinned and shoved him inside.

Joseph stumbled to a halt and straightened under the collection of gazes frozen on him. More than he had anticipated. Rachel stood behind the table halfway through pouring a pot of soup into a crock. Beside her, Hannah waited with the lid, her mouth open, and her eyes wide.

"Papa!" James slammed against his leg and clung tight.

Joseph pulled his son into his arms, and glanced to where Samuel, coat on, crouched with the two little girls on their feet beside him. Martha stared, no longer a baby. With a frightened squeal she lunged to Samuel and grabbed his neck.

"Oh, Joseph, you're home." Rachel was by him before he realized she'd even moved. She leaned forward to hug him over her stomach. She was close to having her baby. When she pulled back to look at him, tears ornamented her cheeks. "Praise the Lord for keeping you safe. After so many months, and then when Hannah and Samuel came with news of what you'd done, and Yorktown…."

The rest of her words faded to the muffled background as Joseph looked again at Hannah. Hands clasped, she watched. He ached to pull her into his arms and kiss her soundly—if he could only be sure that she'd welcome such from him. Had she forgiven him? Is that why she'd returned?

"Let's get you something to eat. Your hands are like ice." Rachel pulled him to the table and pushed him into a chair.

He kept James on his lap and his eyes on Hannah as she dished him a bowl of the soup and knifed some butter onto some bread. "You came back."

"So did you." She smiled and handed him the bread.

Joseph caught her fingers, warm and soft. "Why?"

"I made promises."

"Then you—"

The door burst open and Nora rushed in. "Hannah, I've been riding the countryside trying to find—" Her gaze darted to Joseph. "You're alive! We were so worried. When they told us you were marching with General Washington, we prayed that you'd be safe."

"Thank you." Perhaps those prayers were what

kept him alive. Was he still only the answer to other's pleas?

No. God had brought Hannah back to him—He'd answered Joseph's prayer.

Nora looked at Hannah with a pained expression. "I hate to say what I came for now, with Joseph barely returned, but Lydia begged me to find you, to beseech you to come."

Hannah drew her hand from Joseph's. "The baby?"

"Yes. The pains started this morning. They are quite regular now."

Hands wringing, Hannah looked at Joseph. "I…I promised her I'd come—that I'd attend her. But I…if you prefer, I could…"

Stay. That was his preference. There was so much they needed to talk about. So much he needed to know. But her expression showed such agony—the choice between her duty and what she wanted. Joseph only wished he knew which he was. He would make one last sacrifice for her sake. "You go on. Keep your promise."

She opened her mouth, then sighed, and shook her head. "Very well."

But it wasn't well at all. He wanted to hold her and kiss her with all the passion he'd ever felt for her—with a longing that had only grown in the months apart. Instead he watched her don her cloak and disappear through the door with Nora.

Joseph slumped back in his chair, James cuddled on his lap and his hand still feeling the warmth Hannah had left him…along with so many unanswered questions.

~*~

Hannah's heart bled as the wagon jostled over the frozen road taking her away from Joseph. She gripped the edge of the seat to keep from falling off, but she wished she could clasp her hands together and thank God for hearing her and bringing Joseph home. If only she could've stayed longer with him, but this would give him time with his family. She was the one who'd taken him from them for so long.

Besides, Lydia had become a dear friend since she'd returned to the valley, and Hannah had assured her she'd be present when the baby came. Joseph was the only one who could have swayed her. But he hadn't even tried.

You were my neighbor.

Even after all these months, Joseph's words still stung. Had she…would she ever mean anything more to him?

The Reid cabin was a bustle of activity and girlish chatter, the two younger girls folding blankets on the makeshift bed in the main room. Hannah wished Daniel had stayed in Joseph's cabin for Lydia's sake, giving her some privacy. He'd insisted Joseph would want the cabin for Hannah and Samuel. He'd also suggested Lydia would be able to rest more with his mother and sisters there to meet her needs and instruct her on how to keep a home. Lydia obviously hadn't confided to him how uncomfortable she was under his mother's expectations and watchful eye. Not to mention, the hustle and bustle of a crowded house was not what a woman needed when giving birth.

"Lydia's in the larger bedroom," Nora said. She pulled off her shoes and led the way. The three girls had given up their room while an addition was being built onto the side of the cabin for the newlyweds. In the room, two narrow beds pushed together held a larger mattress and Lydia.

Abigail Reid stood at the head of the bed with a pinched expression, while Daniel sat beside his wife.

"You came."

The relief on Lydia's face eased some of Hannah's regret for leaving Joseph. He wasn't going anywhere, and she was wanted here.

"Of course I did."

Daniel stood and let Hannah take his place. He helped her with her cloak, but passed it to Nora to take out.

"Joseph has returned," Nora said in her retreat.

"Oh, Hannah, maybe you should not have..." Lydia sucked a breath and clenched her jaw as pain twisted her face.

Hannah braced Lydia's arm until she relaxed back into the bed. "Do not worry about me or Joseph. Now I know he's safe. That's all I asked." Though she wanted so much more, she couldn't think about herself right now. "How regular are the tightenings?"

"Like waves. They pause for just long enough for me to catch my breath and begin again."

"That's good." Hannah smiled and focused on the present. "Then all we have to do is wait while your body prepares itself."

The burst of girlish gigging made everyone glance at the door.

Abigail sighed. "I should go find something else for those girls to do."

"Why don't you close the door on the way out?" Hannah suggested.

Lydia's head made a tiny jerk toward her husband.

Hannah set a hand on his arm. "And Daniel, please give Lydia and me a moment."

He looked at his wife for affirmation, and she gave a sad nod…and then braced against another contraction.

Daniel clung to the side of the bed until she finished, before he looked at Hannah, as though questioning how he could leave.

"I'll call you back in a few minutes."

He dragged his heels to the door and closed it gently behind him.

"The pain feels so much worse with him leaning over me so concerned," Lydia said. "And his mother. Is it not bad enough that I can hardly cook an egg, brew coffee, or keep a house? Must I prove myself in birthing, as well?" She ground her teeth against the tension clenching her abdomen, and Hannah took her hand.

"Deep breaths." Hannah stroked her shoulder until the pain eased. She could only imagine what a woman felt while giving birth. She'd seen the agony on the faces of other women, but had never experienced it for herself. Though, maybe now that Joseph was home…

"I cannot do this. I cannot pretend to be strong when I have never been more afraid." Lydia's eyes shone. "I am trying so hard to trust right now."

Hannah stood and pulled back the blankets. "You don't have to be strong right now." She guided Lydia to her feet.

"What are we doing?"

"Don't worry about Daniel or his mother. Or life

or death. As Andrew says, only God can control that." Something Hannah was still striving to believe. "This moment, all you have to think about is you and that baby. Your body knows what to do. Listen to it. Find what it wants."

Lydia's face began to tighten, and Hannah ran her hands down her arms. "Do not fight yourself. Embrace the pain. It's trying to help you. Think of yourself opening wide to welcome your baby."

Lydia slowly lowered to her knees.

Hannah smoothed Lydia's hair back from her face, remembering Mama's words to a birthing mother in their village. "Find what is most comfortable for you. No one else is here, but you and your child. Fill your lungs. Embrace life."

As the tightening eased, Lydia leaned her head into Hannah's shoulder. "Can we pray?"

"Of course." There was so much Hannah wanted to thank God for right now. And a couple more things to ask.

32

Hannah paced the floor with Lydia between the tightenings. The minutes between had lengthened again, but hopefully some movement would encourage the baby lower. The rumble of male voices filtered through the closed door. It was difficult to differentiate between Daniel and his father, but one voice stood out clearly from the others.

The door opened a crack, and Nora poked her head in. "Joseph's here."

"Go, Hannah. Nora can help me for a while," Lydia said.

She should argue—the thought of a real conversation with Joseph tied her insides into knots—but she couldn't. "I'll return shortly."

Hannah slipped past Nora and closed the door. Everyone looked at her with expectance. Daniel came to her side, and she patted his arm. "Lydia is fine. Everything is fine." Except the fact that Joseph stood watching her, and she had no idea what to say to him—no idea what he expected or wanted from her. "Why aren't you with your family?"

Joseph returned his hat to his head. "Will you step outside with me?"

"I shouldn't leave Lydia for long."

He already held her cloak out for her. "It could be hours before the baby comes. She can spare you for a few minutes."

Hannah turned so he could place the cloak over her shoulders, and then let him lead her out. The sun off the snow blinded her after so long in the dimness of the bedroom.

They walked a ways from the cabin before Joseph cleared his throat. "After what I told you about your Pa, I didn't expect to see you here."

Hannah pulled the cloak tighter around her arms. Why did he have to start with that? "I wasn't sure if I ever wanted to see you again either. For a while."

The corner of his mouth twitched. "Does that mean you did hope to see me again?"

"After a while." She paused at a rail fence. "Otherwise I don't think I would have returned here."

"There's a cabin and land here. You could have hoped I wouldn't survive and you could call it your own." The vibrato of his voice suggested he did question whether or not such was possible.

Hannah faced him, an ache rising within. "Joseph…I could never want you dead."

"But do you want me here? With you?" A muscle in his jaw flexed. "I need to know if you've found a way to forgive me."

An overwhelming peace settled over Hannah, and her chest swelled with all the love she'd ever felt for him. And more. "I have."

The door slammed, and they both turned to see Rose, one of the younger girls, racing toward them. "Lydia has started pushing."

"I have to go." Hannah turned, but only made it two steps.

Joseph caught her arm. "It's her first baby. She could be pushing for another hour." He grabbed her other arm and pulled around, a desperation in his eyes.

"First tell me that you're staying."

"Cyrus Acker and his friends backed down after Andrew showed them Colonel Hardy's letters, so there seems no reason for us not to stay. I promised to be your wife and help raise your children, Samuel likes farming…and we love the valley." *And I love you.* But last time she'd said that much, he'd thrown it back in her face. Her eyes burned at the memory, and she tried to jerk away. "Now let me go. Lydia needs me. I promised her…"

"She has a whole family to help her. And *I* need you."

Need? The word probably best summed up what he felt. He needed a mother for his children, someone to work at his side and fill the emptiness of his home. Never had a word felt so shallow.

Hannah settled her shoulders back, determined not to let him see the hurt. "I already told you, you helped me find my brother, and I will keep my side of the agreement as well."

His grip fell away. "So this is still just an agreement to you?"

Of course it wasn't just an agreement to her, but this wasn't the time or place to discuss her feelings. She was already on the brink of coming unraveled and Lydia was in the middle of birthing her baby. "I have to go, Joseph. I'm sorry." Hannah started back to the cabin.

Rose had already disappeared inside.

~*~

Joseph leaned against the fence, weeks of marching, battle, and his journey home laying their full weight over him. "Maybe it would have been better if I didn't come back," he mumbled into the wintery air.

Hannah glanced back. "What?"

He blew out his breath. Better she not hear the depths of his doubts, but he had to know. "You made it clear that you don't want me dead—which I can appreciate—but would you have preferred I hadn't come back? Do you want me to leave?"

"Joseph…" She turned to face him again. "This is your home. Everyone hoped and prayed for your return. Nobody wants you to leave."

"Maybe not." He forced a shrug. "But they'll continue on well enough without me."

Her jaw slackened. "Is that what you think?"

Joseph turned back to the fence. He shouldn't have said anything.

"What about your children? Did you see James when you walked through that door? I'm surprised he let you out of his sight again."

It hadn't been easy to slip away.

"And Rachel. All she did was talk about you and how much like your pa you are. She needs you. And Andrew. He tried not to say much, but he feels he still has much to learn from you."

Joseph pinched the bridge of his nose. It hurt as much as if he'd just lost a fist fight. His eyes watered.

"And me. I need you, Joseph." The tenderness of her words gave way to an exasperated laugh. "And I need to get inside that cabin."

Better he be left to himself for a little while anyway. "That's fine. Go on." Joseph listened for her to leave.

Instead she came closer. "You don't believe me, do you?"

He wouldn't answer that. "You need to go help Lydia have her baby." He thumbed away the excess moisture from his eyes. Hopefully she'd heed him, because he didn't need anyone to see him break apart. He was tired. He should have gone home.

"I do need you." She tugged on his sleeve until he looked at her. "I need your warmth. Your reassurance. I need you to hold me when I'm angry…and kiss me when I'm sad. But most of all…" Her eyes welled. "Oh, Joseph, I need you to love me. I want to be more than just a responsibility you've taken on."

"You stopped being that a long time ago, Hannah."

"But you said you wouldn't have agreed to this marriage if you'd had any other choice." A tear tumbled down her cheek and she swatted at it. "You said I was just your neighbor."

"Hannah…" Joseph reached for her. "I meant it like in that parable Jesus told—from Andrew's sermon. Not a literal neighbor, but healing, forgiving. Loving."

She rammed her fist into his bicep. "You expected me to understand a reference from a Bible story I've never read and only heard about briefly more than a month earlier?"

"Forgive me, Hannah." Joseph dragged her into his arms. "I—"

The door to the cabin slapped open again and Nora appeared looking much too happy. "It's a girl! Daniel and Lydia have a baby girl." She gave a shy smile and hurried back inside.

Hannah slumped against him. "I feel so terrible. I should have been there for her. I promised her—"

Joseph tipped her chin up and covered her mouth with his own. There was no time for regretting the past ten minutes. The future was on his mind. Taking his bride home and starting their marriage, a real marriage. They still had a lot to talk about but that was pretty far from his thoughts, as well. After so long apart, it felt so good to hold her like this.

His kiss was cut short by an elbow in his ribs.

"Now what's wrong?"

Hannah shook her head at him. "You still haven't told me anything—haven't told me what you really feel for me. If anything."

Joseph smiled at his little Mohawk warrior. She definitely kept him on his toes—while filling every part of him. "I love you, Hannah Garnet." He kissed her again to chase all doubts away. "I love you."

Thank you

We appreciate you reading this White Rose Publishing title. For other inspirational stories, please visit our on-line bookstore at www.pelicanbookgroup.com.

For questions or more information, contact us at customer@pelicanbookgroup.com.

White Rose Publishing
Where Faith is the Cornerstone of Love™
an imprint of Pelican Book Group
www.PelicanBookGroup.com

Connect with Us
www.facebook.com/Pelicanbookgroup
www.twitter.com/pelicanbookgrp

To receive news and specials, subscribe to our bulletin
http://pelink.us/bulletin

May God's glory shine through
this inspirational work of fiction.

AMDG

You Can Help!

At Pelican Book Group it is our mission to entertain readers with fiction that uplifts the Gospel. It is our privilege to spend time with you awhile as you read our stories.

We believe you can help us to bring Christ into the lives of people across the globe. And you don't have to open your wallet or even leave your house!

Here are 3 simple things you can do to help us bring illuminating fiction™ to people everywhere.

1) If you enjoyed this book, write a positive review. Post it at online retailers and websites where readers gather. And share your review with us at reviews@pelicanbookgroup.com (this does give us permission to reprint your review in whole or in part.)

2) If you enjoyed this book, recommend it to a friend in person, at a book club or on social media.

3) If you have suggestions on how we can improve or expand our selection, let us know. We value your opinion. Use the contact form on our web site or e-mail us at customer@pelicanbookgroup.com

God Can Help!

Are you in need? The Almighty can do great things for you. Holy is His Name! He has mercy in every generation. He can lift up the lowly and accomplish all things. Reach out today.

Do not fear: I am with you; do not be anxious: I am your God. I will strengthen you, I will help you, I will uphold you with my victorious right hand.

~Isaiah 41:10 (NAB)

We pray daily, and we especially pray for everyone connected to Pelican Book Group—that includes you! If you have a specific need, we welcome the opportunity to pray for you. Share your needs or praise reports at http://pelink.us/pray4us